STAR WARS

FATE OF THE JEDI

OMEN

BOOKS BY CHRISTIE GOLDEN

Books published by The Random House Publishing Group
are available at quantity discounts on bulk purchases for
premium, educational, fund-raising, and special sales use.
For details, please call 1-800-733-3000.

STAR WARS®

FATE OF THE JEDI

OMEN

CHRISTIE GOLDEN

DEL REY • NEW YORK

Star Wars: Fate of the Jedi: Omen is a work of fiction. Names, places, and incidents either are products of the author's imagination or are used fictitiously.

2016 Del Rey Mass Market Edition

Copyright © 2009 by Lucasfilm Ltd. & ® or ™ where indicated. All rights reserved. Used under authorization.

Excerpt from *Star Wars: Fate of the Jedi: Abyss* copyright © 2009 by Lucasfilm Ltd. & ® or ™ where indicated. All rights reserved. Used under authorization.

Published in the United States by Del Rey, an imprint of Random House, a division of Penguin Random House LLC, New York.

DEL REY and the HOUSE colophon are registered trademarks of Penguin Random House LLC.

Originally published in hardcover in the United States by Del Rey, an imprint of Random House, a division of Penguin Random House LLC, in 2009.

This book contains an excerpt from *Star Wars: Fate of the Jedi: Abyss* by Troy Denning This excerpt has been set for this edition only and may not reflect the final content of the book.

ISBN 978-0-345-50913-0
ebook ISBN 978-0-345-51871-2

Printed in the United States of America

randomhousebooks.com

11 10 9 8 7

This book is dedicated to my parents,
James R. Golden and Elizabeth C. Golden.
All those afternoons you dropped me off at the movies
when *Star Wars* was playing have now borne fruit.

Acknowledgments

There are many people who contributed to the birth of this amazing project. First, thanks go to my agent, Lucienne Diver, and my editor at Del Rey, Shelly Shapiro, who approached me for this series and who has been so very supportive and enthusiastic. Thanks also to Sue Rostoni at Lucas Licensing Ltd., who has kept her fingers on many pulses to help coordinate the direction of Fate of the Jedi, and Leland Chee, who is both prompt and cheerful when bombarded with questions. Aaron Allston and Troy Denning both made me feel welcome and part of the team almost immediately: I'm excited to be working with both of you, and am appreciative of your help and guidance as I navigate this brave new world. Jeffrey R. Kirby, my "creative consultant" (and favorite Sith), helped make sure I nailed the feel of the *Star Wars* universe. Finally, thanks to my husband Michael Georges for all his support, and to George Lucas, for making this world so darn captivating in the first place.

THE STAR WARS NOVELS TIMELINE

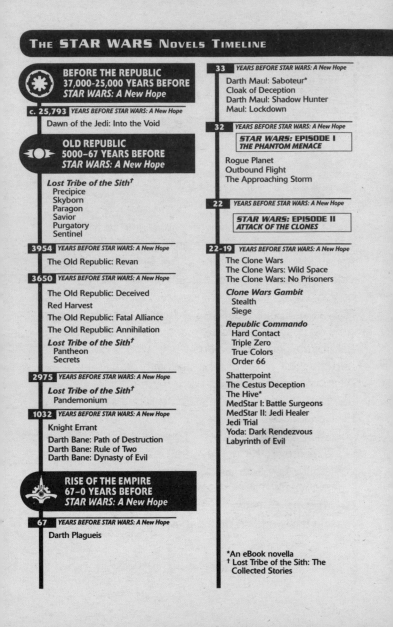

BEFORE THE REPUBLIC
37,000–25,000 YEARS BEFORE *STAR WARS: A New Hope*

c. 25,793 *YEARS BEFORE STAR WARS: A New Hope*

Dawn of the Jedi: Into the Void

OLD REPUBLIC
5000–67 YEARS BEFORE *STAR WARS: A New Hope*

Lost Tribe of the Sith†
Precipice
Skyborn
Paragon
Savior
Purgatory
Sentinel

3954 *YEARS BEFORE STAR WARS: A New Hope*

The Old Republic: Revan

3650 *YEARS BEFORE STAR WARS: A New Hope*

The Old Republic: Deceived
Red Harvest
The Old Republic: Fatal Alliance
The Old Republic: Annihilation

Lost Tribe of the Sith†
Pantheon
Secrets

2975 *YEARS BEFORE STAR WARS: A New Hope*

Lost Tribe of the Sith†
Pandemonium

1032 *YEARS BEFORE STAR WARS: A New Hope*

Knight Errant

Darth Bane: Path of Destruction
Darth Bane: Rule of Two
Darth Bane: Dynasty of Evil

RISE OF THE EMPIRE
67–0 YEARS BEFORE *STAR WARS: A New Hope*

67 *YEARS BEFORE STAR WARS: A New Hope*

Darth Plagueis

33 *YEARS BEFORE STAR WARS: A New Hope*

Darth Maul: Saboteur*
Cloak of Deception
Darth Maul: Shadow Hunter
Maul: Lockdown

32 *YEARS BEFORE STAR WARS: A New Hope*

*STAR WARS: EPISODE I
THE PHANTOM MENACE*

Rogue Planet
Outbound Flight
The Approaching Storm

22 *YEARS BEFORE STAR WARS: A New Hope*

*STAR WARS: EPISODE II
ATTACK OF THE CLONES*

22–19 *YEARS BEFORE STAR WARS: A New Hope*

The Clone Wars
The Clone Wars: Wild Space
The Clone Wars: No Prisoners

Clone Wars Gambit
Stealth
Siege

Republic Commando
Hard Contact
Triple Zero
True Colors
Order 66

Shatterpoint
The Cestus Deception
The Hive*
MedStar I: Battle Surgeons
MedStar II: Jedi Healer
Jedi Trial
Yoda: Dark Rendezvous
Labyrinth of Evil

*An eBook novella
† Lost Tribe of the Sith: The Collected Stories

THE STAR WARS NOVELS TIMELINE

NEW JEDI ORDER
25–40 YEARS AFTER
STAR WARS: A New Hope

35 YEARS AFTER STAR WARS: A New Hope

LEGACY
40+ YEARS AFTER
STAR WARS: A New Hope

43 YEARS AFTER STAR WARS: A New Hope

45 YEARS AFTER STAR WARS: A New Hope

*An eBook novella

Dramatis Personae

Allana Solo; child (human female)
Bazel "Barv" Warv (Ramoan male)
Ben Skywalker; Jedi Knight (human male)
Cilghal; Jedi Master and healer (Mon Calamari female)
Han Solo; captain, *Millennium Falcon* (human male)
Jagged Fel; Head of State, Galactic Empire
  (human male)
Jaina Solo; Jedi Knight (human female)
Javis Tyrr; journalist (human male)
Kenth Hamner; acting Grand Master of the Jedi Order
  (human male)
Leia Organa Solo; Jedi Knight (human female)
Luke Skywalker; Jedi Grand Master (human male)
Natasi Daala; Galactic Alliance Chief of State
  (human female)
Natua Wan; Jedi Knight (Falleen female)
Tadar'Ro; Aing-Tii liaison (Aing-Tii male)
Vestara Khai; Sith Tyro and apprentice (human female)
Wynn Dorvan; assistant to Admiral Daala (human male)
Yaqeel Saav'etu; Jedi Knight (Bothan female)

A long time ago in a galaxy far, far away. . . .

Prologue

ORBITING ZIOST
TWO STANDARD YEARS AGO

DICIAN FELT THE PLANET EVEN BEFORE IT APPEARED ON THE main bridge monitor of the *Poison Moon*. She sensed it had seen her, as she now saw it, this seemingly harmless world of blue and white and green, and she smiled gently. The pale geometric tattoos on her face, standing out in stark contrast with her dark skin tones, crinkled with her smile. This was the destination she had beheld in her mind's eye a short while before, the unvoiced answer to the question of what she was hoping to intercept here. She had ordered the crew of this frigate to make all speed, and only hoped she was in time.

Where are you going, charming one?

To unopened eyes and dead senses, this planet would seem a world much as any other: a world with oceans and landmasses, heavily, practically entirely forested, with two white, ice-capped poles on either end. White clouds drifted lazily above it.

But it was not a world like any other.

It was Ziost. Homeworld of the Sith.

What was left of the Sith Order now remained silent and in hiding on Korriban. She would return there soon, but not without the prize she had come to claim.

Dician realized she was leaning forward slightly in anticipation, and settled back in her command chair. She gently pushed her excitement down lest it interfere with her mission.

"Wayniss, take us into orbit." In her role as an intelligence gatherer, the light, musical tone of her voice often deceived others into thinking her much, much more harmless than she was. Her crew knew better.

"Yes, Captain," the chief pilot of the *Poison Moon* replied. Wayniss was a laconic man, not at all Force-sensitive, pleased enough to do as he was told in exchange for the generous pay he was receiving. In his own way, the graying ex-pirate was as fair, honorable, and hardworking as many so-called upstanding citizens. He had done well by Dician on this mission already.

"Any sign of the meditation sphere?" she asked Ithila, her sensor officer. Ithila leaned forward, her face, which would have been beautiful in the traditional Hapan manner if not for the horrific burn scar that marred the right side, furrowed in concentration.

"Negative," Ithila replied as Ziost appeared in the forward viewports and the *Poison Moon* settled into orbit around it. "No indication of it on the planet surface." She turned to regard her captain. "Looks like we beat it here."

Dician smiled again. No mistakes. All that remained was to capture the small vessel itself.

Dician settled in to wait, her dark eyes on the slowly turning planet in front of her. It gazed back at her, and she felt a tug in her heart. She wanted to land the *Poison Moon,* to walk Ziost's forests as other Sith had done in ages past. But that was not why they were here. She must think of the good of the One, the Order, above her own yearnings. One day, perhaps, she would stand upon the surface of this world. But that day would not be today.

They did not have long to wait. Only a few moments

later, Ithila said, "Picking it up on long-range sensors, Captain."

Dician sat up straighter in her chair. "You have all served well and brilliantly. Now, as our smuggler pilot might say, it is time to close this deal."

It was time for her, Dician, to be perfect. She could not afford a mistake now.

She felt it even as Ithila transmitted the image to her personal viewscreen. There it was, the Sith meditation sphere. She regarded it for a moment, taking it in—the orange-yellow-red hue, the spherical shape flanked by twin sets of bat-like wings. It resembled an enormous eye.

"Hello again, charming one," she said in her most pleasant voice.

Silence from the sphere.

"As you see, we have anticipated your arrival. Why have you come to Ziost?"

Home.

The voice was inside her head, masculine and intensely focused. A little thrill of exhilaration shivered through Dician. This was not a pet to be coaxed, but a mount to be broken. It respected strength and will.

Dician had plenty of both.

There is a better place for you than on an abandoned world. Dician did not speak the words. Her melodic voice was no asset in this negotiation; the focus and strength of her thoughts were.

The vessel continued its approach to Ziost, not wavering in the slightest, but Dician sensed she had its attention. It would listen.

You are a Sith meditation sphere. Come with me to where the Sith are now. Serve us, as you were designed to do. She let herself visualize Korriban: with not just two Sith, but many who were One, with apprentices in need of focus and training in the power of the dark side if they were to achieve the glory and power that were rightfully theirs.

"It's slowing its approach," Ithila said. "It's come to a full halt."

Dician didn't bother to tell the Hapan woman that she already knew that; that she was intimately connected with this meditation sphere, this . . . Ship.

It seemed particularly interested in the younglings, and she understood that this had been the focus of its design. To protect and educate apprentices. To prepare them for their destinies.

You will come to Korriban. You will serve me, Dician, and you will teach the younglings. You will fulfill your intended purpose.

This was the moment upon which everything hinged. She sensed scrutiny from the vessel. Dician was unashamed of her strengths and let it see her freely. It sensed her will, her drive, her passions, her desire for perfection.

Perfection, said Ship. It mulled over the word.

Nothing less serves the dark side fully, Dician replied. *You will help me to attain perfection for the Sith.*

Perfection cannot be obtained by hiding.

Dician blinked. This had caught her by surprise. *It is wisdom. We will stay isolated, grow strong, and then claim what is ours.*

Ship considered. Doubt gnawed at the corner of Dician's mind like a gizka. She crushed it utterly, ruthlessly, and poured all her will into the demand.

The Jedi grow strong and numerous. It is not time to hide. I will not serve. I will find a better purpose.

She felt it shut down in her mind, close itself off to her in what was tantamount to a dismissal. Dician felt her cheeks grow hot. How could it have refused?

"Captain," said Ithila, "the ship has resumed course to Ziost."

"I can see that," Dician snapped, and Ithila stared openly. Ship was a rapidly disappearing sphere on her screen, and as she watched it was lost to sight.

Dician returned her attention to her crew, who, she realized, were all looking at her with confused expressions on their faces. She took a deep, steadying breath.

"The vessel would not have been appropriate for us," she said, her pleasant voice challenging anyone to disagree. "Its programming is antiquated and outdated. Our original message was successful. It is time to pick up the shuttle crews and return home. Plot a course through hyperspace for Omega Three Seven Nine," she instructed Wayniss. He turned around and his fingers flew lightly over the console.

The *Poison Moon*'s original mission had not been to recover Ship, as Dician had begun thinking of the sphere. Dician had initially been sent to track down a Twi'lek woman named Alema Rar and her base of operations. Rar had somehow inherited a lost Force technique that enabled her to project phantoms across space. Dician had been ordered to destroy both the woman and the dark side energy source lest either fall into Jedi hands. And then she had been forced to choose between two unexpected prizes.

When the *Poison Moon* arrived at Alema Rar's base, coming in stealthed, Dician had discovered they were not alone. One of the two vessels already at the asteroid was none other than the *Millennium Falcon*. Subsequent observations of her operations revealed that it was more than likely her notorious owner Han Solo was piloting—and quite possibly his wife, Leia Organa, traitor to the noble name of Skywalker, was with him. Her crews had placed bombs on the asteroid that had been Alema's base, and Dician, not about to let such a victory slip away, was turning her attention to the destruction of the Corellian freighter.

But before Dician could issue the orders to detonate the bombs and attack the *Falcon,* Ship had emerged from the base—without Alema Rar.

Dician had made the decision to follow and attempt to capture Ship, forgoing an attack on the *Falcon.* She had ordered the bombs to detonate and the crews that had placed them to await her return on the largest asteroid in the system, designated Omega 379. No doubt they were anticipating her swift return.

Dician pressed her full lips together. She had chosen tracking Ship over blowing the *Millennium Falcon* out of the skies. She had done exactly what she had threatened her crew not to do—made a mistake. And now she could claim neither victory.

Let Ship remain isolated on Ziost. It would find no one to serve, no one to permit it to do that which it was designed for.

In her irritation, Dician allowed the thought to comfort her.

Chapter One

JYSELLA HORN FELT LIKE A PART OF HER, LIKE HER BROTHER, was encased in carbonite. Frozen and isolated and unable to move. Yet somehow she forced her legs to carry her forward, toward the Jedi Temple that would, she hoped, have some answers for her today.

Ever since the inexplicable and horrifying moment when her older brother, Valin, had turned on their parents, eyes wild, teeth bared, screaming nonsense, part of the youngest Horn had gone with him into the cold prison in which he was now encased.

She had always been the baby of the family, the tagalong, the *me too!* little sister. Three standard years separated the Horn siblings, and it had only been recently that they had begun relating as friends and not just as brother and sister. Jysella had always idolized her easygoing, levelheaded big brother. The lives of her rather famous family had been fraught with danger almost since the day she was born. Often, she and Valin had been separated from their parents and even from each other for long periods of time. Three Jedi in a family did not make for much time spent doing traditional familial things. But the challenges and the separation had always brought them closer, not driven wedges between them.

Jysella shivered. Cold, she was cold; he was cold and in carbonite, her kind, grinning brother, the gentle and loved one, whom they said was criminally insane. He had attacked both their parents, claiming that they had somehow been stolen away and replaced by *fakes*. How could such a thing have happened? But it had, and Valin had been caught, arrested, and imprisoned in the most horrible way possible.

Bazel Warv laid a heavy jade-green hand on her narrow shoulder as they climbed up the long ceremonial staircase of the Processional Way toward the Jedi Temple. A series of grunts and squeaks issued from his tusked mouth as he offered reassurances.

"I know, I know," Jysella said to the Ramoan with a sigh. His small, piggy eyes were full of compassion. "Everyone's doing their best. It doesn't make it any easier."

Bazel, "Barv" as his little circle of close friends called him, considered this and nodded agreement. He squeezed her shoulder, putting all his concern into the gesture, and Jysella forced herself not to wince. Around his fellow Jedi, Bazel tended to forget how strong he was. With little Amelia, the young war orphan who had been adopted by Han and Leia Solo, though, the Ramoan was gentle to a fault. Amelia often went for rides on Barv's huge shoulders, laughing and giggling. The little girl was fond of everyone in "the Unit," as Barv, Yaqeel Saav'etu, Valin, and Jysella called themselves.

"The big guy's right," Yaqeel, walking on Jysella's other side, commented. "Don't underestimate what a group of top Jedi can do when their backs are against the wall."

Jysella had to force herself again to refrain from wincing, this time from the coolness of the Bothan's words. She'd known both Barv and Yaqeel for a long time.

They had been Valin's friends first, but had drawn Jysella happily into the circle as she grew older.

Yaqeel used words in the same controlled, deadly way she used her lightsaber. Normally the acerbic, cynical comments she was fond of drawling didn't bother Jysella in the slightest. But now she felt . . . raw. Like her emotional skin had been flayed away, and even the slightest breeze caused agony.

Barv oinked, annoyed, and Yaqeel's ear twitched slightly. Barv was convinced that the Jedi were working hard to find a cure for Valin's condition not because their own necks were threatened, but because it was the right thing to do. Because that's what Jedi *did*.

Tears of gratitude stung Jysella's eyes as she smiled at her friend. Yaqeel's ears lowered slightly, a sign that Barv's simple faith had gotten to her as well. That wasn't unusual. Everyone—well, everyone except dear, slightly dense Barv himself—knew that Yaqeel had a soft spot for "the big guy," and no one blamed her for it. Barv was uncomplicated and true, with a heart as big as the galaxy and an unshakable sense of right and wrong.

Jysella desperately wanted to believe him in this case, but the fear, fluttering at the back of her throat like a living thing, prevented it.

"Anyway, honey, we know your brother's got his head screwed on right," Yaqeel said in a gentler tone of voice. "Whatever's happening to him, I'm convinced it's only temporary. What you need to do is stop watching newsvids. They're all about reporting whatever sounds juiciest. And that's usually *not* the truth."

They'd reached the Temple entrance. Once, the Jedi Temple had been notable for its five spires, a unique feature of the Coruscant skyline. But much of that had been destroyed during the Yuuzhan Vong War. A great deal of the interior of the Temple had been restored to its former appearances—right down to the marble patterns on the floors in some cases—but the exterior, a collection of stone and transparisteel pyramids in a variety of sizes, was aggressively modern. Jysella found she missed the familiar statues of four former Masters that once stood guard over the main entrance.

She sighed. She'd just turned around to speak to her friends when she found herself caught up in a nearly crushing hug. A grin curved her lips despite herself and she hugged Barv back.

"Thanks, Barv," she said, using up the last bit of air he'd left in her lungs.

He released her and she gulped oxygen, smiling up at him. Yaqeel embraced her then, all warm, slightly spicy-scented fur and a softness that most people never really got to know. "You'll feel better once you're doing something," Yaqeel said.

Barv allowed that he himself always felt better when he was doing something. Usually that involved attacking bad guys. Yaqeel patted Jysella's cheek. "Sure you don't want us coming in with you?"

"No, it's okay. You two have done enough. I—I don't know what I would have done without you, honestly," Jysella said, the words burbling out of her. "Mom and Dad have been so focused on Valin—and I mean, of course they *should* be focused on him. I am, too. Just—"

"You don't need to say it," Yaqeel interrupted her gently, sensing, as Jysella now did, that if the human girl continued she'd lose what tenuous control she had. "We're the Unit. And the Unit can always rely on each other. You'd have done the same for us."

Barv nodded vigorously. And it was true. Jysella and Valin would have done the same for either of these two friends and fellow Jedi Knights. Done a lot more, as she knew they would have if they had to.

"Well," she said, trying to put a brave face on it, "with you two and the whole Jedi Order, I'm sure we'll have Valin out of that carbonite slab in no time. Though I have to admit, when I was a kid, there were plenty of times when I'd have loved it if he'd been a caf table that didn't talk back."

It was a feeble attempt at humor, but they all seized it and laughed. *Gotta laugh or I'll cry*, Jysella thought. And Valin wouldn't want her to cry. She'd done altogether too much of it in recent days.

Grinning, Yaqeel slipped her arm through Barv's. "Come on. I'll buy you a caf. We still on for lunch, Sella?"

Lunch. She'd forgotten about that. She seemed to be forgetting a lot these days, except the overwhelming longing for everything to be all right again.

"Oh, right. Yes, come back in a few hours. I'm sure I will have annoyed Cilghal sufficiently by then." She laughed, a genuine laugh this time.

It was a good note to end on, and the three remnants of the Unit waved at one another. Jysella watched Barv and Yaqeel walk off, then sighed and turned to enter the Temple. She smiled politely at the five apprentices who were stationed there as guardians.

How many times had she been here before? She had lost count. It had always been a special place, as it was to every Jedi. For long stretches, when she was not out on assignment, it had been home. But now it seemed even more to her to be a bastion of hope. Somewhere within this vast repository of knowledge, some information that could help her brother had to be housed. Some clue as to what had happened to him, and how to put it right.

Barv thought so. Jysella clung to that hope as well.

Her booted feet rang in the vast, open space of the Temple entrance hall as she headed toward the turbolift that would take her to the First Wing of the archives.

She crossed her arms, fidgeting slightly, as the turbolift hummed softly and bore her to the top floor.

She found Cilghal in a small alcove in the depths of the stacks, seated at one of the tables and surrounded by tall piles of glowing blue datatapes and datacards. Her smooth brown head was bent over an ancient text, and her flipper-like hands were encased in gloves to protect the delicate old flimsi. She looked up at Jysella's approach.

"Jysella. Right on time," she said, her gravelly voice warm.

Jysella offered her a weak smile in return and slipped into the seat across from her. Even though this was the arranged time for them to meet, it was clear that Cilghal had been here for a while already.

"I . . ." Jysella sighed and reached out for a datapad, holding it in a limp hand. "I'm sorry, Master Cilghal. I don't even know where to *start* trying to help."

Cilghal regarded her sympathetically, slightly turning her head to fix Jysella with a single large, bulbous eye. "You know everyone is doing everything they can. It is important to us all that your brother recover fully—and that we understand what happened to him. With understanding will, we very much hope, come a cure, and the ability to negotiate his release from Galactic Alliance custody."

Jysella winced and brushed back a lock of reddish brown hair that had escaped the haphazard bun she'd pinned up that morning.

"I know. It . . . it's upsetting that this is only serving to damage the Jedi in the eyes of the public. Valin—he would never have wanted that."

"Of course not," Cilghal soothed. "This is in no way a reflection on your family, Jysella. It is simply a tragic and, temporarily I hope, an inexplicable event."

Cilghal sounded utterly earnest, and Jysella believed

that the Mon Calamari healer meant every word. She knew that Cilghal was, to some degree, against the idea of Jedi having attachments. And yet she was still so kind and supportive to Jysella. It meant a lot.

Still . . . She wished Master Skywalker were here. Although Luke had done everything he could to make sure the transition of power was smooth, the Jedi Order had been thrown into tumult upon his departure. She knew Master Hamner was doing his best in the thankless role of trying to handle everything tactfully, but also knew he wasn't succeeding. The last thing the Order needed was a crazy Jedi Knight running around claiming that people weren't who they were.

And now Valin was encased in carbonite in a GA prison, unable to be with those who loved him, to even comprehend that those who loved him were trying to help him. Empathetically feeling the cold that enshrouded Valin, Jysella wrapped slim arms around her own body and shivered slightly.

Oh, Valin. If only you could tell us what had happened . . . why you looked at Mom and Dad and thought they weren't themselves. How could you not know your own parents?

Tears leaked past her closed lids, and she brushed them away angrily. *Stop it, Sella,* she told herself sternly. Grief and worry would not serve Valin, or the Order, now. Only calmness and knowledge would. She opened her eyes and reached for the discarded datapad.

"That looks like a very old record," she said, lifting her eyes to Cilghal. "Do you have any theories on—"

Jysella felt the blood drain from her face.

The Mon Cal was apparently done with the old flimsi and now was intently studying the information on a datapad. Her large eyes were fastened on it, unblinking in her concentration. The alcove was quiet, save for soft voices talking and the sound of footfalls some distance away. All was as it had been just a moment before.

Except everything—everything—had been turned upside down.

Valin had been right. She saw it now . . .

Jysella inhaled swiftly. It *looked* like Cilghal. Whoever had done this had not missed a detail. It even moved like the Mon Calamari healer. And it had certainly acted and sounded like her. But Jysella suddenly and sickly understood exactly what her brother had meant.

The Not-Cilghal turned to regard Jysella, cocking her head curiously. "Jysella? What is it?"

"N-nothing. I . . . you know what?" She gave a shaky laugh. "I think I may be too upset to help you out much," she managed. She rose. She had to get away, and fast, before this doppelgänger realized she was on to its deception. But where would she go? Who could she tell? If Valin had been right, then everyone except for her had been taken and replaced by their doubles. How could she not have seen this earlier? *Oh, Valin, I'm sorry I didn't believe you—*

The imitation Cilghal looked fully away from the datapad she had been studying and fixed Jysella with one huge, circular eye.

"You've held up very well indeed throughout all this, Jysella," the doppelgänger said gently. "It's not surprising that you might now be finding you cannot carry it all. Do you wish to talk about this? Speaking one's worry and fears can be as healing as bacta tanks, in its own way."

The rough voice was warm and concerned. It only rattled Jysella more. Stang—whoever it was, she was good; she had mastered Cilghal's voice, her inflections, her movements. No wonder she was succeeding at fooling everyone.

But Valin hadn't been fooled, although in his confusion he had mistaken his sister and parents for doppel-gängers like the one before her now.

Oh, no . . . what if he'd been right about Mom and—

"I think I had just better go." One hand dropped casually to her waist, resting on the lightsaber hilt that was fastened there. As a full Jedi Knight, she was authorized to carry the weapon throughout the Temple except in a very few restricted areas. She'd almost forgotten it this morning in her stress over Valin. Now she was tremendously glad she had gone back for it.

Cilghal's eye followed the gesture, and she got to her feet. She had her own weapon, of course, but made no move to draw it. "Jysella, why don't you come with me and we'll—"

Terror shot through Jysella, and a sob escaped her. She stepped back, her hand gripping the lightsaber hilt so hard her knuckles whitened.

"Get away from me!" she screamed, her voice shaking.

"Jysella—" It reached out to her imploringly.

"I said get *away*!"

Jysella drew the lightsaber in one hand and shoved the other in the false Cilghal's direction. The males in her family were unable to use telekinesis. Jysella was not so hampered, and she used that ability now. She put all her fear, all her focus, in the gesture, and Not-Cilghal was caught unawares as Jysella Force-shoved her back into a stack of datapads.

She didn't pause to watch as Cilghal crashed into the stack. By then Jysella Horn, quite possibly the only real person left on the planet—maybe in the galaxy—except for her brother, was racing down the aisle toward the turbolift as fast as she could go.

Cilghal recovered quickly, using the Force to steady the stack and prevent it from toppling entirely. A few datapads clattered to the floor as she rose and reached for her comlink with one hand and her lightsaber with the other. She'd been utterly taken by surprise and mentally rebuked herself.

"Temple security, this is Master Cilghal," she said even as she began racing after the fleeing human. "Jedi Jysella Horn is to be captured and retained. Do not harm her if at all possible. She is not herself. Notify Master Hamner immediately. Tell him—tell him we've got another one."

"Acknowledged," came a crisp, cool voice. Cilghal clicked the comlink off. Time enough for more details once Jysella was safely apprehended.

It was obvious what had happened. Like her brother, Jysella Horn had lost her reason. But unlike Valin, who had been irrationally angry, Jysella was pouring utter and abject fear into the Force. Whatever her mind might be telling her, it was terrifying her beyond anything Cilghal had experienced from a human before.

Compassion combined with a grim determination to prevent the frightened young woman from harming anyone lent the Mon Calamari speed. One way or another, they would stop her. After all, this was the Jedi Temple, and Jysella, although quite a capable Jedi Knight, was hardly unstoppable, even if fueled by insane fear.

Where could she possibly go?

Chapter Two

WHERE COULD SHE GO?

Jysella was trapped, trapped like an animal, and she had to get out, she had to. *Oh Valin, Valin, I'm so sorry I didn't believe you, I'm so sorry I—*

She couldn't take the turbolift. It was too slow, and besides, *they,* the doppelgängers, would shut down the power to it and trap her inside. She'd have to get down to the main floor another way, and she knew exactly how.

The turbolift shaft was located in the center area where the hallways of the Archives came together. Four ramps led over an open space from the halls to the turbolift. There were carved stone banisters at waist height, more for decoration than function. Any Jedi walking over these ramps could glance down and see the corresponding hallways of the floor below.

Jysella did not hesitate for an instant. Clutching her activated lightsaber in one hand, she reached out with the other, placed it on the cool marble of the banister, and vaulted diagonally to the other walkway on the floor below. Using the Force to control the leap, she landed easily. She had just turned her head and was about to jump to the next level when she heard Not-Cilghal's voice.

"Jysella, wait! What you think is not true! No one has stolen us away. We—"

Terror flooded Jysella so that her sweaty hand almost lost its grip. She sprang for the next level, haphazardly and inaccurately, and slammed her knee hard against the marble banister as she clung to it from the side.

She felt the presence of the Jedi rushing toward her, and her head whipped up. She knew this Jedi—or rather, knew who she was supposed to be. The doppelgänger looked exactly like the Falleen female Natua Wan, right down to Natua's preference for blue beads woven into her long black hair. Her lightsaber was activated and she was shouting something at Jysella. Some nonsense about how she didn't want to hurt her, that something wasn't right with Jysella's thinking but that they wanted to help her. And this doppelgänger's skin was changing color, just like a real Falleen's would when she was exuding pheromones in order to trap Jysella—

"Right," she muttered. Jysella couldn't release either the railing or her lightsaber, but Not-Natua had to be stopped before the pheromones took effect. Her eyes lit on a bust that sat on a small table at the end of this hallway. With a quick snap of her head, Jysella threw the carved stone bust of a long-dead Jedi at the being who was impersonating a living one. It slammed hard into Natua's double and she fell.

Jysella didn't want to see if the false Falleen got up. Grimly she dropped down, landing easily on the balls of her feet.

Jysella was on the main floor now. Escape, and safety, temporary though it might be, was just a few moments away. She turned and saw the exit from this wing. It opened onto the huge main hallway. Beyond that, the Promenade, and freedom. Jysella gulped and started running.

She swore under her breath as another Jedi emerged from one of the side stacks. This one looked like a

Brubb, but she didn't recognize him. They were *every-where*, these false ones. So desperate was her need to get out that she didn't even slow. With a snarl, she made a gesture as if she were running her fingers horizontally along one of the shelves. Hundreds of datatapes sprang forward as if thrown from where, a heartbeat before, they had been safely ensconced. They showered down on the Jedi Knight, momentarily distracting him as he tried to deflect them. Brubb were strong, and no doubt this doppelgänger had that quality as well. Little that Jy-sella could throw at him would harm him, but all she needed was to buy a couple of moments—

Coming at the Brubb at a dead run, Jysella threw her lightsaber directly at him. She saw his slitted eyes widen in his pitted yellow-skinned face as the glowing weapon hurtled end over end toward him. He barely got his own lightsaber up in time to bat the blade away. By then Jysella was in the air, vaulting easily over him, extending her hand to call her weapon back to her.

She landed lightly, raced through the entrance, then whirled and touched the button that caused the door to this wing to slam shut.

He could open it from the other side, she knew. To prevent that, she shoved her lightsaber hilt-deep into the controls. They crackled and hissed, and her nose wrinkled at the acrid burning smell.

It wouldn't hold them for long, but she'd bought herself a precious moment to *think*, blast it; clear her head and think. She was prey, trapped in the rancor's lair, and she had to get out—

She took a slow, steadying breath, and with the control of a Jedi Knight she calmed her racing, terrified thoughts. Jysella closed her eyes for a moment, breathing in through her nose and out through her mouth, and then slowly opened them.

And saw something very strange.

* * *

Cilghal caught up with Radd Minker as the Brubb was using his lightsaber to cut a hole in the door. She reached out into the Force, trying to sense Jysella, startled to realize that the young woman was still on the other side of the door.

"Cilghal to security," she said on her comlink. "Jysella Horn is directly outside the Archives on the south side. She has closed the door and destroyed the controls. Jedi Minker is currently cutting through the door with his lightsaber. My guess is that once she catches her breath she'll head straight for the Promenade exit. She's frightened, and I anticipate she'll take the most direct route. Expect her to bolt."

"Acknowledged. She won't get past us."

Cilghal replaced the comlink on her belt and extended her thoughts into the Force, trying again to see if she could reach Jysella and calm the panicked human.

She braced herself for the expected, almost animalistic fear that had buffeted her the first time she'd reached out to Jysella. Instead, she found something else entirely. The fear was still there, yes, but over and around it was something that was only vaguely familiar to Cilghal, and the Mon Cal healer couldn't quite place it. She frowned, letting herself drop in deeper.

Jysella saw *herself*, racing down the hallway toward freedom. The hallway was flanked by large pillars on either side, supporting the beautifully carved roof. Before her astonished gaze, hitherto concealed doors in two pillars opened and two security droids emerged.

They started attacking her at once. Jysella watched, trying to understand what she was seeing, as her other self batted back bolts so quickly her lightsaber was nothing more than a blue blur. Was this really her, or just her imagination? What was going on? From the entrance, the five apprentices she had seen half an hour before—had nodded to in greeting—came rushing in. One of them was shouting something into a comlink.

The other Jysella lunged forward and brought her lightsaber down on one of the security droids. It sliced clean through the metal and wires. She flipped just as the other droid was firing, executing a one-handed cartwheel and lashing out with her lightsaber.

This droid, too, was disabled, slowing to a halt, black smoke emanating from it. By then the other Jysella was on her feet, and the apprentices were on her.

She watched, amazed at her own courage and determination, as she fought wildly. She did not escape unscathed. One blow dragged across her cheek, searing in a black burn. Another blow nearly severed her left arm.

Still, the other Jysella fought on. One by one, she slew them, dropping the false apprentices until there were none left. She did not mourn them; they were not really apprentices, simply more imposters. In agony, she stepped quickly over the bodies and made for the doors.

Jysella cried out as she watched what happened next. So close—she was so close to making it. But even as the other Jysella was bathed in sunlight from outside, the shield at the entrance to the Temple was activated. Jysella let out a sob as she watched herself writhing, trying to escape, caught as surely as an insect trapped in a spider's web.

"No!" Jysella cried aloud. She had been mesmerized, watching this strange scene unfold, and was suddenly seized with a realization. And there was a way for her to prove this realization right.

She knew, as all Jedi knew, that there were all kinds of security measures in place at the Temple. The past had starkly shown that even a Temple with Jedi in it could still be violated. Jysella, like all the Jedi Knights and probably most of the Masters, wasn't privy to exactly

what many of these security measures were. At least, she
had never been before, but if her guess was correct . . .

She sprinted to the pillars. If she had indeed somehow
been granted a glimpse into the future, then a droid was
ensconced within. With a grunt, she thrust her lightsaber
in at the exact spot where she suspected the droid's
center would be. The lightsaber cut through the marble
pillar—and into the metal and wiring of a security droid.
With a whiny hiss and crackle, it was disabled before it
was even alerted to attack her. Elated, Jysella leapt across
the main hall to the other pillar and repeated the process.

She turned her head to the exit. She didn't see the apprentices coming at her yet—which meant she had a
chance. Quickly she turned back the way she had come
and saw the telltale outline of the door to a service corridor, opened it, and ducked inside. She closed the door
behind her, then dived behind the large outline of one of
the larger, more industrial-duty cleaning droids. She
curled up, trembling, hugging her knees to her chest as
she had when she was a little girl, and concentrated on
masking her presence within the Force.

Jysella had bolted, and Cilghal didn't know where. She
only knew that the presence on the other side of the
door, so very frightened and yet tinged with that strange
sense of there-not-there, was gone.

Quickly she clicked her comlink. "Jysella is on the
move," she said. "Get people at the main entrance immediately. I think she may be heading for it."

There came a few seconds of silence interrupted only
by the protesting sound of the door as the lightsaber
slowly cut a circle through it. The doors were meant to
be activated in case of an intruder in the Temple, to protect the Archives, or in case of another disaster such as
fire. Thus these doors were not the easiest to get
through, not even for a lightsaber, and Radd Minker's

blade was dragging, like a stick through poured and setting duracrete, as he determinedly kept going. It would
take several more precious seconds before they were
through, and Cilghal didn't think Jysella Horn had several more seconds. She was dreadfully worried that the
confused young woman would get herself killed.

"It's impossible!" came a sudden yelp from the comlink. Cilghal, who had seen enough to know that the
word *impossible* was one not to be bandied about
lightly, didn't comment on the exclamation. She asked,
"What's happened?"

"She—the locations of the security droids are strictly
on a need-to-know basis." This was true—even Cilghal
didn't know where they were ensconced. "There's only a
handful of my team who have that information. And yet
Jysella targeted and destroyed the two we were just
about to activate. She couldn't *possibly* have determined
their locations at all, let alone in so short a time."

Cilghal thought about the strange resonances she had
sensed from Jysella a few moments before, and unease
stirred inside her as a suspicion began to form.

"Go on," said Cilghal, her enormous eyes on the
slowly moving blade.

"And she's not heading for the main entrance. We
don't know where she's heading."

"She's going to want to get out, I can assure you of
that much," Cilghal said. "I would send the security
teams to every other exit."

"Yes, Master Cilghal."

Cilghal sighed. Radd threw her an apologetic glance.
"I'm sorry this is taking so long, Master."

"Perhaps I can assist," said Cilghal. Her lightsaber activated with a *snap-hiss*. She stepped forward and plunged
it into the door, feeling the resistance, and began to slowly
pull it through the material to meet up with Radd's inci-
sion. It was tricky, doing this in tandem. There was the

risk of suddenly feeling the metal yield and having both lightsabers collide while surrounded by white-hot metal, which was why Cilghal hadn't stepped forward before. But Jysella's life possibly hung in the balance.

Cilghal would just have to focus.

Jysella felt them rush past her, sensed their concentration on reaching the exits, their focus so great that they failed to search the immediate area in the Force. That was why they were still just apprentices.

No, she thought. They weren't. They were imposters. That was why they hadn't sensed her. A shiver ran through her and for a moment she was so frightened she couldn't move. Then, through sheer will, she forced her legs to unfold and got to her feet.

She pressed the door with her hand, and it slid open. There was no one, nothing, between her and the exit. The guardian apprentices had gone off elsewhere. What about the shield that had been the downfall of her future self?

Wait—one of the apprentices had been speaking into his comlink as he ran toward her. Was it then that it was activated, when they knew she was heading for it? Had he already contacted security?

There was no time to head for another exit, no time to sit and concentrate to see if she could again find her future self to learn what had happened. Jysella took a deep breath, grasped her lightsaber firmly, and ran down the empty hall.

She tensed as she approached the entrance, the daylight coming through and pooling on the carpeted floor, expecting at any moment to feel the energetic net being dropped around her.

Nothing happened.

Jysella bit back a sob of relieved joy and raced out to freedom.

Chapter Three

YAQEEL SIPPED THE HOT, DARK BEVERAGE AND GLANCED AT the newcomer to the tapcaf. He was human, slender but not scrawny. He had a full head of hair, tawny and immaculately styled, and his clothing was fashionable but tastefully understated. His face was quite handsome by human standards, but the full lips seemed to her to be held in a constant smirk. Yaqeel's sensitive nose detected some sort of musky scent about him. She had learned that humans liked to adorn themselves with "perfume" or "cologne," as it was called, apparently not trusting in their own natural scents to attract the opposite sex. Bothans had no such concerns. They all smelled unique and almost all smelled appealing. At least to other Bothans. She cast a glance at Barv and wondered what he thought of her scent.

Barv was enjoying his caf in silence, his oversized hands holding an appropriately oversized mug. His jade face, with the thick, boxy snout and strong chin that often made him look so glowering and imposing to others, was relaxed in what Yaqeel recognized as comfortable good cheer.

Yaqeel turned her eyes back to the stranger, noting the well-manicured hands that accepted a portable cup. Now that she looked again, he seemed familiar to her somehow. Not the scent, she'd have remembered that, but his looks. Was he a holovid star? She watched the occasional one that Valin and Jysella had recommended to her and found them passably entertaining, but she couldn't identify him. The stranger paid and walked out. He strode off briskly, and a droid that had been patiently waiting outside suddenly lifted and floated after him.

A Hologlide J57 cam droid.

And Yaqeel realized where she knew the stranger from. Her eyes narrowed and she growled softly, her fur rippling in displeasure.

"A *journalist*," she spat, infusing the single word with the same disgust and loathing with which she would have said *A Sith*.

Barv grunted, but he allowed that journalists, despite Yaqeel's personal opinion, were beings, too, and they should be allowed to buy a cup of caf if they felt so inclined.

A pedestrian hurtled through the tapcaf's window right about then, transparisteel folding about him as he hit a table, and the conversation was dropped.

Both Jedi Knights leapt to their feet, weapons in hand but not activated, and raced outside as the customers inside screamed and ducked. A soft, pudgy Ortolan, screaming and flailing his blue arms and legs, ears flapping wildly, hurtled toward Barv. Still calm, he lifted a massive hand and Force-caught the Ortolan, lowering him gently to the ground. Yaqeel's lightsaber *snaphiss*ed to life and she extended her senses, reaching past the chaos and fear to identify the source of the disturbance.

It took less than a second, and her eyes lit upon the miscreant at the same instance the Force directed Yaqeel's attention toward her. Her feline jaw gaped for a precious second.

"Jysella?"

She was there, just outside the Jedi Temple, her lightsaber lit and clutched in one hand while her other was extended, clearing a path through the crowd and battering back any would-be attackers. Jysella's eyes were huge, and even at this distance her friends could see the combination of terror and determination in them.

"*Stang,*" muttered Yaqeel. Barv was right beside her, and moving as one, the two raced toward their friend and fellow Jedi. Barv rapidly began to outpace the Bothan, moving much more swiftly than most would expect of the large Ramoan. Neither he nor Yaqeel knew who was attacking Jysella, but it didn't matter. She was Sella, a member of the Unit, and—

Time seemed to slow. In that stretched-out moment, Yaqeel watched as Jysella tensed. The human Jedi could not possibly have seen Barv running to her side, and somehow Yaqeel didn't think Jysella sensed him in the Force. Jysella didn't seem to react so much as she simply leapt and sprang. Barv was suddenly and unexpectedly jostled by a fleeing crowd member—that was something he needed to work on, Yaqeel thought disconnectedly, he tended to hyperfocus in moments of crisis—and ended up several steps to the right of where he had been running.

And yet Jysella was there.

The lightsaber descended so fast that Barv barely was able to block it with his own in time. Yaqeel stared, stunned into inaction for a moment. Why was Jysella—

"It's not you!" Jysella was screaming as she pressed the attack. She seemed to know exactly when Barv would duck, would parry, would push forward, would execute a Force leap. It would have been astonishing to watch, almost balletic, if it weren't for the horror that Jysella Horn was fighting another Jedi, and not just any Jedi, but one who was among her best friends in the galaxy.

Fortunately for Barv, Jysella's uncanny and hitherto unguessed-at ability to predict where he would be at any given moment seemed mitigated by her panic. She was sloppy, shaking, and Barv, who never seemed to get rattled by anything, managed to defend himself—until Jysella screamed out, "Give me my friend back!" and her glowing weapon sliced across Barv's midsection.

Yaqeel cried out as Barv staggered back. Fortunately Jysella's weapon had barely grazed him. It was a smoking wound, but not deep, and could be treated. Yaqeel's eyes met Barv's. She realized now what had happened. Even as pity and sympathy for Jysella washed through her, the Bothan knew that she had to be stopped.

Preferably by fellow Jedi.

Even more preferably, by Yaqeel.

Crying incoherently, her mouth made ugly by a snarl, Jysella bore down on the Ramoan. Yaqeel's hand shot out, grasped air, and pulled. Barv's huge green body was suddenly invisibly yanked out of the path of Jysella's slicing lightsaber. The weapon made a buzzing sound as it sliced empty air where a fraction of an instant earlier Barv had stood. Had Yaqeel not intervened, the Ramoan would have been sliced in two.

Jysella whirled, her gaze impaling Yaqeel. Then her eyes widened in horror and grief.

"Oh, no . . . not Yaqeel, too!" she cried brokenly, almost whimpering, and if it were not for the fact that the human girl had just almost killed Barv that sound would have cracked Yaqeel's heart. Instead she wrapped it in durasteel and hardened herself to what had to be done.

She glanced around frantically in the instant before Jysella sprang. There was nothing she—ah, the cam droid. There it was, hovering about the now panicking crowd, faithfully recording the incident. And over there, that journalist speaking into something in his hand. It would be all over the newsvids tonight—might already be—actual footage of a Jedi going nuts and attacking civilians and fellow members of her own Order. The GA would have a field day with that.

Yaqeel reached out again with the Force, snagged the cam, and alternately pulled the droid in Jysella's direction and pushed the charging Jedi backward.

Except again, *somehow* Jysella knew it was going to happen. She turned with more than enough time to methodically slice the cam droid into three chunks, which she then directed back at Yaqeel. The Bothan Jedi was dimly aware of the reporter yelling, "Hey! What are you doing? That's valuable property!"

His irritation gave Yaqeel a tiny spark of pleasure. The pleasure quickly vanished when she realized that Jysella was running at her—but then the human Jedi vaulted over Yaqeel's head at dizzying speed. Yaqeel whirled, set to pursue. Jysella had covered a great deal of distance already; clearly, she was more interested in escaping than in fighting.

But it didn't look like she was going to. Even as Yaqeel followed, several GA vehicles pulled up. Their doors slid open and disgorged several men and women clad in the blue uniforms and helmets of Galactic Alliance Security. They immediately started firing on Jysella.

She leapt, ducked, and moved her lightsaber in a blue blur, batting the stun blasts back at those who were firing on her. For a wild second Yaqeel thought Jysella was going to make good her escape. But there came a blast that was either simply one too many for her to handle or else one she had failed with her preternatural senses to anticipate. In midleap, Jysella Horn was struck by a bolt and rendered unconscious. And because she loved her friend, and because she knew that something dreadful had happened to Jysella to make her act this way, Yaqeel reached out with the Force, caught her, and lowered her gently to the pavement.

The GA converged on Jysella like a swarm of insects. Yaqeel glanced back at Barv and was relieved to see that he was on his feet, although he was clearly in pain. He nodded to her and she nodded back, turning toward the guards who had clustered around Jysella.

It would have made for an odd picture, had one not known that Jysella was a Jedi Knight: seven heavily armed officers clustered around one slight human female, their blasters still pointed at her as one of their own quickly bent over the limp form, retrieved her lightsaber, and began to pat her down for any other weapons. One of them snapped restraining devices on her slender wrists.

This was bad. The GA had already gotten their hands on one Jedi who appeared to have gone berserk. They sure didn't need another to encase in carbonite and hang on a wall like some sick trophy or credential. If only Yaqeel and Barv had been able to bring her in.

A thought struck Yaqeel, and she smiled a little to herself. Deactivating her lightsaber and returning it to her belt, she strode briskly up to the nearest GA officer.

"Good work," she said. She extended her thoughts, brushed those of the Quarren male who was speaking into a small handheld device. "A smooth capture. I'm sure your superiors will agree that the Jedi belongs in the Temple. I'll take charge of the prisoner from here."

The Quarren's tentacles twitched in irritation, and even before he spoke Yaqeel knew she'd picked the wrong target. "Not likely, Jedi. Take your mind tricks elsewhere and step back before I have you arrested for interfering with the prisoner's arrest. She was taken down by the GA and will go to them for evaluation."

"You're going to just stick her in carbonite!" Yaqeel burst out, her fur rippling in anger. "She's a Jedi, and the Temple's right here!"

The tentacles twitched, this time obviously in amusement. "Too bad you didn't bring her down a few meters from here then, isn't it? This is not your jurisdiction, *Jedi*."

He almost spat the word. Yaqeel seethed, but the Quarren was right. Legally, the GA had authorization here. The fight with Jysella had taken only a couple of minutes, although it had felt like an eternity, and now she watched as several Jedi, lightsabers glowing, poured from the Temple only to halt in their tracks, as helpless as she. She turned away from the sight of their shocked expressions to watch, impotent and furious and heartsick, as one of her best friends was trussed up and bustled quickly into a vehicle.

The door slammed shut.

Stang.

Accepting, if not liking, the fact that she could do nothing for Jysella now, Yaqeel turned and trotted back to Barv. Some of the other Jedi had already reached him, and Cilghal herself had put a flippered hand on the Ramoan's shoulder and was gently guiding him back to the Temple. No one was going to stop this particular Jedi from receiving Jedi medical aid.

Barv allowed that he had certainly felt better, but had complete confidence in Cilghal's abilities to heal him—and, eventually, to heal Valin and Jysella.

Cilghal caught Yaqeel's attention and sighed. "I saw it happen, right before my eyes," she said quietly. "We'll be debriefing both you and Bazel here. Come back with me to the Temple. We'll take care of Bazel, and then we will talk."

Yaqeel nodded miserably. Her ears twitched at a sound and she turned to see a multipassenger speeder, distinctively marked with the seal of the Galactic Alliance, pull up right beside the cluster of officials.

"Just when I thought it couldn't get worse," she growled.

Chapter Four

THE SPEEDER DOOR SLID OPEN, AND AN ATTRACTIVE OLDER human female stepped out. Her crisp white admiral's uniform molded to a figure that was still fit and toned. Green eyes took in the situation at once, keen as lasers in a face framed by copper-colored hair only beginning to gray, and as Admiral Natasi Daala, Galactic Alliance Chief of State, moved assuredly forward, Yaqeel's heart sank.

A 3PO protocol droid followed her and addressed the crowd that was beginning to quiet down now at the presence of GA Security. All were curious as to what their Chief of State had to say about this event. Yaqeel glanced over the crowd and frowned as she saw the reporter holding a small cam and speaking intently into it, then directing it toward Daala. She had hoped that the coverage of the event would have stopped with the destruction of the cam droid, but apparently the journalist had a backup.

"Your attention please, good citizens," said the protocol droid in its pleasant, crisp voice. "Chief of State Daala has a few words to address to you."

The crowd murmured expectantly, then fell silent. The Jedi supporting Barv stayed where they were.

"This should be good," Yaqeel muttered sarcastically.

Cilghal silenced her with a pointed glare from a single eye.

Daala waited until her staff had set up a makeshift podium, complete with a microphone, then stepped forward. She did not speak immediately, only regarded the crowd intently.

"A short while ago, Valin Horn, Jedi Knight, appeared to go insane," Daala said without preamble. Her voice was slightly husky, but pleasant to the ear. Still, Yaqeel winced at the choice of words. Daala obviously was not going to pull any punches.

"He claimed not to recognize his own parents. He claimed they were doppelgängers—identical replacements of people he had known and loved all his life." Daala paused to let the ludicrousness of the notion sink in to the now avidly listening throng. "And in escaping these evil duplicates, he caused a great deal of property damage and physical harm as he attempted to elude capture. Fortunately—and with little thanks to the Jedi Order, who consistently stood in our way—the GA was able to obtain custody of Valin Horn. Deemed criminally insane, he is now safely imprisoned in carbonite, unable to harm anyone further."

Daala paused to take a sip of water. Yaqeel was willing to bet she wasn't really thirsty, just making a dramatic pause. "Today," the Chief of State continued, "Jysella Horn, Jedi Knight and *sister to Valin Horn* demonstrated identical behavior. Fortunately, her capture was swift and decisive, and she is safely in Galactic Alliance hands. There will be no 'negotiations' for her release with the Jedi this time. She will be taken directly from here to the same facility in which her brother is incarcerated. Once any injuries she sustained in resisting arrest are properly treated, she will be frozen in carbonite."

Cilghal lowered her head and closed her eyes. Yaqeel

felt a lump in her throat. She thought of Master Corran and his wife, Mirax. Both of their children—how would they endure it?

Daala continued mercilessly. "It is becoming brutally clear that there is something going wrong with the Jedi. They are intelligent, trained warriors, with powers that most of us can barely comprehend. Their former leader, erstwhile Grand Master Luke Skywalker, failed in his duty to protect the public from one Jedi who sought to obtain power. As all of you know, he pleaded guilty to the charge of reckless endangerment of a population. For this crime, Luke Skywalker has been sentenced to exile for ten Coruscant years unless he can produce a convincing argument and evidence that he is able to properly control and manage his Order.

"Now we have not one, but *two* Jedi who appear to be having dangerous hallucinations that even the Jedi themselves cannot properly explain. Rest assured, we will investigate and explore all possible explanations for this baffling and unsettling development. In the meantime, the Jedi will continue to come under heavy scrutiny and remain under the watchful eye of the government. I will now accept a few questions."

As Yaqeel had known he would, the reporter shouldered his way to the front, raising his hand. He was not alone—apparently the incident, brief and comparatively bloodless as it had been, had drawn the newshounds like krakanas to chum-infested waters. Daala smiled a little at them. Her emerald eyes flickered over the crowd, and then she pointed at someone.

"Javis Tyrr," she said. "Please ask your question."

"Admiral," the first reporter said, his voice smooth and cultured and perfectly paced and pitched—Yaqeel was really beginning to hate this guy—"do you honestly think it can possibly be coincidence that the two Jedi who have displayed such aberrant behavior are siblings?"

"There are many factors to take into account in our investigation, but certainly we will be looking into any genetic causes for this display of uncontrollable violence and paranoia. We will also consider the environment in which these two Jedi have been raised."

"So would it be fair to say you think that because the Horn siblings are the children of a Corellian Jedi Master and the grandchildren of a well-known smuggler, these factors might have caused this mental condition?"

"Don't go putting words into my mouth, Tyrr," Daala admonished, but there was no real ire in her tone. "I simply said we would consider the environment in which they were raised, that's all."

"Do you think this is a hitherto unknown manifestation of simply being Jedi?" Tyrr plowed on, although Daala had turned away and was looking at another reporter with his hand imploringly raised.

By this point, Yaqeel's hand had closed on her lightsaber, as had Barv's, although he grunted with pain at the effort. A flippered hand touched her wrist, slightly moist, cool, and sending calm through the Force.

"Don't," said Cilghal in a quiet voice. "Don't give them any more ammunition to use against us. I for one have heard enough, and I daresay that we'll be seeing this particular speech played and replayed often enough on the HoloNet that we can pick up anything we've missed. Come. Let us get Bazel treated and we will talk."

Yaqeel growled softly and nodded. Cilghal spoke wisdom, although it pained the Bothan to sit by and listen to such disgusting things being said about Valin and Jysella's parentage.

"To think anyone would stoop that low," she muttered, and turned to follow the other Jedi. She moved to one side of Barv, smiling reassuringly up at him as she slipped his arm around her shoulders to assist him as he walked. Cilghal was on his other side. They and the other Jedi who had emerged from the Temple moved steadily, unobtrusively back toward their sanctuary. But apparently not unobtrusively enough.

"Jedi!" came Javis Tyrr's voice. Yaqeel froze in her tracks. Barv turned his massive head to regard the reporter. In his grunting, guttural language, he chided Tyrr for not covering the news impartially and for clearly harboring a bias. Such behavior, Barv said, was not becoming for a journalist, and Tyrr should know better. While the rebuke was mild, the Ramoan language always sounded as if the speaker were trying to take someone's head off verbally, and Tyrr, clearly not understanding a word of it, recoiled ever so slightly.

"Do you have any comments on Admiral Daala's speech? I witnessed the fight between you two and Jysella Horn. I take it you were trying to stop her? Can you tell us why? How much of a threat is she? How far-reaching is this strange mental illness?"

Cilghal, displaying more patience in her right flipper than Yaqeel had in her entire furry body, stepped forward before the Bothan could retort.

"The Jedi are obviously very concerned about the current state of events, and have been since the first incident. We are doing everything we can."

She gave him a smile and then turned decisively back toward the Temple. Yaqeel knew she shouldn't, but she couldn't resist casting one more glowering glance over her shoulder at Javis Tyrr.

"This can't be good," she murmured.

Daala leaned back into the comfortable nerf-hide upholstery of her chauffeured speeder and sighed, running a hand through her hair. Across from her sat her personal assistant, Wynn Dorvan. Slight, nondescript, but always looking completely pulled together with not a brown hair out of place, he had become invaluable to her over the last year and a half. So invaluable that she had relaxed regulations and permitted him to allow his pet chitlik to accompany him from time to time. It perched on his shoulder now, a small, orange-striped marsupial from Ord Cestus that had become all the rage as a pet. It was quiet, litter-trained, and had a tendency to find a dark place to sleep most of the day, so the little creature was not much of a distraction for either Dorvan or Daala.

It had been Dorvan who had been scanning the HoloNet when the coverage began, and he who had notified her of what was happening. Now he glanced up at her, calm and yet eager, his datapad in his hands as he awaited her comments and perhaps further instructions. The chitlik snuffled at his ear, then jumped down and curled up quietly beside him.

"Well done, Dorvan," she said. "I don't know how you managed to get the GA on this so fast. It was completely under control by the time I even got here, and we didn't waste a moment."

"Jedi mind tricks," he deadpanned, his thin lips only cracking into a smile when he saw the amusement on his employer's face.

"Careful who you joke with about that," Daala said, sobering. "While I can't complain about the political leverage incidents like this provide, it is . . . troublesome. I have always had my issues with the Jedi." There were many things, and people, and organizations, she'd had issues with. The Jedi had almost had to get in line, but she'd had her eye on them for a while.

"Keep them in their box, away from politics, and certainly *never* arm them," she'd once said to bounty hunter Boba Fett. Now that she was in a position to do precisely that, it seemed more and more like a good policy. "It is certainly convenient that there's reason to tighten the reins on them, but it's more than that. What's going on with them now . . ." She sighed and shook her head, her unbound hair waving gently, and peered out the tinted reinforced transparisteel window. Dorvan dropped a hand to pet the sleeping animal beside him, and waited patiently as she gathered her thoughts.

"This is dangerous and unpredictable. And I don't like what I can't predict. They're far too powerful to simply be allowed to run amok like this. If they can't even control their own members, they are a very real threat. One that has to be contained for the greater good."

Wynn nodded, not necessarily agreeing—his approval carried no weight, and both he and she knew that—but in acknowledgment of her words.

"Master Kenth Hamner wishes to meet with you tomorrow. Will you be available?"

Daala considered for a moment. "No," she said. "Isn't my schedule too tightly booked for that?"

Again, the ghost of the not-quite-grin. "It is indeed. You couldn't possibly spare him any time for at least . . ." He entered some data and looked up at her inquiringly. "Three more days?"

Jysella Horn would be locked away like her brother within the hour. Hamner would have to arrange a meeting with his fellow Masters, and probably, frankly, contact Luke Skywalker, even though it violated the terms of Luke's exile. That shouldn't take more than a day or two, given that most of the Masters seemed to be sticking close to Coruscant these days.

So that would give her one, two days to leave the Jedi Council stewing and fretting. Long enough to work in her favor, not so long that she looked like she was neglecting a duty.

"Perfect," she said. "I wonder if I should promote

you, Wynn." She graced him with the smile that still managed to disconcert men of almost all ages.

"Oh, please don't, ma'am," he said, sounding utterly sincere. "Right where I am is just perfect. Any higher and I'd have to have someone under me, and that just wouldn't do."

Daala laughed.

Chapter Five

THE OCEAN SIGHED AS IT RUSHED FORWARD AND RECEDED in a rhythm even more ancient than what was unfolding on its lavender-sand shores. While the sun was bright and warm, a breeze came from the sea to cool the heated faces of the two figures standing there.

They faced each other, as still as if they were carved from stone, the only motion around them that of their hair and heavy black robes as the wind toyed with them.

Then, as if by some unheard signal, one of them moved. The soft sound of the ocean was punctuated by a sharp *snap-hiss*. The almost perfectly symmetrical, light purple features of Vestara Khai's adversary were abruptly cast into sickly green relief. Vestara activated her own weapon with a fluid motion, saluted her opponent with it, settled into position, and waited to see who would make the first move. She balanced lightly on the balls of her booted feet, ready to leap left, right, or straight up. Still her opponent did not move.

The sun was at its height and its light was harsh, beating down on them like something physical. Their heavy dark robes were stifling hot, but Vestara would no sooner abandon her robes than she would abandon her weapon or her heritage. The robes were traditional, ancient, a deep and valued part of who she was, and she would endure the encumbrance. The Tribe valued strength as much as it valued beauty; rewarded patience as much as initiative. The wise being was the one who knew when which was called for.

Vestara sprang.

Not at her opponent, but to the left and past him, leaping upward, turning in the air, and slashing outward with the blade. She felt the blade impact and heard its distinctive sizzle. He gasped as she landed, flipped, and crouched back into a defensive position. The sandy surface was treacherous, and her foot slipped. She righted herself almost instantly, but that moment was all he needed to come at her.

He hammered her with blows that were more of strength than grace, his lithe body all lean muscle. She parried each strike, the blades clashing and sizzling, and ducked underneath the final one. Lightness and agility were her allies, and she used them freely.

Her long, light brown hair had come loose from its quickly twisted braid, and the tendrils were a distraction. She blew upward to clear her vision just in time to block another one of the strong blows.

"Blast," she muttered, leaping back and switching the blade to her other hand. She was completely ambidextrous. "You're getting good, Ahri."

Ahri Raas, apprentice, member of the native—and conquered—species of Keshiri and Vestara Khai's close friend, offered her a smile. "I'd say the same about you, Ves, except for the fact that that sand-jump messes you up every single ti—"

She interrupted him with a sudden upward leap, landing on his shoulders, balancing there lightly with the use of the Force, and plunged the lightsaber straight downward, aiming for his back between his shoulder blades. He dived forward, Force-pushing her off, but not before she had touched the tip of the glowing red blade to his robes. Ahri arched, his dive thrown off as his body twisted from the pain; even the training lightsabers inflicted a powerful shock.

Vestara leapt as Ahri dived, using his Force push to her own advantage, turning twice in the air and landing surely, facing him. She smirked in satisfaction as she brushed her renegade locks out of the way. Ahri completed his dive and came to his feet, rolling in the sand. Vestara extended her arm with the grace of a dancer. Ahri's lightsaber was snatched from his hand and flew into hers. She grasped it and dropped into the Jar'Kai stance, ready to come at him with both blades. Ahri looked up and sighed, dropping back into the sand.

"And you get distracted far too easily. Focus, Ahri, focus," she chided. She gestured casually, just a slight jerk of her chin, and a handful of sand flew toward Ahri's face. Muttering, he lifted his empty hand and used the Force to deflect the grains.

"It's just training, Ves," he muttered, getting to his feet and dusting himself off.

"It's *never* just training," she shot back. She deactivated her training lightsaber, hooked it back on her belt, and tossed Ahri's to him. The Keshiri youth caught it easily, still looking disgruntled. Vestara undid her hair and fluffed it for a minute, letting the air penetrate to the roots to cool her scalp. Her long fingers busily rebraided it, properly this time, as she continued to speak, while Ahri shook grains of purple sand out of his own white, shoulder-length hair.

"How often have I told you that? Say that in the presence of one of the Masters and you'll never make it beyond a Tyro."

Ahri sighed and rose, nodding to acknowledge the truth of what she said. Neither of them had been formally chosen as an apprentice yet, although they had been training in classes under the tutelage of various Masters for years, their strengths and weaknesses in the Force noted and analyzed and pushed.

Vestara knew that, at fourteen, it was still possible, even likely, that she would be chosen by a Master as his or her formal apprentice. But she chafed horribly at the delay. Some Tyros were chosen at much younger ages, and Vestara knew that she was strong in the Force.

She reached out for a flask of now warm water and the canteen resting on the sand floated to her, the lid unfastening as it moved. Vestara gulped down the liquid thirstily. Sparring at the height of the sun was exhausting, and Ahri always muttered about it, but she knew it toughened her. Vestara handed the canteen to Ahri, who also drank.

She regarded him for a moment. He was a nearly perfect physical specimen of a species whose physical strength, agility, and harmony of features and form had become an ideal for her own people. He could easily pass for a member of her own species—he would make a striking human, but a human nonetheless—were it not for the pale purple cast to his skin. His eyes, too, were slightly larger than a human's; large and expressive. His shoulders were broad, his hips narrow, and there was not an ounce of superfluous fat on his frame. His face, though, was flushed a darker purple than usual because he was overheated, and his hair had far too much sand in it.

"That's two for two," she said. "You up for another round?" She gave him a wicked grin, which was exaggerated by the small scar at the corner of her mouth. The scar that the Tribe saw as a flaw. It was plain on her face, right out in the open—there was very little she could do to disguise it. Attempts had been made to heal it and to correct it with cosmetic surgery. Those attempts had been mostly successful and now, to be sure, it was not all that noticeable. But this was a world where any flaw, any scar or deformity, was a strike against one's potential for advancement.

The scar added insult to injury, as far as Vestara was concerned—because of its location, the thin line almost always made her look like she was smiling, even when she wasn't. She had hated that about it until Lady Rhea, one of the most respected of the Sith Lords, had told her that deception was actually a very useful thing indeed.

"It mars your beauty," Lady Rhea had said bluntly, pausing as she strolled down the line of potential apprentices after a formal ceremony. "A pity." She, whose beauty was only slightly diminished by the cruel ravages of time, reached out a long finger and touched the scar. "But this little scar—it can aid you. Make others think you are *something you are not.*" She tapped the scar lightly with each of the last four words, emphasizing her point.

That had made Vestara feel a bit better. All of a sudden, looking like she was smiling all the time, even when she wasn't, seemed like a good thing to her.

"I think I've sweated off at least two liters already," Ahri replied. "Can't we continue in the training courtyard at least? It's cooler in the mountain shadows."

At least he wasn't refusing the offer of another round. Vestara dragged a black-draped arm across her own forehead. She had to admit, fighting in the cool shadows of the proud columns, beautiful statuary, and sheer mountain stone in which the Temple courtyard was nestled had a definite appeal right at the moment. While they were not yet formally apprenticed to any of the Sabers or the Masters, as Tyros they would be permitted to spar in the courtyard. That was as far as they were allowed to go, however. Neither of them had seen inside the Temple or, even more significant, inside the Ship of Destiny yet. The ship's name was *Omen,* but the name

"Ship of Destiny" had fallen into common usage. For such it was. Such an ancient, precious part of the Tribe's heritage, with all its secrets and mysteries, was not just for any eyes.

"Well," Vestara said, "we can go back and finish there. But only because you're too fragile to—"

Her teasing insult died in her throat as something passed over the sun.

It was not an uvak, one of the deceptively delicate winged reptiles that were used for aerial transportation. Vestara's dark brown eyes widened in shock.

"Ves," Ahri said in a faint voice, "that's . . . is that a *ship*?"

The hairs on her arms and the back of her neck stood on end despite the heat as she watched, lifting a hand to shade her eyes. She still couldn't speak, but nodded. She was pretty sure that was exactly what the thing in the sky was.

Yet it looked nothing like the Ship of Destiny, or any other vessels she had seen depicted or heard described. Rather than being long and rectangular, or V-shaped, it was a symmetrical sphere. With . . . with wings like an uvak. It moved swiftly and silently, and she now saw that its color was a dark orange-red. Closer and closer it came, until for a wild moment Vestara thought it was going to land right on the beach beside them.

It was coming in for a landing, certainly, but not quite so close as that. It was heading for the sharp, ridged mountains that seemed to spring up from the ocean itself. That was where the Ship of Destiny had crashed so long ago, and for a moment Vestara was alarmed that this vessel would suffer the same fate. Sudden worry suffused her. It couldn't! She had to know who was inside, what sort of beings they were. Perhaps they were a species she had never before encountered. The thought was thrilling.

As it passed over, its shadow fell across her for an instant. A sensation of coldness, much more than the expected sudden coolness of something blocking direct sunlight, brushed Vestara. She gasped slightly as the feeling tingled through her.

It was cold, yes, forbidding . . . but also challenging. Curious. Intrigued.

By *her.*

She no longer was afraid for the vessel's safety. Its pilot knew exactly what it was doing. It was heading directly and quite deliberately for the ruins of the Ship of Destiny, and the Temple, almost as old, that had been constructed around it.

Any fear or trepidation she had experienced a moment before evaporated like water on a hot rock. Vestara reached out in the Force and summoned Tikk, her uvak. Tikk had been basking in the sunlight, craving the heat as all reptiles did, his sharp beak and brilliant green eyes closed. Now he lifted his bright gold head, stretched out his long neck, and spread his red-and-black ruff in the uvak equivalent of an awakening stretch. With an answering croak, he spread his wings, leapt upward, and flew the few meters toward Vestara and Ahri.

She barely paid attention to Tikk, keeping her eyes glued to the strange vessel as it grew smaller and finally vanished from her sight. When she could see it no longer, Vestara took a deep, steadying breath, then gathered up the long hem of her robes, turned to where Tikk patiently awaited her, and began to run as fast as her long legs would carry her in the cumbersome sand, using the Force to stabilize her feet and push her along.

"Come on," she called over her shoulder.

"Where are we going?" asked Ahri, hastening to catch up.

Vestara Force-leapt upward, landing gracefully on the

broad back of the uvak. Ahri followed suit, his arms slipping around her waist as he sat behind her.

"To follow the ship," Vestara said. "Couldn't you feel it? It was for us, Ahri."

Tikk gathered himself, shifting his weight from one clawed foot to the other, then sprang upward.

"For us?" Ahri shouted over the beat of the membranous, veined wings—wings so very like those of the vessel that had brushed Vestara's thoughts only a few heartbeats earlier.

"For us," Vestara repeated firmly. She didn't know how she knew, only that she did.

The vessel had come for them. For younglings. For apprentices.

It had come for Sith.

It was not a very great distance as an uvak flew to the Sith Temple. Accessible only from the air or by a perilous climb, the Temple had been created to protect and watch over the Ship of Destiny and house the survivors of the crash. Vestara had visited here many times before, ever since she had become a Tyro. But she was more excited now than she had been even on her first trip so long ago.

Tikk's leathery wings beat steadily, and the Temple came into view. It had been hewn from the very rock that had been the destruction of the Ship of Destiny— the *Omen*. It was very much like the Sith, Vestara thought, to take that which had been responsible for their greatest hardship and make it serve them. She knew the history of its creation; how the original Sith crew, equipped only with lightsabers and a few handheld energy weapons, had cut into the mountain's heart and shaped the spires, walls, and windows of the massive central Temple. Other wings were added as the centuries crawled past.

Most of the initial work had been done by the Sith, who could move huge chunks of rock with the power of the Force. Later, here and many kilometers away in the capital city of Tahv, the Keshiri—Ahri's people, the native humanoid species of this world—were put to work, with the Sith in charge. Tahv bore the stamp of a place that had been expanded by a people who had the luxury to appreciate art and beauty; the Temple, while beautiful in its own right, as the first home of the Sith was more functional than decorative. The statuary, of early Sith leaders, including Captain Yaru Korsin, the first commander of the *Omen,* had been brought in much later, and the lovely carvings were an almost delicate counterpoint to the hard beauty of the Temple architecture.

Not visible from the air, but housed protectively within a special, highly secured section of the Temple, was said to be the *Omen* itself. Some muttered that the vessel was nothing more than bits and pieces of twisted metal, preserved only for sentimental reasons. Others believed that much of what it had once been still remained, its knowledge hoarded and shared with only the select few who ascended to the lofty ranks of the Sith Lords or the Masters.

But Vestara was not interested in admiring the black spires and functional, simple terraces of the Temple, or the beautiful figurines of its courtyard. And for once, her thoughts did not drift toward wondering what secrets the *Omen* contained. This time, her eyes were on the sphere of livid orange-red that sat in the middle of the courtyard of the Sith Temple.

Vestara's breath caught in her throat again, and she stared, not even wanting to blink. Suddenly she felt as if all her life had simply been spent waiting until the moment when the spherical vessel had soared over her and caressed her with the cool brush of darkness, calling her to follow it.

The . . . Ship . . . was a perfect circle, its wings now folded in on itself, its surface rough and hard looking. Dark-side energy seemed to flow from it. Dozens of Sith were milling about in the courtyard already, and Vestara saw that more were approaching on uvak-back.

She wanted to land, to leap off, to rush up to the Ship and caress its knobbed, pebbly surface. A soft sob escaped her; embarrassed, she tried to turn it into a cough. But Ahri knew her too well. He tightened his arms around her waist.

"Ves, you all right?"

"Yes, of course I am. I just . . . this is an unusual situation, don't you think?"

She knew that Ahri was fond of her, and while she found him attractive—he was a Keshiri male, of course he was gorgeous—she had no desire to start a romance. For one thing, despite the fact that the Sith were firm believers in merit over birth, there was still a stigma attached to being Keshiri. No doors were closed to them by their unfortunate birth—indeed, one of the current High Lords was Keshiri—but there were never marriages between them and the Sith, and they had a narrower window of opportunity to prove themselves.

Some Sith did take Keshiri lovers, of course, although the species were sufficiently different that no children could be conceived. The physical beauty of the Keshiri was difficult to resist, but Vestara knew she would not be one of those who succumbed to it. She was utterly devoted to the Force, to her studies, to practicing and training and honing her skills until her body quivered with weariness, until she was drenched in sweat, until she crawled into bed and slept the dreamless sleep of the exhausted.

And now this Ship had come, and she did not care about anything else.

Again she felt the cold perusal, and shivered. Ahri's arms tightened about her, mistaking the gesture for a physical chill.

You sensed me.

I—I did, she sent back through the Force.

She was being . . . examined. Appraised.

You seek to become a Sith Master. To harness the power of the dark side.

I . . . I . . .

Vestara straightened to her full tall height atop Tikk's back and deliberately banished her childish hesitancy. Never mind that she had never before beheld a spacefaring vessel—never even seen the diagrams and schematics that were purported to rest inside the forbidden hull of the crashed *Omen.* She was of the Tribe, the daughter of a Sith Saber. She was exceptionally strong in the Force and knew it.

And the ship—Ship itself, not its pilot, she realized now it had no pilot, not yet—was testing her. She would not shrink before its probity.

I do. I shall. I am Vestara Khai, daughter of a proud heritage. I have what is necessary to command the dark side and bend it to my will. To use it for the good of the Tribe, and the People.

For the good of all Sith, Ship suggested.

She nodded automatically, though even as she did so she realized the vessel couldn't see her.

Except somehow it *could.* Or rather, she realized, it could sense her agreement in the Force. She felt it approve and then withdraw. Without the coldness of its presence in her mind, she somehow felt bereft, but she refrained from seeking it out again.

At that moment, as her gaze wandered from Ship to the throng of Sith crowding around it, in that sea of dark robes she saw a pale blond head turn in her direction. It was Lady Rhea, one of the members of the Sith Circle of Lords, and her blue eyes were fixed upon Vestara. Even from this height, Vestara could see that Lady Rhea's eyes were narrowed, as if she was considering something.

Slowly, Vestara smiled.

Chapter Six

THE *JADE SHADOW* WAS FULL OF ALL THINGS MARA.

Once or twice, during the long silences that filled too many hours spent simply traveling, with the quiet, controlled hum of the engines the only sound, Ben Skywalker could have sworn he felt his mother's presence. And he did not dismiss it every time as wistful imagination; he was a Jedi, and he knew better. If her spirit was to linger or visit anywhere, surely it would be here, with her husband and son, in the ship that had been designed especially for her.

In a way, it was like having almost everyone who'd cared about Mara Jade Skywalker present. Their love and labor had gone into turning an ordinary space yacht into something unique, formidable, and unexpected, like the woman for whom it was intended.

The basic vessel itself had come from Lando Calrissian. Tendra, Lando's wife, had given it the name *Jade Shadow*. The name was ostensibly because of the vessel's hull, gray and nonreflective, but Ben thought it an apt choice. Mara's shadow was everywhere in it. With all the extras, Mara could have piloted the vessel herself. The bridge, however, was originally designed for a pilot, copilot, and navigator. Three, just like the Skywalker family had once been three.

Upgrades, some astonishing and cutting-edge, had come. Lando and Talon Karrde gave the vessel teeth in the form of retractable AG-1G laser cannons and two concealed Dymex˙HM-8 concussion missile launchers. Each had a magazine of eight high-yield torpedoes. The whole defense system could be controlled manually or by a targeting computer that did everything except send consolation notes back to the next of kin. The ship might be a shadow, but it was quite substantial when it came to fighting back.

Han Solo himself had souped up the engines, replicating many of the tricks he'd learned over the years on his own beloved vessel, the *Millennium Falcon.* On top of that, he'd given the *Shadow* an advanced long-range sensor suite that anyone seeking to avoid detection or beat a hasty retreat would salivate over. Port and starboard visual scanners, sensor decoys, jamming devices, fake transponder codes, and what Ben had always thought of as the jewel in the crown—a remote-controlled slave circuit that summoned the *Shadow* over short distances.

After that, Luke and Mara had worked together on many aspects of the vessel, just as they had worked together on a marriage that had been dedicated and true. They'd complemented Han's contributions by adding an autopilot capable of admirably evasive maneuvers, and retrofitted the aft docking bay to accommodate a modified starfighter.

Mara herself, at not insignificant cost, had installed an extremely sensitive holographic communications array that could send and receive messages all the way from the Deep Core to the Outer Rim. Ben now viewed that almost as a prescient gift, though of course Mara could not possibly have known how vital a lifeline it would one day be for her son and husband. The places Ben and

Luke were going to could hardly be considered a quick trip.

Ben was leaning back in the copilot's seat, hands clasped loosely behind his head, gazing up through the transparisteel canopy at the velvet blackness punctuated by stars.

"Thinking of Mom?" Luke asked quietly.

Ben nodded. "Yeah. Spending so much time in her ship—it's hard not to."

"I know what you mean."

"I'm glad we took the *Shadow*. Not just for the practical reasons."

Luke glanced over at his son and gave him a quick grin. "Me too. It feels appropriate. As if part of her is making this journey with us."

Ben nodded. He didn't mention the feelings he'd had, almost as if she'd been present. If it was real, Luke was doubtless already feeling it, too; if it wasn't, it was his own imagination and he'd keep it to himself.

In a way, this was a memorial journey. The immediate reasons were very pressing and very dire. They were attempting to gather information that would help demystify and hopefully cure the strange mental illness that was affecting Jedi Knights Seff Hellin and Valin Horn, and also figure out what had gone so badly wrong with Jacen Solo so that Luke's ten-year exile would be commuted. But Ben was also finding that the many hours of comfortable silence or quiet conversation the journey allowed him to have with his father had been honoring Mara Jade Skywalker in some way. He knew they wouldn't have had these times together on Coruscant. In a way, Luke's exile and this journey upon which they had embarked had been and promised to continue to be something that brought them together, slowed things down a little bit, despite the urgency of the mission.

Mara's expensive holographic communications array

chimed softly. Luke frowned. Ben did, too. Cilghal wasn't expected to make contact for another four hours; one could set one's chrono by her. Luke reached forward and tapped the controls.

A diminutive image of the Mon Calamari healer, about a third of a meter high, appeared on the little dais of the holoprojector. Mon Cal expressions were hard to read, but both Luke and Ben could tell from the way she moved her body that she was agitated.

"Cilghal, what is it?" Luke asked.

Cilghal inclined her head in a gesture of respect, observing the proprieties even when Luke was in exile and disgrace, even when she was obviously in distress.

"Much has happened in the last few hours, Grand Master. Shall I tell you the good news or the bad? Both are important."

"Let's start with the bad news," said Luke.

"Very well. There has been another incident with a Jedi Knight," she said.

"Oh, no." Luke breathed. "Who?"

"It was Jysella Horn."

The Skywalkers exchanged glances. Two thoughts slammed into Ben's brain at once. One was *Poor Jysella;* the other, *What's this done to their parents?*

"I witnessed it, Master Skywalker. She had come to the Temple to assist me in researching a cure for her brother. She seemed agitated and did not appear to have slept well, but I assumed that was to be expected, considering. She was seated beside me in the research room, when suddenly she stiffened and began to make excuses for why she had to leave immediately. I realized something more than simple worry was affecting her and attempted to engage her in conversation."

Cilghal's enormous eyes blinked rapidly, a sign of agitation. Luke listened, not interrupting, and Ben followed his father's example although he was burning to ask questions.

"She rose and activated her lightsaber, accusing me of absconding with the real Cilghal."

"Just like Valin," Luke said.

"Exactly. Then—she fled the Temple."

"She escaped from the Temple? How? There's Jedi all over the place!" Ben had blurted the words before he could censor himself.

Instead of reprimanding him, Cilghal sighed. "An excellent question, Jedi Skywalker. Jysella is a trained Jedi Knight, certainly, but nonetheless, in our own Temple, we ought to have been able to capture her. Master Skywalker . . . Jysella Horn . . . flow-walked."

Luke looked startled. "You're certain?"

"I am reasonably so, yes. She seemed able to know exactly where each of us would try to confront her and took routes to avoid us. I can't think of any other explanation than her seeing into the future."

"That's hardly incontrovertible evidence of flow-walking," Luke said. "That could be tactics, smart use of the Force, and just plain luck. Part of being a Jedi is being able to anticipate what others will do."

"It could be those simple things," Cilghal agreed mildly, "had she not known exactly where two security droids—the very droids about to be activated to attack her—were hidden and disabled them. Two of her dearest friends tried and failed to capture her when she fled the Temple. They were in a tapcaf right outside and came out when the fighting began. Both Bazel Warv and Yaqeel Saav'etu report that she knew where they were going to be, knew what tactics they were going to use, and was able to counter every single blow before it landed."

Luke looked skeptical. "Cilghal, that's a very basic

Jedi technique—anticipating your opponent. Knowing what they're going to do."

"Not like this," Cilghal said earnestly. "This was beyond the ordinary. It was almost—choreographed. Too precise. The only thing that saved Bazel's life was the fact that Jysella seemed so distressed, she was not thinking clearly.

"Also," Cilghal added, "I felt something in the Force. Something involving time and space. I have not tried to sense when anyone is flow-walking before, but if I had to guess—that is what I would have assumed even without knowing what Jysella had done with the droids and in the fight."

Ben's eyes were enormous. Even his father was hard-put to conceal his shock. "Go on" was all Luke said.

"Unfortunately, as I said, Bazel and Yaqeel were unsuccessful in their attempt to capture her. The GA has her, and Chief of State Daala reports that she is going to be put in carbonite."

"Without even an exam or trial," Luke said. It was a statement, not a question, and Cilghal nodded.

"GA Security was on the scene immediately," she continued, "and Daala wasn't far behind them. And Master . . . there was at least one reporter who broadcast almost everything."

Ben felt a knot in his gut. This couldn't possibly have gone worse. Unless—

"Were there any casualties?" he asked.

"Thankfully, no. Many civilians received injuries, most minor, and Bazel was wounded. He will make a full recovery."

Ben thought that the same could not necessarily be said for Valin or Jysella.

"Well, that's something to be grateful for, at least," Luke said. He rubbed his eyes. "You said the attack was recorded?"

"Yes. Transmitting the broadcast now."

Luke and Ben watched in increasingly sickened silence as one Javis Tyrr, "Reporting live from just outside the Jedi Temple in Galactic City, Corsucant," proceeded to interview passersby while feeding them transparently leading questions like, "How long do you think the Jedi have been hiding this issue?"

At one point, Ben actually snorted in disgust. His father might have been trying to smother a smile at the sound, but he quickly sobered as the footage continued.

It was damning. There was Jysella, in full Jedi robes and brandishing a lit lightsaber, shrieking at pedestrians and Force-hurling them out of her way. And the commentary as the cam zoomed around, always seeking out the perfect angle: "Another Jedi has gone crazy! She's attacking people right and left!"

Jysella's hair had come undone, and dark strands flew about her head. The cam zoomed in on her at one point and revealed brown eyes wide with terror.

"She *does* look crazy, Dad," Ben said softly, the admission paining him. Luke said nothing, his expression sad as he stared at Corran Horn's little girl.

"Even her fellow Jedi think she's dangerous," came Tyrr's voice, still remarkably calm. "I can see one, no, no *two* Jedi heading to intercept the rampaging Jedi now. And it looks like several are emerging from the Temple as well."

Ben stared raptly, thinking that this was like watching a speeder crash. He couldn't tear his eyes away, even though the sight made him sick.

What he saw next he couldn't believe. A Ramoan whom he recognized as a Jedi Knight charged forward. He was suddenly slammed into by a fleeing pedestrian and, apparently caught unawares by the impact, stumbled several steps to the side.

And that was precisely where Jysella leapt even before

he'd begun moving. Her lightsaber came down in a blur of motion, and Jysella shrieked, "It's not you!"

"Pause," Luke said. The recording stopped obediently. "Replay." Both Skywalkers watched the encounter again. Ben felt a shiver chase up and down his spine.

Flow-walking. This was more than Force anticipation.

The fight continued. Ben realized that Cilghal was right. At every turn, Jysella predicted exactly where Barv would be. Sometimes she seemed to be two steps ahead. Ben had never seen that kind of Force anticipation, not even from his father. His skin crawled. He paid no attention now to the reporter's running commentary, only dimly aware of words like "so young and attractive" and "tragic family" and other bantha poodoo. He was much more interested in the fight. He heard a snarl. Jysella's head whipped around.

"There is another on the scene, a young Bothan Jedi, who seems to—"

And suddenly the cam was flying at Jysella, who whirled. There was a perfect, beautiful shot of her insane face as she lifted the lightsaber, then the transmission ended.

Luke heaved a heavy sigh and ran his hand through his hair. "While I confess I'm pleased that Yaqeel was able to take out the reporter's holocam, a lot of damage has been done. I'm certain that last image of Jysella is going to be all over the newsvids."

"It was good thinking on Jedi Yaqeel's part, but it did little in the end. It turns out the reporter had a backup cam," Cilghal continued miserably. "Here's what else he was able to record."

The quality of the holovid was greatly reduced in this version, but the words came through loud and clear. There was Chief of State Daala, as usual looking stunning for someone her age, telling everyone in a calm, reassuring voice that Jysella Horn, like her brother, would be "safely imprisoned in carbonite." That there was "something going wrong with the Jedi," and that her government would "investigate and explore all possible explanations."

Tyrr piped up with another leading question similar to the ones he had posed to the civilians earlier. Ben uttered an oath that his mother would have winced to hear—even though she had probably taught it to him unwittingly—and Luke's lips thinned as insinuations were made that it was the Horn blood that was responsible for the madness.

"Oh, Master Horn's going to love *that*," muttered Ben. "I feel really bad for him, having to listen to garbage like that. It's like rubbing salt in a wound."

"*I* feel bad for whoever he runs into," Luke said.

Daala responded with the finesse of a natural politician, managing to smear the Jedi and the Horns both without actually saying anything that could be pointed to as inflammatory, even going so far as to chide the reporter for "putting words into my mouth."

Luke sighed as Daala finished up and returned to her speeder. The reporter went on to try to get quotes from Bazel and Yaqeel, and finally Cilghal herself stepped into the frame.

"The Jedi are obviously very concerned about the current state of events, and have been since the first incident. We are doing everything we can."

"I apologize, Master Skywalker," the live Cilghal said, her gravelly voice deep with regret. "I would have preferred not to speak for the Jedi until after we had had the chance to discuss this and present a united front."

"You were on the spot, don't worry about it," Luke assured her. "When are the Masters gathering?"

"Within the hour. The question is, how much of what the reporter said is correct?"

Ben's auburn brows drew together. "Dad," he started to protest, but Luke held up a hand to forestall his comments.

"These are two Jedi who are closely related," Luke said. "That is something that's going to come up—repeatedly—and we need to have an answer for that. Is it possible that it's a genetic cause? The Horns won't like it, but I bet they'll know we need to check it out."

"What about Seff Hellin?" Ben pointed out. "He's not a Horn, and he was the first one to have manifested any of these symptoms."

Luke smiled at his son. "Good point, and correct." He turned again to the holographic image of the Mon Calamari. "And you were right, Cilghal. It certainly did look as though Jysella could have experienced flow walking. She wasn't concentrating enough to simply be landing good strategic blows."

Cilghal inclined her head. "I would rather it be the latter, frankly," she admitted.

"Me too."

"Three for three," Ben said.

"Three for three what?"

"Three Jedi displaying the same kind of paranoid behavior and abilities they shouldn't have."

"Abilities that Jacen learned, but that they couldn't possibly have learned themselves," Cilghal said, nodding.

"Exactly." Ben started counting them off on his fingers, rising, his agitated body, weary of being in the confined space, needing to move to assist his thinking. "One: Seff was able to freeze his adversaries and snatch their weapons from them in the middle of a fight. Two: Valin was able to fake a seizure—alter the impressions his brain waves emitted well enough to fool everyone. And three: Jysella flow-walked. It's circumstantial evidence, but it's the best we've got right now. It's the only common thread I'm able to see."

Ben paused and turned around to see both the holographic Cilghal and his father staring at him. He flushed a little, wondering if he'd been babbling, but he saw approval in his father's blue eyes.

"Agreed," Cilghal said. "Your decision to explore the connection with Jacen appears, tragically, to continue to be validated. We still have no indication that Jacen had any sort of contact with these three Jedi Knights."

"But there's got to be a link," Ben blurted, then amended, "Well . . . logic dictates that there should be anyway."

"The Baran Do Sages weren't able to shed any light on this," Luke said. "I wonder if we're not herding the wrong nerf. Chasing the wrong lead." He leaned back in his chair, his eyes narrowed, thinking. "A link with Jacen—" Luke's eyes widened. "No. Not Jacen . . . at least, not with the physical one."

"But . . . there's been no trace of him in the Force," Ben reminded his father. As always, the thought saddened him. For all the rage he had once borne toward his late cousin, Ben had learned to forgive him, although like Luke, he still needed to understand what had happened to him. For a few seconds at the end, Jaina had assured them all he'd been Jacen again, not Darth Caedus. And Ben had loved Jacen. Ben felt an uncomfortable, slightly awkward sorrow, as of something left forever unresolved, at the thought of never sensing his presence again.

Luke shook his head. "That's not what I meant," he said, and his voice held a trace of the same sorrow that Ben was feeling. "I was wondering if Caedus somehow was able to see that his reign as a Sith would eventually come to an end. And if he saw that . . . maybe this entire situation is something he set up by flow-walking into the past."

Ben stared at his father, wide-eyed. "You can do that?"

Luke's face showed disapproval. "You can influence the future, to a certain degree, yes. Caedus didn't have the chance to find and train an apprentice to carry on his work after he was killed. He couldn't break you, and he wasn't able to fully corrupt Tahiri. Maybe he took this route to leave a legacy of some sort."

Ben had followed Jacen more than a slight way down a very dark path, but he had not gone to the dark side. He knew that Caedus had thought him too weak. In the end, though, he'd learned to realize that what Caedus had dismissed as weakness was that which the Jedi realized was their greatest, truest strength.

"I—I imagine it would be possible," Cilghal was saying, distaste evident in her voice. "It certainly bears investigation, unsettling an idea as it is."

"He did study with the Aing-Tii," Ben offered. At one point, he'd known just about every place Jacen had been during his five-year galaxy-hopping adventure. He'd desperately wanted to emulate it, and now it was beginning to look as though he was going to, under far different and much sadder circumstances. "Maybe we should go talk to them."

Cilghal gave a raspy, gurgling laugh. "That will be much easier said than done. The Aing-Tii are notoriously unwelcoming of strangers, and there's very little information about them even in the Temple files."

"I think Ben is right," Luke said. "It's more than just investigating a Force trick that Jacen used. The flow-walking could be the key to understanding the entire situation. If Caedus flow-walked and laid this . . . this mental instability as some sort of bomb rigged to go off if he failed, then understanding how he did it may help us understand how to undo it. I know we don't have a lot of information on the Aing-Tii, but please send me whatever you find."

"They live in the Kathol Rift, that much I know," Cilghal offered. She sighed and closed her large eyes for a moment. "I'll send you everything I learn, Grand Master."

Luke whistled softly. "The Kathol Rift? I'll *need* everything you can learn, then. This just keeps getting better and better."

"What's so bad about the Kathol Rift?" Ben asked.

"I'll tell you later," Luke said. "Thank you, Cilghal. Now, didn't you say there was some good news? I think I could use it along about now."

Cilghal smiled faintly. "Ben mentioned Seff Hellin earlier. I am pleased to report that he has been captured— by the Jedi. We are currently holding him deep within the Temple for analysis."

"Well, that *is* good news. Does the GA or Daala have any idea about this?"

"None whatsoever. Jaina, Tahiri, Mirax, Winter, and Jag took him down."

"Tahiri?" Ben was pleased. He knew Tahiri Veila hadn't been willing to fully rejoin the Jedi, but he was glad to know that she was cooperating with them.

"Indeed. It would seem that she is not opposed to aiding us. Perhaps she will decide to rejoin at some point."

Ben hoped so. It had been his choice to spare Tahiri, believing she could come to her senses, be redeemed.

Cilghal hesitated. "I said that the GA and Daala do not know about Seff's capture. Nor do any of the Masters save myself. No one has any desire to place Master Hamner in a compromising position."

Luke frowned, then nodded. "If this comes out, he can in all honesty deny any knowledge of it, and the Order is not affected. I still don't like it." He sighed, and then shook his head, seeming to refocus on the matter at hand. "What have you learned about Seff so far?"

"He does not demonstrate Valin's ability to blank the encephaloscan, and thus we were able to successfully take brain scan readings. The parts of his brain that are active while dreaming also appear to be active while he is awake, to a certain extent. In other words, there is a definite dream state occurring, although he is wide awake and cognizant of what is going on. Our investigation continues."

Investigation. Even Cilghal was starting to use Ben's terms. Ben suddenly was hurled back in time in his mind to when Master Cilghal had been conducting the investigation into the murder of Mara Jade Skywalker. The detachment had helped. Ben had burned with the desire to do everything exactly right, so that the investigation into his mother's death wouldn't be compromised. He'd been the one to prove what had happened to her, even when things seemed to point in another direction entirely. And now here was another investigation, not into a murder but into something that was most assuredly a mystery.

"What is his behavior like?" Luke asked.

"Exactly as you'd expect. He thinks everyone's been taken and replaced by doubles. He is scared and angry and determined to kill us all. Captain Solo and Jedi Organa Solo will be arriving within a few hours to offer what insight they can, as they were the ones who encountered Seff Hellin first."

"I remember," Luke said. "I'm not sure they will be able to give us any additional insight, but who knows? Anything else?"

"I would have thought that this would be quite sufficient for one conversation, but if you insist, I'm sure I can come up with something else."

Luke laughed. The sound surprised Ben. There was so

much bad that was going on, it seemed hard to find anything to be amused about. But now Cilghal was grinning, too, and he mentally shrugged.

"No, I think you're right," Luke said. "That's more
than enough for one day. Let me know when you find
anything on the Aing-Tii, and brief me after the Council
meeting. In the meantime, Ben and I will set course for
the Kathol Rift." He hesitated, then added, "And please
give my deepest sympathies to Corran and Mirax. This
is an especially difficult time for them."

"Of course, Master Skywalker." Cilghal inclined her
hairless head. Her image disappeared.

Luke settled back in the chair, folding his arms behind
his head. His blue eyes were distant, unfocused. Ben
held his tongue for a while, but finally he couldn't help
himself.

"Do you really think that Jacen—that Caedus set all
this up?" he asked. "The Jedi going crazy, the stuff they
know—do you really think he planned all this?"

Luke sat back up and began laying in a course for the
Kathol Rift. "It's a possibility, and it would explain a
lot."

"Wouldn't explain how he was able to actually do it."

"With any luck, we'll find the Aing-Tii in a congenial
frame of mind, and they'll choose to enlighten us."

Ben couldn't help what escaped his lips next. "Do you
think we'll have to flow-walk in order to find out?"

"I hope not, Ben. I truly hope not."

Chapter Seven

"YOU KNOW," BEN GRUMBLED, "WHEN I SAID I WANTED TO come with you, I didn't realize that I was signing up for the Mobile Chapter of the academy."

Luke, his eyes on the holographic star chart that looked like someone had spilled watered-down blue milk all over it, chuckled softly.

"Studying is good for you," he said. "Builds character." He adopted an old man's creaky voice. "Why, when I was your age, my young apprentice, all I wanted to *do* was go to the academy. Uphill, both ways, in a sandstorm."

"Yeah, Uncle Han told me about that," Ben retorted, his own mouth twitching as he suppressed a grin. "You didn't want to get a good education. You wanted to go hang out with your friends."

It was a bittersweet joke; Luke indeed had ended up flying with his best friend Biggs Darklighter, but under completely different circumstances. It had not been a joyride or race or friendly competition; it was an assault on the Death Star, and it had cost the lives of everyone in the Red Squadron except Wedge Antilles and Luke Skywalker.

But Luke smiled fondly at the comment. The memories he held of Biggs were all good ones. Biggs had not been the first to die for a cause he devoutly believed in, and he wouldn't be the last. But he'd died making a difference, and that was the way Luke knew his friend had wanted it.

So it was easy for Luke to shoot back to his son, "Too bad you don't have any close friends that aren't your family. Maybe you'll become friends with an Aing-Tii kid."

Ben grimaced. "I'm . . . not too sure about that."

A few hours before, Cilghal had transmitted everything she had been able to learn so far about the Kathol Rift and the Aing-Tii. It wasn't a lot, but the two Skywalkers had divvied up the research between them. Luke had given Ben the information on the Aing-Tii, while he had studied the complex and extremely dangerous spatial phenomenon that was the Rift. Ben was certainly a capable pilot, though one could always be better and Luke had often given his son the helm during the journey in order for Ben to have more flying hours under his belt. But the Rift was something else again, and Luke felt more comfortable managing it himself.

It was difficult to navigate for a whole host of reasons. To begin with, it was huge—a cloud of wildly unstable gases, the birthplace of thousands of stars, that was several parsecs wide. *Several parsecs* was about as precise as one could be, considering that the cloud was constantly shifting. At first glance, this place of powerful electromagnetic lightstorms and sensor-distorting radiation seemed impossible to traverse. But the Aing-Tii, who were thought to live on one of the thousands of planets believed to lie inside the Rift, seemed to navigate it just fine. Uncannily fine, as a matter of fact. They seemed completely able to avoid the lightstorms that were quite capable of destroying entire fleets of ships in a matter of minutes, and by all accounts their vessels appeared untouched by particle buildup that could render sensors pretty much useless and weapons systems utterly nonfunctional.

They could do this because there were currents in the Rift—the literature referred to them as "corridors"—that twined throughout the stunningly beautiful, colorful, and incredibly dangerous gas cloud. The trick was that the corridors changed position. Frequently. One report stated that they changed as often as dozens of times in a twenty-four-hour day. The logical conclusion was that there was some kind of predictable pattern to how and when these corridors shifted, and that the Aing-Tii had figured out the mystery. So far, though, no one else had, at least no one whose recollections and observations could be found in the Jedi Archives.

Even if one did happen upon one of the corridors, no pilot or crew could possibly call such a passageway "safe." These areas were simply less dangerous than the rest of the Rift because the concentration of radiation and charged particles was slightly less.

Moving through the Kathol Rift, for non–Aing-Tii vessels, meant placing one's ship in constant danger. Even in the corridors, weapons ranges were cut in half, shields were weakened—and as for communications systems, Luke figured he might as well resign himself to not hearing from Cilghal again once they entered, even with Mara's incredibly sophisticated equipment upgrades.

Then, once they did enter the Rift, they'd be targets. Not just for the xenophobic Aing-Tii, who were infamous for disliking anyone sticking their noses into their business, but for the energy discharges of the Rift itself. A ship acted like a lightning rod, so for the entire duration of their trip the *Jade Shadow* would be pounded by energy bolts. It would be quite a show visually, but an extremely bumpy ride.

And there was another reason the Rift was so dangerous.

A stigma was attached to the place, a stigma that went above and beyond the fact that it was simply a bad place for a ship to be. Cilghal had seen fit to enclose in her transmission a whole host of first-person reports that came uncomfortably close to being classified as "ghost stories." At first Luke was confused as to why Cilghal had included them. He was inclined to lump them into the same categories as cabin fever and spacesickness, but then he realized that report after report insisted that Force-sensitives were more strongly affected than others.

Most planets here would not thrive particularly well, Luke supposed. The constant high levels of radiation were not exactly conducive to the vast majority of lifeforms. He wondered how the Aing-Tii managed to survive as well as they seemingly did.

Luke stretched, rose, and went to the small area that served as a galley. "Hungry?"

Ben looked up from the hologram. "I'm sixteen. Of course I'm hungry."

Luke grinned and selected two bowls of brogy stew and a nerf steak, programmed the requisite amount of time into the pulse oven, and returned to where his son was sitting.

"So, brief me," he said, leaning back in his chair. He put on his old-timer voice again. "And remember, young apprentice, your continued progress depends on this report."

That got a full-fledged grin from Ben. "Well," he said, "I'm not quite done going through it all yet. Cilghal sent me a metric ton of information."

"When faced with an overwhelming amount of information, begin at the beginning. Start with the basics. What are they like physically?"

Ben touched a pad, and a holographic image about a third of a meter high appeared. It was bipedal, standing squarely on feet that had two clawed digits in front and one in the back. A large tail swept behind it; its forelegs had two digits and seemed disproportionately tiny. It was covered with overlapping bony plates, from the long tail to its skull. Large eyes peered out beneath a plate that resembled a helmet. Each of the jointed plates had some kind of markings that were either painted, etched, or tattooed on; it was hard to tell at this size.

"They look reptilian, but actually they're edentate mammals," Ben said. "They're about two meters tall and—"

The pulse oven announced that their meals were ready with a soft chime. Ben—suddenly reminding Luke that, even though his son was a Jedi Knight and had been through more than Luke had even imagined at his age, he was also a ravenous teenager—practically sprang from his chair to get their food, leaving his sentence unfinished. Luke continued to study the three-dimensional, animated model and raised an eyebrow when the small image suddenly shot forth not one but six long, thin, squirming tongues.

A few moments later Ben brought their meals back on trays, along with two steaming cups of caf and four sweetcakes that looked evilly gooey.

"Thanks, Ben, but I don't want any sweetcakes," Luke said as he reached for the caf and sipped it.

"Oh, I know, those are for me." Ben began cutting his steak as he talked, his eyes still on the Aing-Tii. For all his joking complaints, he was clearly very interested. In his role as the son of the Jedi Grand Master, he had attended several diplomatic functions and met a staggering variety of beings. He was no backplanet farm boy seeking novelty, as Luke had been at his age. But the

Aing-Tii were mysterious, unknown, elusive, and intriguing.

"So, yeah, about two meters tall, and they can apparently use those tails quite effectively in combat," Ben said, then took a bite of steak and chewed.

"Speaking of combat, what are their tactics in battle? That seems to be what we know best about them, from the brief glance I had at Cilghal's summary."

Ben paused in midchew, his green eyes narrowing. "She gave you a *summary*?"

Luke chuckled and took a bite of the stew. "Instructor's prerogative. Keep going, you're doing fine."

Ben swallowed, scowled, and continued. "Well, like I said, they can slap you with that tail pretty good. They also have these—well, they're like clubs, or sticks, wrapped up in some kind of wiring that delivers a very powerful stun."

He popped another bite in his mouth, talking as he ate. Luke was mildly amused. Leia knew the etiquette of dozens of species and had done her best, along with Mara, to instill manners in the boy. And when it mattered, Luke knew that his son was capable of behaving impeccably in a formal situation. But right now, they were simply two bachelors eating dinner and talking, and formality had gone out the air lock, and Luke didn't mind one bit. He resisted an impulse to ruffle his son's red hair affectionately.

"Now, their ships—" Ben swallowed, extended an arm, and tapped another key. The image of the Aing-Tii was replaced by that of their vessel. "These things are *really* astral."

Luke took another spoonful of stew, looking at the miniature holographic vessel that turned slowly. Roughly ovoid, it resembled the beings who presumably built it in that it, too, was covered with thick hull plates that bore similar designs to what the Aing-Tii sported on their bodies. Conical projections jutted seemingly at random from the hull. The whole thing struck Luke as organic in some fashion, and for a moment he was uncomfortably reminded of the Yuuzhan Vong.

"It's huge," Ben said with a mouthful of stew, having already devoured the nerf steak. Luke remembered when he'd had an appetite like that and marveled silently as Ben continued. "They're called Sanhedrim ships. Half the size of an *Imperial*-class Star Destroyer. The Aing-Tii have some kind of technology or Force knowledge that enables the ships to appear out of nowhere—literally just pop from one place to another. They use a variety of attack styles, the least pleasant of which is when they suddenly turn and smash your ship across their bow. The most benevolent is bathing your ship with some kind of ray that apparently distorts your perception of time. By the time you recover your wits, their ship is long gone."

Luke frowned, the bowl of stew forgotten for the moment. "Distortion of time . . . I wonder, does it just stun the victim somehow, or does it really alter time? After all, these are the beings who developed the knowledge of flow-walking. There could be a connection."

"Maybe. You going to eat that?"

Luke shook his head, his eyes still on the miniature Aing-Tii. "Go ahead."

"Thanks." Ben scraped what Luke had left of his stew into his own bowl and continued eating.

"We know they are fiercely isolationist and xenophobic. What about their belief system?" Luke knew the answer to this, but wanted to see how far Ben had gotten in his research. To be fair, there had been a lot to dig through. Right now, though, they had nothing but time on their hands, and he wanted Ben to learn everything he could.

"It's a little odd sounding. I think—I'm not sure—but

I think the term *Sanhedrim* means 'pilgrim,' or maybe 'monk.' I've run across the term *Aing-Tii monks* in various notes from eyewitness encounters. It seems as though the few ships and aliens that anyone's encountered are either the explorers among their people or on a quest or pilgrimage or something. I don't think they as a people are casual spacefarers, not like humans are. So that raises the question, what are they looking for? And why?"

Ben paused for another quick bite, and Luke asked, "What's your conclusion from what you've learned?"

"Talon Karrde actually ran across them once, did you know that?" Ben grinned as his father's blond eyebrows lifted.

"No, Cilghal failed to mention that in her summary."

"Aha!" Ben pointed his spoon at his father in a victorious gesture.

"Son, that just supports my theory that research you do yourself is more useful than research someone else does for you. Continue, my young apprentice."

Ben mock-scowled. "Karrde's report didn't say much, so we might want to contact him directly if we can. But what interests me is that he met the Aing-Tii through his former boss, Jorj Car'das, who actually lived among the Aing-Tii. He was, it seemed, very ill—dying in fact—and Master Yoda sent him to go and ask the Aing-Tii for aid."

This much, at least, Cilghal had included in her overview. She'd also included the complete document Car'das had written about his sojourn with the aliens. Luke fully intended to read that from start to finish himself.

"They healed him, but asked that he sort of be their chronicler. So he wrote down everything he learned about them. Which is a lot."

"I have to say," said Luke, reaching for a sweetcake

despite his earlier claim that he was not interested, "that that strikes me as strange. Everything we know about the Aing-Tii says they are very intent upon maintaining their privacy. They'll attack and even kill to defend it. So why admit a human they've never met—one in dire need of a huge favor from them, no less—into their innermost circle? And then let him write about his experiences?"

"Well, if Yoda sent *you* someone and asked you to take care of him, wouldn't you do it?"

Luke laughed at that. "Yes I would, as fast as I possibly could. But I'm a Jedi, and Yoda was a Jedi Master. That's a bit different."

"We don't know what their personal relationship with Master Yoda was. Maybe it was just as close or even closer. Even if they're not Jedi—and it seems pretty clear by all accounts that they're not—they're Force-users on an impressive scale. Who knows what kind of relationship they had with him?"

"You raise an excellent point."

"Thanks. I wish I could have met him."

"I wish you could have, too," Luke said quietly. "I wish I'd had more time with him myself. He was . . ."

Luke's voice trailed off. A silence fell, broken only by the sound of Ben's spoon scraping the bottom of the bowl.

There were not really words sufficient to the task of describing the deceptively small, large-eared, green-skinned being, as wise as he was wizened. He had opened Luke's eyes to so very much in the brief time Luke had been with him. Luke missed him and his other teacher and friend, Obi-Wan Kenobi, "Ben," after whom his son was named. Obi-Wan had also been taken from Luke after too brief a time. That they were part of the Force now, he knew; he had seen them. Anakin Skywalker and Mara were with them, and one day he and Ben would both join them.

But not today.

"Well, let's put it this way," he said. "Anyone Yoda trusts enough to send a dying human to for help, I could learn to have warm fuzzy feelings about. Continue with your theory about why they're going on these quests or pilgrimages."

Ben set aside the empty bowls and plate and reached for a sweetcake. "According to Car'das, the Aing-Tii believe in elusive, mysterious deities they refer to as 'Those Who Dwell Beyond the Veil.' Your guess is as good as anyone else's as to what they are and what *veil* means."

"It might refer to the Rift."

Ben shrugged and ate half the sweetcake in a single bite. With his mouth full, he said, "Maybe. But one thing we do know is that they are collecting artifacts."

"Artifacts to offer to these beings, or artifacts *from* these beings?"

Again Ben shrugged. Luke was suddenly struck by how broad those shoulders had gotten over the last two years. *Oh, Mara, you'd be so proud of him. He's a fine young man.* A ghost of a smile curved Luke's lips as he imagined Mara rolling her eyes at both him and Ben. Yes, her presence was definitely here in this ship that had been so uniquely hers. He returned his attention to his son's slightly crumb-enhanced discourse.

"One of the records said they utilized a human to retrieve an artifact for them. It was called the Codex. No one's sure how they got him to cooperate. The best guess is that they brainwashed him, but they kinda messed up and he went insane from it."

"It's difficult enough for an experienced Jedi to do such things without causing damage," Luke said. "I imagine it must be almost impossible to try something on a species you're unfamiliar with."

Ben paused in midchew for a second before resuming eating. His reddish brows drew together for a moment, and a shadow passed over his face. Luke knew without even having to sense his sudden disquiet in the Force what his son was thinking. Ben was recalling a moment three years ago when Jacen had inadvertently killed a prisoner while mentally torturing her for information. Ben hadn't been present, hadn't seen it happen with his own eyes—but he had been just outside the room, had heard and felt things through the Force that had forever and irrevocably altered his opinion of Jacen Solo.

"Well, sounds like you're off to a good start," Luke said lightly, reaching out to squeeze Ben's shoulder. "Time for *my* report."

He filled Ben in on the basics of the challenges addressing them. "I think that we may have an extra card to play, though. I'm wondering if the *hassat-durr* technique I learned could be useful here."

Ben had the proper teenager's dubious expression, but he also looked as if he wanted to be impressed. "Really?"

"Really. Think about it. *Hassat-durr* means 'lightning rod' in their language, right?"

"Right, you told me," Ben said. "Because if you're not perfect in your mastery of it and perform it during a storm, you'll be repeatedly struck by lightning and killed."

"It stands to reason therefore that if you *are* a master of it, you could use it to be a sort of anti-lightning rod. To deflect energies, at least to a small degree."

"I guess," Ben said. It sounded like the dubious part was winning.

Luke grinned. "Well, it's worth a try anyway. I'm pretty sure I know enough to not be a lightning rod."

"That's good. I'd die horribly embarrassed."

"Where'd you get that sarcastic sense of humor?"

"From Mom."

"Ah, right. How do you like spiders?"

The change of topic caught Ben off-guard. "What do you mean?"

"Spiders. Giant glowing ones, or hundreds of small ones crawling on every centimeter of the ship." Luke was enjoying this.

Ben shrugged. "Not pleasant, of course, but I don't have any particular fear of them. Are you telling me that giant glowing spiders lurk in the Rift, too?"

"In your mind," Luke said. "Apparently this part of space is known for causing hallucinations. Force-sensitives in particular are affected. Spiders—from the large and glowing to the small and plentiful—are one of the recurring hallucinations reported. So, too, are sightings of little hairless beings with large eyes, slit noses, and tiny mouths. Other side effects are nausea and severe headaches."

". . . I don't think I like the field trips the Mobile Chapter of the Jedi academy provides," Ben said.

Luke grinned. He pointed at the last sweetcake. "You going to eat that?"

"I'll split it with you."

"Deal."

Chapter Eight

JEDI TEMPLE, CORUSCANT

MASTER KENTH HAMNER, ACTING GRAND MASTER OF THE Jedi Order, made sure he was the first to arrive in the High Council Chamber.

He needed the time to think.

Hamner went to one of the windows and looked through it. When the Temple had been rebuilt, so had this tower. Except now the tower was enclosed within a so-very-modern transparisteel pyramid. Therefore one was not able to look out directly into the skies of Coruscant as one used to. Instead, one was treated to the far less scenic sights of painted duracrete or transparisteel walls, with the occasional tiny figures of Jedi moving about their business. Doubtless the architect had been proud of the "stylish" design. Hamner sighed and wished they'd simply stuck to what had worked so well for so long.

He had done his best to navigate the Jedi through one of their most trying times. He was good at the game of politics; he had a flair for it, a deftness when it came to dealing with people. Luke Skywalker had known that about him, and had also known that Hamner was respected in many quarters. He himself knew he was a good choice for interim Master.

And yet everything he did, every order he gave, every

stance he took, seemed to drive the Jedi he was trying to protect—both as individual beings and the Order as a whole—even deeper into a very ugly pile of bantha poodoo.

Daala in particular seemed to confound him. She had initially struck Hamner as a good choice for Chief of State of the Galactic Alliance. The Imperial connections didn't seem to matter so much after the war, not when Jagged Fel was the Imperial Head of State and was clearly involved with Jedi Knight Jaina Solo, daughter of two famous erstwhile Rebels. It was—calming, actually. Natasi Daala herself seemed rational and composed. Things had been going well.

Until Luke Skywalker had been arrested, and Valin Horn had gone—and Hamner himself realized he agreed with the choice of words—criminally insane.

He'd done his best to cooperate, thinking to hunker down and ride out the storm. He'd let the GA assign their "observers," at least until Nawara Ven had been able to overturn that order. He'd let GA Security into the Temple itself to physically remove the raving Valin, in full view of the observers. He'd opened up areas of the Temple to the public, even the press, for scrutiny. And yet Daala was still riding the Order, pressing down on them like an assassin pressing a thumb on the carotid artery until blackness descended.

He shook his head. That was an unkind image. And yet—he had requested a meeting with her immediately, and she had put him off for three days.

Three days.

He ran a hand through his fair hair and sighed, turning away from the window and crossing the marble floor, which had been almost perfectly reproduced. He eased into the carved stone chair, relaxing slightly. The view might be different, but this room still bore its link to the past. Although this was not the exact same room that had served the Jedi Masters well through centuries, the restoration had been painstaking, and the spirit was still here.

Kenth Hamner gave a ghost of a smile and wondered how Grand Masters past would have dealt with the predicament in which he now found himself.

Over the next several minutes, the Jedi Masters currently at the Temple came trickling in, sometimes one at a time, sometimes in pairs or small groups. He nodded to them quietly as they entered: Kyle Katarn, Octa Ramis, Saba Sebatyne, Cilghal, Kyp Durron. Leia Organa Solo and her daughter, Jaina, entered, their heads together, quietly talking. They were not officially Masters—not yet, though Hamner suspected that one or both might be elevated sooner than either woman expected—but this was not the first time their insight and positions made them welcome guests at a Masters meeting.

But there was one Master present whom Hamner did not see, one who most assuredly ought to have been. And he had had no word from this particular Master about appearing via hologram in lieu of in person. Hamner waited a moment, letting the Masters settle in and murmur among themselves, then discreetly clicked his comlink.

"Master Horn," he said. "We are all assembled and awaiting your arrival. May I ask when we might expect to—"

"I'm on my way." The voice was strained and sharp. Such was to be expected, Hamner thought to himself. The Horn family did seem singled out for misfortune during this trying time.

"I'm glad to hear it. Shall we wait or—"

"Wait or go ahead, I don't care." There was the distinct sound of Corran's comlink being deactivated.

Hamner blinked, feeling the eyes upon him, and exuded calm in the Force. "Master Horn will be joining us shortly," he said. "As the main topic of conversation concerns him quite intimately, I suggest that if anyone else has other business to bring before the meeting, we address that first."

He spread his arms, indicating that they should take seats. Those who could not be physically present were here in holographic form. An uncomfortable silence stretched out.

Finally Kyp Durron spoke. "Well, *I'll* mention the bantha in the room if no one else will. Master Hamner, with all due respect, there *is* no business to be put before this assembly other than that of the Horns. Specifically Jysella, what happened to her, and how long it's going to be before Daala and the GA do something else to us."

Out of the corner of his eye Hamner saw Jaina relax. Clearly if Durron hadn't spoken up, she would have.

"I do not think it appropriate or considerate to begin discussions on that subject until Master Corran Horn—"

"I'm here."

Corran Horn stepped inside. He looked terrible. His vivid green eyes were bloodshot, and the creases around them, not unexpected in a man of middle age, seemed to have been carved by an unkind hand. He looked scruffy, as if he had not shaved in days, and there was a simmering feeling of suppressed, righteous anger hovering about him in the Force.

"Master Horn. It's good to see you. Please, come join us."

Corran strode toward an empty seat and dropped heavily into it, rubbing his eyes. Jaina and Leia—as they were not yet Masters, they had opted to stand rather than take one of the stone chairs—moved to stand behind Corran. Leia dropped a hand on his shoulder and squeezed it in a silent gesture of reassurance.

Hamner turned to Cilghal. "Master Cilghal, since you

were present when the . . . incident occurred, and have debriefed the two Jedi Knights who fought Jysella"— Hamner saw Corran flinch, ever so slightly, at the words—"I would appreciate it if you told us what you know thus far."

Cilghal glanced compassionately at Corran Horn, then twisted her body in the Mon Calamari equivalent of a human nod. Hamner, of course, had heard her report earlier. Most of the other Masters had heard about the incident, but not the details. He wondered how much Corran Horn himself had heard, and kept his eyes on the man as Cilghal spoke.

In her gravelly voice that nonetheless held a world of kindness, Cilghal recounted the painful events: Jysella's irrational fear and firm belief that everyone was an imposter; her pausing outside the locked door and subsequently escaping using knowledge that she could not possibly have had; her fight with her friends outside the Temple; the fact that this was on all the newsvids on what was apparently a brutal, endless loop.

"The inescapable conclusion, given the evidence," Cilghal finished up, "is that Jedi Jysella Horn was afflicted by the same mental disorder that affected her brother. Her reaction is virtually identical. I am convinced that if I had been given the opportunity to study her, the diagnoses would have been the same."

"Except you weren't," Horn said, his voice low and calm—deceptively so, Hamner suspected. "She was hunted down and dragged off, a holocam catching every minute of it. Her guilt and sentence were determined before anyone had even examined her."

"Yet there is a difference between Valin and Jysella, one that fortunately I was able to witness—to sense in the Force," Cilghal continued. "And it could be an important clue. As I said, I dearly wish I could verify whether or not Jysella's brain wave pattern is similar to her brother's."

"By that you mean if she was able to project artificial readings?" asked Kyle Katarn.

"Exactly," Cilghal said. "Because if my theory is correct, she would not be using that Force ability. It is my belief, from everything I experienced, that she is using another Force ability entirely." She turned to Leia and Jaina, her large eyes expressive. "I believe that Jysella Horn flow-walked."

Leia and Jaina exchanged glances. Hamner waited. Jaina frowned and looked down, and Leia sighed.

"That's . . . another ability that Jacen had that most Jedi don't," Leia said. "You're certain she flow-walked?"

"I am," Cilghal said gently. "Both the evidence and what I felt in the Force confirm it."

Hamner turned to Corran. "Master Horn, I've no wish to cast aspersions, but in light of the evidence—"

Corran, who had been listening with increasing emotion, now spoke. "You don't even have to say it. Of course Mirax and I will come in for a thorough medical examination. Don't you think that was the first thing that popped into our minds when we were told about Jysella? Whether this sickness was something she or I had passed along to them?"

"Thank you, Master Horn," Cilghal said gratefully. "The more information we have, the better. Currently, I confess, no one has any idea what might be causing this tragedy. I must eliminate what possibilities I can." She turned to Hamner. "Master Hamner, I and a team must be permitted to examine Jysella. It is vital to our investigation into what is causing this."

Corran laughed, a short, harsh bark. "Good luck with that, Cilghal," he said. "Mirax and I aren't even being permitted to see her."

"What?" The single word erupted from several throats. Some of the Masters literally rose from their seats. Saba Sebatyne hissed.

Hamner held up a calming hand. "That's utterly inexcusable, Corran, and I'll make a formal request that you and your wife be allowed to see your daughter before she is put in carbonite. I'll be seeing Chief of State Daala in three days and—"

"Three *days*?"

"I am endeavoring to persuade her that this is a matter that requires her immediate attention."

"She shouldn't keep you waiting for three *hours*, let alone—" Kyp burst out.

"Master Hamner." The voice was feminine, cool, reasonable, and it cut through the raised voices and tension in the room like a vibroblade through cheese. After all these years, Leia Organa Solo still had what it took to draw the attention of a room full of people.

"If I may—my husband and I have been allowed to act as go-betweens before. With your permission, I would like to contact Chief of State Daala and speak with her on this subject. She is a grandmother herself. I'm convinced that she's not as callous as this action would indicate."

It wouldn't do to have Leia undermining his efforts. Hamner thought for a moment before responding. "While I am grateful for your offer, I think that the Order needs to speak with a united voice."

"You misunderstand," Leia corrected him gently. "I do not intend to speak with the authorization of the Order, merely as myself. This would not be in the place of your meeting with her, but in addition to it."

Hamner pressed his lips together. He liked and respected Leia, and she had certainly been able to help out the Order on more than one occasion. It would be foolish and, worse, arrogant to refuse her help now.

"Then of course. Thank you. So," he resumed, mentally ticking things off, "I will endeavor to speed up my meeting with Chief of State Daala. At that meeting, I will request that Cilghal and any team she chooses to accompany her be permitted access to Jysella Horn before she is encased in carbonite, and also that her parents be allowed to visit her. Any information that the GA has obtained on her during their initial examination is to be shared with the Order, and we will, of course, do likewise in the spirit of cooperation. Master Horn and his wife, Mirax, will report immediately following this meeting to the medcenter for whatever tests Cilghal deems necessary. The Horn children's maternal grandfather, Booster Terrik, will also need to—"

"No."

The single word, blunt and stubborn, caused Master Hamner to blink.

"I beg your pardon, Master Horn?"

"No. Mirax and I are *not* going to report immediately after this meeting to the medcenter. And I think it highly unlikely that any order you issue to Booster Terrik will be obeyed like he's a loyal pet, either. What I will be doing after this meeting is finding my wife, kissing her, and trying yet again to find a way to see my *own child before she's frozen in carbonite like a common criminal.*"

Corran Horn had always been forthright. His was not a delicate or diplomatic tongue. But always before, he had come down firmly on the side of focusing on what was important. This sudden divergence on his part to putting his offspring first—an understandable desire, and one that everyone here felt sympathy for, but one that could not be accommodated—was unsettling and perhaps dangerous.

Before he could speak, Cilghal said quickly, "We have much data that needs to be processed before we are ready for you and Mirax. Perhaps in a few hours? And if you could speak with your father-in-law, I am certain he would wish to do everything he can to help his grandchildren."

Corran's posture did not relax, but his anger dissipated somewhat. He nodded curtly. "A few hours then. And Mirax is already talking to Booster."

The tension had been defused, but Hamner sighed inwardly. He suspected it was only a momentary reprieve.

Chapter Nine

JEDI TEMPLE, CORUSCANT

IT WAS, LEIA MUSED AS SHE STOOD BATHED IN FLATTERING blue light, not all that unpleasant a place as far as prisons went. She herself had been in worse. More than once.

She was currently in an isolated corner of the detention center located deep within the Jedi Temple, along with her husband Han, their daughter Jaina, and the person they had come to see. This particular Asylum Block, a two-story cellhouse with a barrier field erected around it, could almost be taken for a comfortable apartment at first glance. The interior had flowform couches, tables and chairs, and a state-of-the-art holographic center that her gadget-loving nephew Ben would likely envy. Two doors opened from the main living area to a bedroom and a refresher.

Just a pleasant apartment—if one's apartment had transparisteel walls in the living area, had all its furniture bolted to the floor, and was surrounded by Force-suppressing ysalamari housed in olbio trees, expensively and swiftly brought from their native Myrkr. Leia and her family were standing on an observation balcony with a barrier field safely between them and the inmate.

"Where can *I* sign up to be a Jedi prisoner?" Han said. "This place is nicer than my first living quarters."

Standing within a centimeter of the transparisteel wall, Seff Hellin, square-jawed, curly-haired, stared stiffly up at the Solo family. He gave no sign of recognition. His arms were folded across his chest, and his eyes were like chips of ice.

Jaina, Jag, Tahiri Veila, Winter Celchu, and Mirax Horn had taken him down a few days earlier. He had been spotted disguised as a worker outside of the Armand Isard Correctional Facility where Valin Horn was contained. It was one of the rare strokes of luck they seemed to be having that they were able to capture him both alive and without the Galactic Alliance knowing a thing about it, although a great deal of damage had been done to the prison during the incident. It had been all over the newsvids, but thus far no member of "Darkmeld," as Jaina had dubbed the team, had been identified.

Leia kept her eyes on Hellin as she spoke to Jaina. "I'm glad you removed him from the medcenter. This feels better."

Jaina and Leia had commed Han right after the exquisitely uncomfortable Masters meeting and asked him to meet them here. Now Jaina stood between her parents, small and dark-haired like her mother, vitally energetic like her father, watching not the prisoner she had helped to bring down but Han's and Leia's reactions.

"He's a patient, not a prisoner, but of course we have to keep him contained. The incident with Valin Horn painfully demonstrated the need for that."

Han frowned. "Although I gotta say, I think the blue light would start to bug me. Hey—is that a PV-One-Eight-Seven holographic display unit?"

"Dad," Jaina said. She turned to her mother and continued. "The bedroom and the refresher are screened off to give him some amount of privacy, although we have the ability to check them if we feel there's a need. We want to make him as comfortable as possible while making certain he's absolutely confined. And we hoped the change of venue might calm him."

"Oh, he looks calm," Han said. "Calm and contemplating how best to dismember us."

"Dad," Jaina repeated.

"I gotta say, I never thought we'd see this guy again," Han said, smoothly shifting from acerbic humor to deadly seriousness. "And we're not so glad about it, to be honest."

"You're certain it's the same man you saw?" Jaina asked, directing the question to both parents.

"Yep. I recognize him."

Seff did not move.

"And I recognize his feel in the Force," Leia said quietly.

"Has it changed at all?" Jaina inquired.

Leia sighed, peering down at the tall, attractive young man whom she'd known since he was fourteen. She and Han had run across Seff Hellin just a few months before. He had alarmed their granddaughter, Allana, by how he felt to the girl in the Force. Allana had fled, screaming, to Leia, crying out Jacen's name. The girl was perceptive . . . there was indeed something dark and dangerous in Seff Hellin's energy.

And about ten minutes after that encounter, Hellin had shocked everyone by tearing loose a dozen blasters from the hands of GA Intelligence, throwing them against the wall, and then paralyzing his enemies as if literally freezing them dead in their tracks. A neat little trick, one that he shouldn't have been able to do.

But one that Jacen Solo had.

"It's gotten more intense," Leia said, wishing she had better news to report. "Stronger. Darker."

"Sounds like a cup of caf," Han said. He ran a hand over his stubbled face. "You know, I could use one."

They had left Kessel as soon as word had reached them about Seff's capture, and little things like food, drink, and sleep had been pushed aside. Leia had to smile. "Me too. I think I've seen enough here. Let's go upstairs, get some caf, and take it somewhere private, where we can talk."

They had all turned and were about to leave the prison via the catwalk that surrounded the cell block and led down to the main level when Seff spoke, startling them all.

"Yes," he said, his voice laced with hatred. "Pretend to be just like us. Drink your caf, eat your nerf steaks, swing your lightsabers like real Jedi. But we'll stop you. We'll stop and get back the people you've stolen."

Leia fixed him with a compassionate gaze, her brown eyes soft. He stared back. And without another word, the Solo family turned as one to leave.

"Han, you and I need to meet with the Horns. They could use some support now."

"After caf," Han muttered, but his expression was troubled, and he added, "I can't imagine how Corran and Mirax must be feeling."

The Solos had had to mourn the deaths of two of their three children: Anakin and Jacen. Jaina, who had been their only daughter, was now their only living child. Beside her, walking swiftly like her mother in order to keep pace with the longer strides of Han as they headed to the security door, Jaina frowned.

"It's been very hard on them. First Valin, now Jysella. And Daala's comments didn't help." Her mouth was a thin line as she punched in a code and pressed her face to a small aperture for a retinal scan. She stepped back and let her parents emulate her.

"Yes," said Leia grimly. "We saw the newsvids."

"It's disgusting," Jaina blurted as the door opened and they headed toward the turbolift. "She all but declared that the reason Valin and Jysella went crazy is because of who their family is."

"Well, come on, honey, not everyone can be Solos," Han said, reaching out a hand to squeeze his daughter's slender shoulder as the turbolift doors opened.

Being born a member of the Solo clan had never been easy, although it did have its privileges. Jaina offered Han a small grin, but her brow remained furrowed in righteous anger.

"Seriously, Dad, if you saw it, you know what I'm talking about. And you *know* how steady Jysella and Valin are. Were. Now, I don't know anything about Seff Hellin."

"I have to say, I was surprised at how Corran behaved in the meeting," Leia said. "Han—you remember when we were aboard the *Errant Venture* a few years ago? How Wedge was grumbling about his daughter 'seeing a boy' and it was Corran who steered everything back on topic?"

"I do. Lost it, did he?"

Leia shook her head. Even now, her long hair was only slightly tinted with gray. "No. Not yet, anyway. But he's taking it harder than I expected."

"It was bad enough with Valin, but when Jysella snapped—right in front of Cilghal and her two best friends—and got hauled off and ordered to be put in carbonite before Corran could even see her . . ." Jaina frowned. "It was like something broke in him."

Han said nothing, but his brows drew together. Leia slipped her hand into his and squeezed it reassuringly. She understood that there was a special bond between fathers and daughters. Whether the daughter needed sheltering and protecting, like Allana did right now, or was quite capable of handing said father his rear on a platter, as Jaina unquestionably was, didn't matter in the slightest.

Jysella Horn was a full-fledged Jedi Knight. She had been entrusted with dangerous missions that sent her all over the galaxy.

She would also always be her father's little girl, whatever happened to her.

"Everyone's fond of Valin and Jysella" was all Leia said. "Corran needs to keep hope alive. And so do we," she added, glancing at her husband and daughter. "I'm sure we can get to the bottom of this."

"Hopefully Daala will agree to meet with you two. You did pretty well with the negotiations concerning Valin."

"Didn't stop him from ending up in carbonite," Han muttered.

"We did what we could with Valin and we'll do what we can with Jysella," Leia told her daughter. "And we'll see about that carbonite. For some reason, Daala does seem willing to talk to the two of us. Probably because even though she and I were on opposite sides fifty years ago, she respects the rank I once held as Senator."

"Your rank? Pssh. I think she agrees to meet with us because of my roguish charm," Han quipped.

"Sorry, only one strong and powerful woman in your life, flyboy," Leia said.

"Two," Jaina interjected, slipping an arm around her father's waist and squeezing briefly. Han brightened.

"It's Seff I'm worried about," Leia continued, still thinking of the prisoner.

"Yeah, me too," Han said. "I know the Masters needed to know. But it shouldn't go beyond that group. This guy needs to be protected. We're the ones who need to study him and figure out what's wrong with him and, presumably, Jysella and Valin. All the GA wants to do is slap him in carbonite, and that doesn't help anything."

Jaina grimaced. "While I am delighted beyond belief that I no longer have an official observer practically following me into the refresher—particularly not one who looks like my dead younger brother—that doesn't mean we're not all being watched. One journalist in particular seems very keen on chatting with Jag and me. Trying to ditch him is like trying to shake a mynock off the hull."

"Anyone I know? I'm so terribly fond of the press," Leia said drily.

"You might," Jaina said. "Guy named Javis Tyrr. He's gotten very popular recently and he's been a total pain to Jag and me."

"Javis Tyrr," Han said. "Average size, perfect hair, smirk that begs to be wiped off with a blaster?"

"That'd be him. He was right across from the Temple when Jysella came tearing out of it and fought with Bazel Warv and Yaqeel Saav'etu. He got some very clear images before Yaqeel destroyed his cam droid in her fight with Jysella." Jaina looked slightly pleased as she spoke.

"She did?" Han said. He looked impressed. "Good for her."

"The entire situation played straight into Daala's hands, right down to the press being present," Leia said. "It almost sounds orchestrated, but I don't see how that could be possible."

"No, it's just a really lousy coincidence." Jaina sighed. "Like I said, Tyrr has been buzzing around me and Jag. He's almost always either near the Temple or the Senate chamber."

"Ah, good old Jagged Fel. How *is* old Durasteel-For-A-Spine anyway?" Han asked.

"He's certainly got his hands full with the Moffs," Jaina said.

"I should have reduced the number of Moffs he has to worry about when I had the chance," her father said.

Shortly after Jacen's death, Han, Luke, and several Jedi Masters had confronted the Moffs about their role in Allana's supposed murder. Han, his heart full of grief and fury at the death of his son, even though brutal and bitter necessity had forced him to acknowledge that it had to be done, had placed the business end of a blaster to the head of the Moff who clearly had been tapped to take the fall. The Jedi present hadn't stopped him from pulling the trigger. It was Han himself who made the decision to stand down, as the Masters had known he would.

Now, as Han referenced the incident, his wife and daughter both knew he didn't mean the words he spoke. Oh, he definitely *wished* he meant it, of that Leia was certain, but that was an entirely different thing.

"He says it's like babysitting evil intelligent children who take every advantage when the parent is away," Jaina continued.

Despite herself, Leia let out a snort of amusement. "How very apt," she said.

"Fortunately," Jaina continued, "at least for the moment, they are also *behaving* like children. There seems to be enough snarling and sniping among themselves— and the mandatory inclusion of females didn't help *that*, for sure—that Jag hasn't had too many outward difficulties. But it's a strain." She shook her head. "This conflict between the GA and the Jedi . . ."

The turbolift had reached its destination, one of the small cafeterias, and settled to a stop. Jaina leaned forward and touched a pad to prevent it from opening immediately in order to finish the conversation. She looked earnestly up at her parents.

"Mom, Dad . . . it's not helping anything. Not the Jedi who are having these . . . these problems, not the Imperial Remnant or the GA, not the public, not anyone or anything."

"Certainly not young love," Leia said wryly.

Jaina flushed slightly. "Well . . . okay, I admit, it isn't

really conducive to romance. But Jag and I are adults, and we know our duties. Neither of us begrudges the time and effort and diligence they demand. But the extra strain of dodging first observers and then reporters, the finger-pointing . . . well, it certainly doesn't help."

Han slipped an arm around Leia's narrow waist and squeezed. "I don't know about that. I kinda miss the moments when your mother and I had to steal time together." He winked at his wife.

Jaina rolled her eyes and let the doors open as her parents kissed. An apprentice, a human boy about age five carrying a tray heaped with a disproportionate ratio of sweets to vegetables, gaped at them. Apparently Jaina did not want her romance to be a topic of conversation, but didn't care if her parents' was.

Leia didn't much care, either, and patted the blushing boy's fair head as they stepped out.

"Where's the caf dispenser?" Han demanded. "And *stang*, I'm starving."

"Men." Leia sighed.

Chapter Ten

THE WINDOWS OF VESTARA'S CHAMBER WERE OPEN, ALLOW-ing a soft, cool breeze fragrant with the heady scent of dalsa flowers in bloom to waft congenially about the room. Vases containing other varieties of cut flowers were perched on pieces of furniture. Paintings from the finest artists around the world, both Keshiri and human, adorned the walls. Everything in the room bespoke beauty, calmness, and contentment.

Everything except Vestara herself.

She fidgeted on the chair, drawing a soft rebuke from her attendant, Muura.

"If my lady wishes to appear beautiful, then she must be patient," Muura said in the soft, lilting accent of her people. Even after millennia spent with humans among them, the Keshiri had not quite lost the rhythm of their native tongue. Vestara liked hearing it, although the vast majority of humans and the Keshiri themselves regarded it as a liability. Vestara thought it was soft and beautiful and perfect, like so much of the Keshiri.

She gazed at her image in the mirror as Muura's clever fingers braided and pinned her long, light brown hair. The intricate vor'shandi face markings had already been painted on. Their history predated the Sith presence on

Kesh. Each mark of the brush dipped in the dark brown nectar of the s'rai plant had deep significance and was bestowed with heavy ritual. Vestara admired the delicate tracery of a dalsa flower and its trademark thorns trailing up her neck and across her cheek, then frowned a little as the leaves merged with the scar on her mouth. She always ordered the artists to disguise her scar with a design whenever possible. At least this way she could minimize her disfigurement.

She distracted herself from her self-criticism by wondering for the thousandth time why she was being summoned before the Circle of Lords. At first, when the summons had come to her and her parents yesterday, borne by no lesser a figure than a Sith Master in full formal robes, she had thought it had something to do with her application to become an apprentice. But then the summons had stipulated that she appear, alone, at the High Seat in Tahv. If it had been something as traditional as taking on the role of apprentice, she would have been summoned to the Sith Temple.

Her father, Gavar Khai, himself a Sith Saber, exuded surprise and puzzlement in the Force. Lahka, her mother, wasn't Force-sensitive at all, but even she couldn't miss the tension and mystery. She glanced worriedly from husband to daughter, but held her tongue. This was Sith business, and not for her to know about.

Vestara's father had questioned her at length that night, his presence affectionate but concerned. Had she said anything to displease anyone of significance? Had she broken any of the rules Tyros vowed to obey? Perhaps slacked on her training or studies?

Mute with apprehension, Vestara had shaken her head. She had done none of these things.

She did not mention the conversation she'd had two days previously with Ship.

In fact, the subject of Ship had not been mentioned at

all, by anyone. Shortly after Ship's arrival at the Temple, security had taken to the air and demanded that everyone clear the skies around the area. All training had been postponed, and the Temple was closed until further notice, save to those who lived there. No doubt, the Circle of Lords was discussing the strange vessel and what it meant for them, but ordinary Sith had no idea as to what was going on. It was all as mysterious as Ship itself.

Vestara shivered, even though the air circulating through the room was warm. She extended a hand, and a glass of water floated into it. She sipped the cool liquid from a straw so as not to mar the vor'shandi markings so close to her mouth while Muura finished up.

"There," Muura said, smiling, meeting Vestara's eyes in the mirror. "You look lovely, mistress!"

Vestara did not answer. She turned her head this way and that, then rose to view the formfitting green dress that was slit up the side to showcase her long, lean legs. Her arms, sleek with muscle, were also adorned with vor'shandi markings, and every finger on her hands sported a ring of some sort. The markings, painted on by artists who had studied for years under their masters as Vestara would study under hers, would wash off tonight in the bath, leaving her skin pristine and undamaged. The jewelry that dangled from her ears was draped around them, not inserted in the lobes.

Vestara was a member of the Tribe, and as such she would never dream of deliberately disfiguring herself. Her hand again went up to touch the scar on her mouth, then she clenched her fist and deliberately brought it down. All that could be done to remove the scar had been done, and she would simply need to become accustomed to it.

And make sure that every opportunity she got, she covered it up with beautiful artwork.

She glanced over at Muura, who beamed up at her happily from her shorter height, and sighed. Unadorned with jewelry or cosmetics, and wearing only the simplest of clothing, the Keshiri girl seemed to Vestara to outshine her own beauty as the sun did the moon. That, like her scar, was a simple and unchangeable fact that must be endured.

Vestara glanced around at the room. Where was—ah. She extended a hand, and her training lightsaber sprang to it. She had just finished fastening it to her jeweled belt when a knock came at the door.

The knock was for Muura's benefit, not that of Vestara, who could sense at once who was on the other side of the door.

"Come in, Father," she called.

Gavar Khai was clad in his usual attire—full Sith robes, black trimmed with silver. His long hair, as night black as his robes, was pulled back into a topknot. Vestara dropped a curtsy, then stood quietly. His dark eyes narrowed as he examined her, then he nodded and held out his arms.

She slipped into them and felt them close around her comfortably, as she had when she was a little girl. He was guarding his emotions well, but Vestara was strong in the Force, and this was, after all, her father.

"What's wrong?" She drew back to peer at him searchingly; she was almost as tall as he was now.

"Nothing you need to worry about," he said, not denying that there was, indeed, something amiss. She frowned, confused, sensing sorrow, worry, and . . . pride? Something was definitely not right.

But she was Sith, of the Tribe, and she hoped one day to become a Sith Master, and Sith Masters did not fall apart when their parents seemed worried. So instead Vestara smiled at him, and he cupped her cheek and smiled back.

"Tikk is waiting. I had one of the servants give him a bath. Can't have you attending such an important meeting on a dusty, smelly uvak, now can I?"

Vestara laughed and hugged him. "I suppose not."

Gavar pushed her away gently. "Off with you then. You don't want to be late."

"You're not—" Vestara caught herself. She had thought her father would see her off, but he made no move to leave with her. Too, he would have been in his formal robes, not his everyday garments. Indeed, Gavar did not seem to intend to leave the room.

"No. I have some things I need to discuss with Muura." He smiled and squeezed her shoulder. "Hurry, child."

Vestara was still standing there, puzzled, when Gavar gently closed the door. The last thing Vestara saw before the door shut was Muura looking at her master with a confused expression on her face.

So puzzled was she by her father's behavior that for fully half the flight to Tahv, Vestara wasn't even thinking about standing before the Circle of Lords. But as soon as the walls of Tahv appeared below her, her thoughts immediately turned to what might happen.

The walls of Tahv had been built centuries before as a pragmatic measure; five thousand years ago, there had been dangerous beasts that needed to be kept at bay, and nearly every large habitation of Keshiri was enclosed within walls. With the arrival of the Sith and their knowledge of superior technology, even though they did not have the means to craft much of what they knew how to fabricate and operate, the Keshiri—and their new Sith allies—were able to drive off some of the dangerous, predatory creatures and domesticate others. The ever-practical uvak had been tamed for centuries, but hitherto had been reserved only for Keshiri leaders.

Times had changed. The walls had become decorative rather than functional. Nearly every high-ranking Tribe member possessed an uvak or two. And the Keshiri, whose world this once had been, had become second-class citizens.

The city enclosed within the once protective embrace of the walls had changed as well. It was now more beautiful than utilitarian, reflective of a society with sufficient extra resources, power, and time to devote to the arts. The Sith had brought the Force to bear on the place, directing the growth of trees into pleasing shapes—a very popular form was the double helix—levitating fountains, and, most famously, forming sculptures out of glass.

The Sith craftspeople who could simultaneously heat and shape great amounts of the pale lavender sand that stretched for kilometers from the city to the ocean were much in demand. Three guilds had a stranglehold on the craft, and competition among them was fierce. The term *cutthroat* came to mind, quite literally; artisans often had bodyguards in their employ lest they end up with a distinctive shikkar dagger blade—the shikkar being an exquisitely crafted, single-use weapon made of glass, the idea being that it was used for a very specific purpose, at which point the blade was snapped off and left in the victim's body—from a rival guild in their gut.

Their work was everywhere to be seen in Tahv—in windows, as statuary, as jewelry and trendy shikkars, and even as domes and spires in sheltered areas of the city where their fragility was not in danger—or where Force-users, who could protect them, dwelled.

The poorer inhabitants, all of whom had no facility with the Force and most of whom were Keshiri, lived closest to the wall. The areas grew more luxurious and more attractive the closer one came to the center of Tahv, an area known as the Circle. Here was the seat of government, comprising the Grand Lord, seven High Lords, and thirteen Lords. All were, of course, Sith.

And it was the Circle to which Vestara had been instructed to report. There was an open stretch of land just north of the cluster of buildings, including the glass-domed capitol in the exact center, and Vestara saw several uvak and the placid, broad-backed riding shumshur already there. She landed Tikk gracefully, and a Sith dressed in the distinctive ice-blue color that marked him as an attendant to the Grand Lord stepped forward.

"You are?" he asked. He had light blue eyes and reddish-brown hair, and beneath the blue livery his body was obviously heavy with muscle. Vestara wondered why this strong, attractive human was merely an attendant. But then, there were many who considered simply serving the Grand Lord sufficient an achievement.

"Tyro Vestara Khai," she replied. "I was summoned."

He nodded, his face betraying nothing. "Yes. Tyro Vestara. I was told to expect you. Do not keep them waiting. Enter the capitol and speak to the Sabers there; they will take you before the Circle of Lords."

Vestara followed his directions, moving quickly but not too quickly lest she look too eager. The warmth of the day faded as she stepped into the circular capitol building. It was dark and cool inside, and from somewhere came the sound of splashing water. She paused, letting her eyes adjust to the sudden dimness after the brightness of the day outside, and suddenly realized: *I am in the capitol. I am about to go before the Circle of Lords.*

It was then that she heard the sounds of boots on the stone floor behind her and she turned.

Three Sabers, two women and one man, regarded her evenly. She had no idea where they had come from, but she was unsurprised to see them. They were Sith Sabers. She *shouldn't* have been able to sense them coming.

She bowed politely, and they nodded in acknowledgment. "I am Tyro Vestara Khai," she said. "I was summoned."

"Indeed you were," said the tall, dark-skinned woman. "Saber Shura will take you to the Circle Chambers."

"Follow me," the other woman said, and turned. Vestara obeyed, following the woman up several flights of twining stairs, realizing only belatedly that the Council Chambers were held in the glass dome of the building. All her life she had only glimpsed the landmark dome from the outside. Now, she would be permitted to see what was inside.

They reached the pinnacle and stood before a seemingly blank wall. Saber Shura reached out with both her hand and the Force, not needing to touch the wall, and suddenly Vestara could see the outlines of a door that slid open.

One of the great lessons her father had taught her, from an early age, was how to conceal her emotions, if not control them. Gavar assured her that the latter would come with time.

"Soon," he had said, "if you do not wish to be angry, you will not become so. If you do not wish to be afraid, you will cease to be. Even happiness can interfere. You will learn to use your anger, your fear, your hatred. You will choose which emotions you will feel and when. They will become weapons, just like a lightsaber, and you will be their wielder." He had smiled slightly. "But until that time, you must learn to mask them well, so as not to let others have any kind of an advantage over you."

And so Vestara knew that, even as anticipation and apprehension surged through her, her heart did not speed up, her face did not show a flicker of her worry, and no false step betrayed her as she strode with a measured pace up the stone stairs. Even in the Force, she projected a sense of calm expectation.

She reached the top of the stairway, entered the glass chamber, and as etiquette demanded, she dropped to one knee and lowered her head.

"You are Tyro Vestara Khai, daughter of Gavar, son

of Thallis." The voice was masculine, slightly quivery
with age but still deep and resonant. The acoustics in the
chamber were excellent, and the voice came clearly to
Vestara's ears. "Rise and face us."

Smoothly, the shimmery fabric of her gown rustling
with the gesture, Vestara obeyed. She held her head high
on her long, graceful neck, not tilted up in defiance, not
lowered in submission. She controlled the frequency of
her blinking as she regarded those who had summoned
her here.

She recognized them all, of course. The Grand Lord
Darish Vol, sitting upon an ornate throne of metal and
glass, the staff of office clutched in a hand so gnarled
with age that it resembled a claw. His robes were bright
and colorful, appearing even more so in the multicolored
light that came through the stained glass dome. Embroi-
dery that must have taken tailors months to produce ran
throughout the cloth. Lord Vol had permitted the hood
to fall back, revealing a nearly bald pate. Once, he had
been handsome, possibly as handsome as a Keshiri. Even
now, he was impressive looking. His eyes, still bright
with intelligence, shone intensely from a sunken face
painted with the vor'shandi markings appropriate to the
occasion. Vol was a striking, almost heavy presence in
the Force; he was not the Grand Lord without reason.
No one on this world was stronger in the Force than he.

Next to him on either side were seated the High
Lords, two of whom were female and actually addressed
as "Lady." They wore robes that were similar to the
Grand Lord's, but slightly less ornate. Less powerful
manipulators of the Force than Vol, they were nonetheless utter masters of it. Vestara recognized among their
number Lord Takaris Yur, the Lord whose task it was to
run the Sith Temple.

There were no members of the third level of leadership, the Lords, present on the dais, though Vestara had spotted them standing off to the side.

Standing flanking the Lords were the Masters. Their robes were traditionally dark and somber, but were made of expensive material and beautifully tailored. Their faces were shadowed by hoods, but Vestara felt their eyes boring into her, felt them reaching out in the Force to examine, poke, and pry at her. As she turned back to the High Lords her gaze was caught and held for a moment by Lady Rhea, who narrowed her eyes speculatively, as she had two days before when Ship had arrived.

The Grand Lord, the High Lords, and the Masters of the Sith presented an intimidating picture, by design. They wanted to throw her off-guard by keeping her ignorant of the purpose of her summons as long as possible, in the hope that she might accidentally reveal something.

Vestara felt a surge of rebelliousness, which she quickly quashed. They would get nothing from her save that which she chose to give them, and that included revealing such a desire. As she had told Ship, Sith blood pumped in her veins, Sith heritage was encoded in her genes.

A youth not much older than she, wearing the traditional black robes she usually wore but with the bright red sash that marked him as an apprentice, stepped forward.

"Surrender your training weapon, Tyro," he said.

Vestara felt her veneer of serenity flicker slightly, then calmed herself again. Unhurriedly, her fingers not fumbling in the least, she unfastened the training lightsaber and presented it to the youth, who took it and retreated.

She tried not to guess at the meaning of the request. It could be that they were planning to accept her for apprenticeship and would therefore give her a real lightsaber of her own.

Or it could be that they were denying her entirely, rejecting her even as a Tyro.

Vestara forced herself not to swallow hard.

"Tyro Vestara Khai," Grand Lord Vol continued. "Tell this gathering the story of the Return."

Of all the questions she might have been expecting, that one most certainly wasn't it. Vestara couldn't help it—she blinked in surprise and confusion. Tell the Lords and the Masters about a belief that had been part of their history for millennia? The very cornerstone of their existence on Kesh? Was this some kind of trick, or trap?

She clamped down on the uncertainty and the fear that wanted to come along with it and instead allowed herself a small smile.

"I am certain this august body knows the story, but I obey the Grand Lord's request," Vestara said. She was pleased; her voice did not betray her with the slightest quiver. She straightened and clasped her hands behind her back, reciting the details of a story every single being in the room, indeed probably on the planet, knew by heart.

"When the *Omen* first crashed on Kesh, our forefathers were greeted warmly by the Keshiri. They were made welcome, brought safely down from the crash site on uvak-back, and treated almost as gods. The Sith soon learned why. The Keshiri believed that the arrival of the Sith was, indeed, an omen."

Her gaze flickered to Lady Rhea. The older woman regarded her impassively. Vestara reached out, subtly, into the Force, but could glean no hint as to how her recitation was being received. She continued.

"They believed that the Sith were the predestined Protectors, who would protect the Keshiri when the feared Destructors would eventually return. The Destructors, according to ancient Keshiri myth, periodically descend on inhabited worlds to wipe out civilization and return all beings to their natural, primitive states. Research conducted in recent years does seem to confirm that such a planetwide catastrophe has been visited upon Kesh at least once, lending credence to the legend."

Her throat was dry. Gamely, Vestara pressed on.

"The Sith felt that indeed they . . . we . . . were the ones who had been foretold, and know that it is our destiny to grow strong, to gain wisdom, and, when the time is right, to stand firm against the Return of those who would destroy Kesh."

"Destroy Kesh," said one of the Lords whose name Vestara couldn't remember, "and other worlds as well. The Sith destiny is too vast to be confined to one world. Was this not taught to you, Tyro Khai?"

Ah, there was the trap. She cursed herself for not catching it sooner, it was so obvious. She was not yet able to control the blush that rose to her cheeks as she answered.

"Of course, Lord—" *Ai,* what was his name—Workan, that was it! "Lord Workan. But for five thousand years, we have not been—"

No. Oh, no. *That* wasn't the trap. She'd walked right into the real one and mortification flooded her. Then she felt a reassuring presence, almost as gentle as that of her father. An assurance that while it was a trick, it wasn't a trap.

Lord Workan smirked and glanced over at Lady Rhea. Vestara realized that it was she who had sent the brief brush of comfort. Lady Rhea, slender, tall, graceful as a sorumi doe, stepped forward.

"Everything we have known for over five thousand years changed yesterday beyond imagining," Lady Rhea said in her deep, husky voice. "For the first time since the *Omen* crashed in the Takara Mountains, we have found a way off Kesh. A way to fulfill our destiny. This . . . *Ship* . . . has sought us out for that selfsame purpose."

A little thrill went through Vestara when she heard the emphasis put on the word *ship,* as if it was a proper name rather than a simple noun, as she had done when thinking about the vessel.

"It is, as you have no doubt surmised," Lady Rhea continued, almost drawling, moving inexorably forward with a graceful stride in Vestara's direction, "much more than a simple vessel. It is a Sith meditation sphere. I imagine you can tell me its purpose, can you not?"

Vestara hesitated. Should she lie? Would it be dangerous for the Lords and the Masters to know exactly how much she knew, how Ship had spoken to her? Or would it be better for her to tell them everything? It was likely that no one in this room had slept since the arrival of the strange vessel. And it was likely that it had spoken to them as it had to her. After all, these were the very leaders of the Sith, the keepers of all that it meant to *be* Sith. She wanted badly to lick her dry lips but wouldn't let the gesture betray her anxiety.

"It is designed to train apprentices," Vestara replied.

Lady Rhea had reached her now and stood with her hands on her hips. The gesture spread her black cape behind her, and even though Vestara was nearly as tall as she, the overall effect was imposing. It was meant to be.

"Indeed," said Lady Rhea, almost purring. "What did it tell you? And what did you tell it?"

Vestara met Lady Rhea's eyes evenly and told the truth. All of it. Right down to her burning desire to become a Sith Master. Her father had once said that the main thing that differentiated them from Jedi was that the Jedi were too afraid to embrace passion.

"Don't ever be afraid of what you feel, Vestara," he had said. "Just know that you can use it. You *must* use it, or else it will use you."

And she used it now. Ship had contacted her. It had spoken with her. She used that, and her deep wanting—

her need—to be trained. To become a Sith Master. To fulfill her destiny, as the Sith were about to fulfill theirs.

The chamber was hushed as Vestara's youthful voice rang out clear and strong and deeply passionate. Lady Rhea listened raptly, her eyes on Vestara's face. Finally, the girl finished, and stood waiting.

Lady Rhea glanced back at the Lords and the Masters with what could only be called a look of triumph.

"You see? Everything she says corroborates what Ship told us."

"It is . . . an unusual way to pick an apprentice," said Grand Lord Vol, placing the tips of his fingers together and regarding Vestara speculatively.

Pick an apprentice? Vestara's breathing caught for just a second. Could it finally be—

"But I suppose that once, it was not so unusual," the Grand Lord continued. "Ship is, after all, a training vessel."

Lady Rhea turned back to Vestara, smiling, and there was genuine pleasure emanating from her in the Force.

"Yours was the first mind Ship contacted, Vestara," she said. "It was intrigued by you. Far be it from the Circle of Lords to stand in the way of the decision made by such a construct."

She snapped her fingers, and the apprentice who earlier had taken Vestara's training lightsaber from her reappeared. In his hand he bore one of the remaining lightsabers from the original Sith. Vestara gasped, then her teeth clicked together as she clamped down on the wave of joy that surged through her.

Despite her resolve, tears stung her eyes. Usually, apprentices had to make their own lightsabers, and with the limited resources available to them, they were not as fine as these antiques. Every Master had one, certainly, but there were even some Sabers who did not. They were powered by Lignan crystals, one of the great heritages of the Sith. The crystals, thousands of which had crowded the cargo hold of the *Omen* when it crashed, enabled the lightsabers to burn hotter and last longer than the original design permitted. Too, for various reasons, they were perfect for Sith weapons.

And Tyro—no, *Apprentice*—Vestara Khai now owned such a lightsaber.

For an instant, sorrow filled her. That was why, then, her father had behaved so oddly this morning. He had known, and not been able to tell her. For once a Tyro was chosen as an apprentice, she was separated from her family with no warning—and no contact for an entire year.

But that was the order of things, and she and her family knew it. The sorrow was chased away by other feelings she tried to corral, lest she seem arrogant.

But there was no fooling Lady Rhea. The older woman reached out a hand and squeezed her shoulder.

"Everyone here understands what you are feeling, *Apprentice* Khai," she said gently. "Revel in your delight and pride. Know that you have been chosen for this, chosen more surely than most. Come with me now, and I will show you the secrets of the *Omen*.

"And further"—her smile widened, became predatory with anticipation—"Ship will share with you its knowledge and wisdom of the galaxy beyond this world."

Vestara thought her heart might burst from joy and excitement.

"Praise circumstances for the time of your birth, young one," said Lady Rhea. "For you will know the honor and responsibilities and delights of being among the first in five millennia to leave Kesh . . . and rejoin our brethren, from whom we have been separated for so very long, to take your place in ruling a Sith galaxy."

Chapter Eleven

WYNN DORVAN MOVED THROUGH THE VAST CORRIDOR OF power that was the Senate Building with the calm, almost preoccupied stride of one who knew it well. He nodded a courteous but distant greeting to the guards at the various security checkpoints, who politely wished him "Good morning, sir." His pocket bulged, but not with anything more dangerous than a sleeping chitlik, who was as familiar a fixture as Dorvan himself.

Wynn Dorvan arrived hours before anyone else and generally left hours later. He stood in the turbolift, not fidgeting or making any attempt at whiling away the time as others might, until it opened on his floor. He strode down the thickly carpeted hallway and keyed open the door to his office.

Dorvan's office was as free of frills, trappings, and busyness as the man himself. He had no holopics of family, for he had none—well, none outside of the small ball of fur softly snoring in his right-hand coat pocket. There was art on the walls, simply because leaving them bare had proved too unnerving to what few visitors he had, but it was passionless, safe art—unremarkable reproductions of Coruscant's old Galaxies Opera House and the Manari Mountains. The windows had no full, floor-length drapes in rich fabrics, but only shutters that rolled up or down at a touch to emit or prohibit light as Dorvan found it necessary. There was a desk, a chair, and two extra chairs for the rare guests. It was all in all, clean, simple, and tidy.

Which was why the huge bouquet of trumpet and pyro flowers, in its almost obscene riot of red and purple and rich scent, was so dreadfully out of place.

Dorvan blinked. He was not alarmed; no one could gain admittance to this office save himself, Daala, and a few other trusted colleagues. Besides, an intruder was unlikely to leave flowers.

Pocket stirred, poking her nose out and sniffing the overwhelmingly lush fragrance of the gift. Absently Dorvan petted the chitlik with one hand while he stepped forward. There was a card propped up in front of the bouquet, with his name written on the thick, cream-colored flimsi in a bold yet elegant hand. He knew that handwriting. Chief of State Natasi Daala had left this gift for him.

Utterly confused now, he opened the envelope and read three words: "Sorry. A favor."

He frowned slightly. What did Daala possibly have to be sorry about?

"Wynn Dorvan, sir?"

The voice was young, female, and eager.

Ah, Dorvan thought with a sad little smile. He turned around to see the speaker standing, shifting her weight uneasily. She was a Twi'lek, striking as all females of her species. Her skin was green, with darker, forest-green stripes visible here and there. She was dressed demurely in understated business attire, her lekku draped in front of her shoulders. She carried a datapad and smiled a bit hesitantly at him.

"I'm—"

"My new assistant," Dorvan interrupted her.

"Y-yes," the girl stammered. "My name is Desha Lor. Chief of State Daala appointed me."

Dorvan recalled the conversation he'd had with Daala in the airspeeder and sighed slightly. He really, really didn't want an assistant. He functioned so much better by himself.

But he could understand why Daala might have wanted to hire this girl. Once she herself, Admiral Natasi Daala, had been looked on with scorn as little more than Grand Moff Wilhuff Tarkin's "bit on the side." True, she had once been his mistress, and true, she was a strikingly physically beautiful woman. But she was also fiercely intelligent and ambitious, with an exquisite grasp of strategy that often left both allies and adversaries reeling. She had used the underestimation and contempt in which she had been held ruthlessly, calculatedly to her advantage. Now she was the head of the Galactic Alliance. She had insisted that the Moffs include women. It made perfect sense that she'd feel a kinship with a female Twi'lek, who until recent history had fetched high prices on the slave market. Daala would want to give a deserving female the same opportunity she'd had herself to defy expectations and excel.

Dorvan extended his hand. "Hello, Desha Lor. I'm Wynn Dorvan, as you already know. Is this your first government job?"

She nodded vigorously. "Yes. Chief of State Daala is a friend of my family. It was most kind of her to offer me this position."

"Most kind," Dorvan echoed. "You'll have to excuse me . . . your presence here is a bit of a surprise for me. I'm sure we'll learn to work together."

He indicated one of the simple chairs, and she took a seat while he slid into the chair across the desk from her. Pocket squeaked slightly, and he lifted the little animal out and put her in her small bed on a shelf behind the desk.

"Oh, is that a chitlik? They're adorable!"

"Yes, they are, and Pocket has the run of the office. I'll take care of her. All you need to do is watch out not to step on her."

Desha gave him a radiant smile. "I'm sure I'd never do that."

"Not more than once, believe me. She's generally calm, but she bites if she's unhappy. Now . . . tell me about your clearance level and what our good Chief of State said you'd be doing for me."

Desha Lor had a very high level of clearance indeed, which would be necessary if she was to be more to him than a pretty face to greet visitors. He intended her to be. If he was going to have an assistant forced upon him, then he would make her earn her keep. While she spoke, he ran his own check on her, keeping the screen turned away so she couldn't see what he was doing. He nodded in all the right places, listening with half an ear.

Lor, Desha, daughter of a Twi'lek diplomat, had been an intern in the private sector for a year. Stellar student, no criminal record, all her offworld visits checked out. Her family was well known and respected. She was definitely clean. Almost too clean.

Is anyone this innocent anymore? Dorvan wondered, then reprimanded himself for waxing sentimental. He'd better keep an eye on her, make sure she was just the innocent young woman on her first big government job that she seemed to be. Daala was a sharp one, no one knew that better than Wynn Dorvan. But he aided the Galactic Alliance best by knowing the weaknesses of those around him, and Daala's sympathy toward an attractive female trying to earn a place in the galaxy based on more than her looks might just be a weakness. It

would not be the first time he had quietly helped the GA
by moderating Daala's more extreme stances.

Princess Leia Organa was the shining example of a
beautiful young woman with good family connections
and a spotless record turning out to be a rebel against
the current administration.

Oh, yes. He'd definitely keep an eye on her.

MOFF LECERSEN'S RESIDENCE,
SENATE DISTRICT, CORUSCANT

"I'm keeping an eye on him," Moff Lecersen said as he
relaxed back into the tub full of pleasant-smelling water.
"Not, mind you, that it's all that hard to do."

"Indeed." Moff Vansyn's voice over the comm was
amused and wry. The conversation had begun earlier
that night over an excellent meal accompanied by two
bottles of imported gold wine. The hour had grown late,
and Vansyn had an early-morning meeting, so the discussion continued via comm. The serving droid rolled
up to the edge of the tub with a glass and what was
left of the second bottle of gold wine. Lecersen poured
the remainder of the beverage into the fluted glass and
took a sip. It was an excellent vintage, of course, and
Lecersen had several cases of the stuff. There was a bittersweet irony in that the beverage was Hapan. After his
latest dealings with the Hapans, the last thing he wanted
was to be reminded of that particular part of space. And
yet, the beverage went down so smoothly. One could
dislike the Hapans and still admire their skills in viticul-
ture and oenology.

"I'd say all you really need to do is keep an eye on
Jaina Solo," Vansyn continued.

Lecersen smiled thinly and took another sip. "Child's
play itself. Jagged Fel may be the nominal head of the

Empire, and a disciplined soldier, but he is a pathetic puppy when it comes to matters of the heart. He has no concept of how to properly keep a mistress."

Lecersen's thoughts wandered to one such Moff mistress, an infamous one who now ran the Galactic Alliance, and he frowned slightly. He edged down farther into the warm water, letting it soak the tension from him.

She'd been fine enough when Wilhuff Tarkin was alive. He'd known how to keep her properly under his thumb. Now she was causing them no end of difficulties. Female Moffs. What was the Empire coming to?

"Granted, he chose a headstrong one, and I'm not sure who is keeping whom," Vansyn said. Lecersen laughed out loud at that.

"A nerf bull with a ring through his nose can be easily led," he said.

"Jaina Solo is doing the leading, not us," countered Vansyn. "It is unfortunate that he has become taken with a Jedi. Especially one with such a pedigree. He has made his informal and personal relationship with her into a governmental one, and that doesn't sit well with me . . . nor many others."

Lecersen shrugged. The water splashed softly with the gesture. "What you say is true, Vansyn. But if we understand how Solo is leading, we can use that to our advantage. The pup is distracted. You saw him at the last meeting. Kept checking his chrono. He thinks he has brought us in line because he wants to think that, so he can pursue his . . . extracurricular activities without feeling he is neglecting his duty."

No, the Moffs had most definitely *not* been brought to heel the way the Jedi had wanted on that dreadful day when Jacen Solo had been cut down by the very same Jedi female presently under discussion. Han Solo's blaster threat had been empty—the man did not have the stuff for such a cold-blooded, systematic execution simply for revenge. But Skywalker's threat hadn't been empty. It hadn't even been veiled.

Luke Skywalker had very bluntly stated they had two choices: One, become Hapan prisoners of war and face a war crimes trial for the nanokiller attack the Moffs had launched against the royal family. Or two, the Moff Council could join in reestablishing the Galactic Alliance. Skywalker had appointed Jagged Fel on the spot. It had been ease itself to agree to the second option. The first was hardly viable.

But that did not mean the Moffs would stop looking out for themselves. It was good to have gone from the "Imperial Remnant" to "Empire" again, but what exactly did that mean? How to make it more than an empty title? That was the puzzle Moff Lecersen had been gnawing on daily.

"Patience is a virtue, my friend. Let Fel carry on this little love affair. Passion burns hot and fast. It makes mistakes and clouds judgment. And when his judgment is cloudiest . . . we will be there to take advantage of it."

Opportunities were everywhere, all the time, for sharp minds to find. Like credcoins dropped on a pavement. And Lecersen had a very sharp mind. There were so very many enemies to set at one another's throats.

Daala was already doing a very good job of alienating the Jedi. Lecersen didn't think he could have done any better. The Jedi, in turn, were doubtless up to something. He wasn't sure what. Yet. But he did not think for an instant that the elegant, courteous Kenth Hamner spoke for every single Jedi Knight or, indeed, even Master in the Order. The observers who had now been legally abolished had been good for Daala and the GA, not so good for the Moffs. Far better to have the Jedi thinking they weren't being watched.

Two Jedi were now incarcerated. That was good. The

Jedi had been chafing under Daala and all but reveling in their new, legal freedom. That was good, too. Jag was distracted, and so was Jaina, and reporters were apparently annoying the two to no end. Also very good.

The threads were all there. Now to weave them into a tapestry that would illustrate a picture of the Moffs restored to their rightful Imperial glory—without a lovesick puppy of a pilot at its head.

Lecersen drained the wine, looked at the empty glass, and smiled.

Chapter Twelve

JAINA COULDN'T BELIEVE IT, BUT SHE ACTUALLY MISSED DAB Hantaq.

She did not miss the random check-ins that had often interrupted her sleep or other nocturnal activities. She did not miss his following her during her waking hours, reporting on her every movement. And she most certainly did not miss the fact that he was a dead ringer—*nice pun, Jaina,* she thought with a wince—for her late brother, Anakin.

What she did miss was the fact that Dab had tried to do his job with courtesy. He did what he was ordered to do, but he never seemed to particularly relish it.

Unlike the reporters. Jaina was beginning to think the ruling in favor of eliminating the official observers had traded one nuisance for a worse one. At least the observers had had rules of their own. The journalists seemed to have none whatsoever. During the whole "let's give the entire galaxy access to the Jedi" phase that had mercifully come to an end recently, certain areas of the Temple had been opened to journalists. At least a Jedi had accompanied them during their sightseeing, but Jaina had never gotten used to running into the press in the dining room or in the Room of a Thousand Fountains.

She sighed and slipped into her outfit for the night's mission, which Jag had dubbed Operation Caranak, and began to apply the makeup necessary to complete it. She scowled at herself in the mirror and sighed. Time was growing short. It would have to do.

Automatically she reached for her lightsaber, and then hesitated. Sword of the Jedi she might be, but tonight's mission would not necessitate fighting. She hoped. It had a very specific goal in mind, and if she ended up being forced to use her lightsaber, all would already be lost. With a slight frown, she dropped it in her black, stylish nerf-hide handbag anyway. No one needed to see it, and she felt naked leaving without it.

She clicked on her comm. "Gaunt, this is Slicer."

"Gaunt here." Jag, his voice calm as ever but with a slight edge to it that only Jaina, who knew him so well, would have noticed. The mission clearly had him keyed up.

"Everything in order?" she asked.

"Check. Carved is in position."

"So is Curved. I'm preparing to initiate Phase One."

"Copy that," Jag said. "I'm moving into the secondary location."

She took a deep breath, steadying herself for what she might face. "Okay. See you at the rendezvous."

"Watch yourself. They'll be gunning for you."

"I know. You too."

She clicked off her comlink and attempted to put it in its usual position on her belt, then remembered she wasn't wearing the belt tonight.

These stealth missions were annoying.

She dropped the comlink in her bag beside her lightsaber. A final perusal of her outfit and she left the room.

The reporter was waiting for her the instant she stepped outside the Temple.

She had known he would be, and steeled herself for the encounter.

Reporters were forbidden to enter the Temple unless invited to do so, a welcome change from earlier. So instead they clustered like a swarm of insects at the base of the stairs, a milling little knot of salacious beings all clamoring for the exclusive story.

"Jedi Solo! Over here!"

"Solo! Where are you heading?"

"Jedi Solo, what is your opinion on the movement to eliminate slavery on Vinsoth?" This last from a Chev, tall, powerfully built, piercing violet eyes staring at her from under a heavy brow.

Jaina waved a hand airily at all of them, forcing an expression of good cheer.

"Come on, guys, can't a girl go out on a dinner date just like anyone else?" She opened her coat, nerf-hide black to match her evening bag, and mockingly showed off the long, red formal evening dress she wore underneath it, with matching red shoes with high, narrow heels. "See? Not even wearing my lightsaber. And I'm certainly not going to be running in these shoes. Now, unless you are keenly interested in what I'm going to order for dinner, you should really go home. Or bug someone else."

Some of the crowd sighed audibly and backed away. But at least one tagged along after her, shouting, "Shouldn't a Jedi, who respects the Force created by all living beings, be a vegetarian?"

Jaina rolled her eyes and bit back a retort. *Think of the mission, Jaina. Think of the mission.* She ducked into the speeder that had pulled up and was now hovering, waiting for her.

"Go. Now."

Winter Celchu, her distinctive white hair dyed a forgettable shade of muddy brown, her features blunted by a judicious application of makeup, and her figure swathed in the robes of a Jedi apprentice, caught Jaina's eyes in the mirror and grinned.

"Of course, Jedi Solo."

It might be only a dinner, Javis Tyrr thought, but many a secret had been whispered between lovers by candle-light before. Jaina had a head start on him; he would have to move quickly. As he lifted off, his Hologlide J57 cam droid securely in the seat beside him, he was able to catch sight of her vessel.

Had Jaina been piloting, he knew, the speeder would make all sorts of convoluted twists and turns in an effort to elude pursuit. Instead, it remained almost staidly in the proper lanes of traffic, not exceeding legal speeds. And if Jaina wasn't piloting tonight, that meant she might be choosing to imbibe some alcohol with her meal. Tyrr smiled. That would be useful. Intoxication often loosened tongues.

His network's ratings had soared upon his coverage of Jysella Horn's "Jedi Rampage," as it had been dubbed. So had his popularity with his bosses. He'd been given his own exclusive half-hour show, which he had titled *Javis Tyrr Presents: The Jedi Among Us.* Some episodes had been calmer than others. Most recently, in fact, he had aired an educational spot about the history of the Jedi. The ratings were starting to drop as the public lost interest, and his boss had recently indicated that something "a bit livelier" would be preferred.

He was not going to stoop to eavesdropping on pillow talk. Tyrr was, after all, a reputable journalist. But any conversation held in a public place was fair game.

The little red speeder was fairly easily followed, and Tyrr wondered if perhaps this might not be a waste of his time tonight. Jaina Solo and Jagged Fel were highly important personages, but they were beings, too, and it might indeed just be a dinner out. Even so, there could possibly be crumbs dropped that would be worth it. He tapped in a request on the vessel's computer and it came up with a list of several restaurants in the area. As he quickly scanned the list, he realized he thought he knew where they were headed. That information helped make up his mind. He veered into another lane, taking a short-cut in order to arrive before Jaina. If, as he suspected, Fel and Solo were dining at the Indigo Tower, one of the nicest restaurants in the quarter, at least he'd have a good meal at the network's expense.

The Indigo Tower was modeled after the famous Skysitter Restaurant, shamelessly stealing that establishment's concept of a revolving room on a tower high above the Coruscanti skyline. Its exterior was made of shining, blue-black durasteel, extremely modern and chic. Inside the color theme continued throughout the lush décor.

Tyrr pulled into the valet lane, handed a credcoin of decent denomination off to the valet, and lingered at the entrance to the Tower, checking his chrono and looking about as if waiting for someone. He was careful to stay in the shadows as much as possible.

A black speeder with the insignia of the Galactic Empire pulled up. Imperial Head of State Jagged Fel was clearly not attempting to hide his appearance. He also was driving his own speeder, and stepped out briskly, his military bearing obvious. His dark head with its distinctive white streak, a continuation of the scar that ran across his face, was bare, but he wore an elegant cloak, scarf, and gloves in concession to the chill of the altitude. He, too, handed his vessel off to a valet, then stood and waited, his breath puffing in the chill air.

A few moments later the little red speeder appeared. Jaina Solo stepped out, smiling at Jag as he assisted her courteously. He kissed her cheek, drew her arm through his, and together they entered the restaurant.

Tyrr followed, keeping a discreet distance. He was certain he had not been observed. But it wouldn't matter if he *had* been spotted by the two: As a journalist of repute, he would not arouse suspicion by choosing to dine at this establishment. He lingered as they were led off by the maître d' and then told the young female Ortolan who approached him, "I'd like to be close to those two."

He subtly flashed a credcard and winked.

"I'll get you as close as I can, sir," she said, taking the card in her large, stubby hands, running it, and returning it to him just as discreetly. He followed her as she led him through the dining room, and wondered if her dark blue skin had been an asset during the hiring process at a place called the Indigo Tower. The carpet was thick and plush; over in the corner, a musical trio—a Bith, another Ortolan, and a human—was playing a soft tune. A sultry-voiced Pa'lowick stepped up to the microphone and began to sing.

The Ortolan led him to an area where secluded booths extended into corners and the blue light made everything look mysterious and cool. He watched Jag and Jaina, her arm still through his, their heads bent close together as they spoke quietly.

And then the maître d' opened a door, and they disappeared.

"Here you are, sir," the Ortolan said blithely. "This is the closest table to our private rooms."

He stared at her.

"I'd have given a lot to see the look on Tyrr's face," Jaina said.

"We must, alas, content ourselves with imagining it," Jag said.

"Anything else I can do for you, sir? Madam?" the maître d' inquired politely.

"Not at the moment. Just keep up the façade. Open the doors from time to time to let him have a look," Jag said.

"Of course, sir. You'll have five minutes before the waiter comes in with the wine list." He went to the door and waited for everyone to take their positions.

Sitting at the cozy, romantic, candlelit table for two were two humans who at first glance—and probably second—looked exactly like Jaina and Jag. Jag had first given Jaina the idea when Darkmeld had gone after Seff Hellin. "Like all sensible Chiefs of State, I have a double, hard at work pretending to be me back in my quarters," he had said after they'd successfully brought down the troubled Jedi.

Leia hadn't used a double, as Jaina had pointed out to Jag, but she would. It was just too useful an idea.

Jag's double, Karn Valanti—code-named "Carved" for the decoy he was—was positively uncanny, Jaina thought. It wasn't so much the looks, although he did strongly resemble Jag, especially around the eyes, but the man had gotten his movements down pat. She wasn't so sure hers would pass close inspection, but everyone else assured her that Lina Zev—code-named "Curved," not for her figure but for a fishing hook—had captured Jaina to perfection.

"Wait till you see her demonstrate your trademark annoyed scowl," Jag had said once. Jaina had frowned at him. "That's the one. She's nailed it."

Now the two doubles were helping Jag out of his outfit and Jaina into hers. Jag had worn a close-fitting, dark, nondescript tunic and pants beneath his formal wear, and Karn was now draping a hooded cloak over Jag's broad shoulders. Jaina had shucked the high-heeled shoes and slipped a pair of trousers on beneath her dress. She turned away and wriggled out of the gown while Lina draped a shirt over her. She shrugged into her own cloak, demanding, "Time?"

"We have exactly one minute and thirty-three seconds," Jag assured her.

"Let's go," Jaina said. They turned and ducked into the side door that led into the kitchens, which had doubtless been pressed into use as an escape route before. As the door closed, she glanced back just in time to see the main door to the dining area opening.

Stang . . . those doubles *did* look convincing. The door slid shut and Jaina smiled at the kitchen staff. Some of them smiled back at her, but most appeared disinterested. Trysts between high-powered couples were apparently nothing new at one of the most popular restaurants in the Senate District.

Jaina sniffed appreciatively. Her stomach rumbled and she eyed some of the prepared dishes wistfully.

"One of these days," she said, "we really will have to come here just for dinner."

"I promise," Jag said. "But for now—we have a mission, remember?"

Tyrr fumed quietly for a few moments, but then resigned himself to the situation. It could still be turned to good use, and an evening spent dining on nerf steak and thakitillo, washed down with a nice glass of Crème D'Infame, was not one to be regretted.

He caught glimpses of them from time to time as the door opened and the waiter brought in wine, appetizers, and the main course. They didn't look like two high-ranking figures in deep discussion about politics, or Jedi principles, or anything. They looked like . . . a couple out on a date.

His opportunity came when the serving droid tweetled past, a small unit bearing a sinful-looking array of pastries, puddings, and candies. It paused to permit an elderly couple to leave, and in those few seconds Tyrr removed a tiny cam, the size of a pinkie fingernail, from his pocket. He activated it with a remote in his other pocket, and the little cam sprouted legs like a spider and scurried onto the serving droid. It hastened up and embedded itself beneath the napkin on the tray, and Javis Tyrr grinned.

The Pa'lowick singer stepped up to the microphone and began to croon a currently popular love song. Her Basic was surprisingly good.

> It's all just a dream, isn't it?
> This thing we call love . . .
> A marvelous scheme, isn't it?
> This thing we call love . . .

Javis listened with half an ear. He liked the song, and the performance was a good one, but his attention was most definitely elsewhere. A moment later, the droid paused before the closed door of the private dining room and bleeped a few times. The door opened to let it through, then slid shut behind it.

> It's just an illusion,
> A trick of the heart,
> A pleasant delusion
> When two are apart—

Tyrr nursed his own dessert and after-dinner drink, pulling out what looked like an ordinary datapad and perusing files. To all observers, he looked like the newsman he was, reading up on notes his assistant had gathered for his latest story. And indeed, that was what was on the screen—at the moment. But in a small corner, which could be enlarged with a tap of the finger, was an up-close-and-personal glimpse of . . . white napkin.

He manipulated the controls in his pocket and the tiny cam droid scurried down to the thick carpet. He could hear them talking:

"Oh yum . . . Vagnerian canapés. Mom loves these. Have you ever had one?" Jaina. Tyrr frowned. Perhaps the audio receivers were maladjusted—she sounded *off*, somehow.

"No." The sound of a fork clinking on plate, and then, "Mmm . . . okay. That's pretty amazing."

Yes, the audio was definitely off. Jag's voice sounded slightly deeper than normal, and more nasal. Oh, well, at least their words were being recorded. Tyrr again touched the controls and the little droid climbed up the table leg as the two continued to chat about the merits of various desserts and whether or not caf or Cassandran brandy was the proper beverage to consume with them. Tyrr sighed. It was an utterly banal conversation. He was about to write the evening off as a waste—except for the lovely meal—when the cam finally made it to the top of the table and raced to hide itself amid the fronds of the bouquet that served as a centerpiece.

The woman was not Jaina.

Oh, at first it looked like her, but the mouth was too wide and the nose too pinched. And the voice—there was nothing wrong with the audio receiver. It was the voice itself that was wrong.

Quickly Tyrr directed the droid to maneuver to the opposite side. Was Jag—

He zoomed in on the scar, and realized it was cleverly applied makeup. Doubles. They had gotten doubles. It was a fine old tradition, and he'd fallen for it.

It was all Tyrr could do not to pound his fist on the table in frustration.

It's all just smoke and mirrors, darling;
A pretty lie, and nothing more.

Smoke and mirrors, indeed. It was time to take off the gloves. His ratings needed a boost. He needed a scoop, a story that would eclipse anything else.

And he was determined to get it.

The small, nondescript speeder was waiting outside the rear door. Tahiri Veila opened the doors and Jaina and Jag jumped inside, barely making it before Tahiri lifted off.

"How'd it go?"

"Smooth as shimmersilk," Jaina said.

"Catch any in the net or was it just a good general slip?"

"Javis Tyrr followed us," Jag said. "At least we know he's wasted an evening."

Tahiri smirked a little. "Good. He's tried to interview me, you know."

"I'm not surprised," Jaina said, wrinkling her nose in distaste. "You'd boost his ratings through the roof."

Jag clicked on his comlink. "Hoth, this is Gaunt. Is the bantha in position?"

"In the cave as promised," Winter Celchu replied. "Ready to travel."

"Great. Mynock has been effectively neutralized for the evening. Operation Caranak will proceed as planned."

"Good luck. Hoth out."

Jaina listened, her lips curving in a smile. Jag had come up with the name *mynock* to describe their parasitic journalist. It was just perfect. She sighed and leaned against him. One more "bantha"—speeder—to pick up, and the mission would be accomplished. She and Jag would spend the night under aliases in a small, out-of-the-way inn halfway around the planet.

"By the way," asked Tahiri, "why Operation Caranak?"

"A caranak," Jag said, slipping an arm around Jaina as she rested her head against his shoulder in the backseat, "is an aquatic fowl native to Endor. It is notoriously difficult to domesticate."

Tahiri was silent, then she said slowly, ". . . a wild goose?"

"Just so."

Another pause and then, "And they say you don't have a sense of humor, Jag."

"They," said Jag, his voice completely serious, "do not have a sufficiently good espionage network."

THE SOLOS' PRIVATE APARTMENTS, CORUSCANT

"I'm worried about Allana," Leia said. She was curled up next to her husband, her petite frame nestled against his larger one as they spooned together in their bedchamber. They had opted to leave the large, military-grade-thickness transparisteel viewport open. At all hours of the day or night, they could watch the colorful, constantly changing images of Coruscant traffic. Some might have found the view stressful. The Solos, with their love of vessels, found it reassuring.

"What about her?" Han mumbled. He had almost fallen asleep, but he could feel the tension, the wakefulness in his wife's body. "She dealt okay with the spiders on Kessel. Just like a Solo granddaughter should."

"I'm not talking about repercussions from Kessel," Leia said. Her voice was soft, quiet, and Han could barely hear her. He frowned and propped himself up on his elbow, gently turning her to face him.

"This some kind of Force thing?"

"No, not at all. In fact the opposite." Leia sighed.

"Han, she needs something . . . ordinary. And we're most definitely not."

"Well, you got that right, but neither is she. She was born the Chume'da, the heir to the Hapan throne. She's the daughter of Tenel Ka and Jacen Solo, two very powerful Jedi. She's about as far from ordinary as you can get."

Leia sighed and snuggled against him, idly stroking his chest. "Even so, when she was Chume'da, she had her routines. Her place. Her droids."

"She has droids here. And that feels nice, so keep on— Ow!" Han glowered at her as, annoyed, Leia tugged on his chest hair with the intent to irritate.

"She does. But with all that's going on right now, I can't help but think back to my own childhood. What made me feel happy, safe, and loved."

"Oh, yeah, you had a very ordinary life. Forgot about that, Princess and Senator."

Although he was being sarcastic, Han knew that he was also correct, and Leia, who was usually fair about these things, did not reprimand him by tugging again on his chest hair.

"No, I absolutely did not have an ordinary life. But I never felt unsettled. And I'm afraid that's what's happening with Allana."

The faint light from the never-dark Coruscant skies fell upon her features, still beautiful to him—and others—after over forty years. Her eyes, that rich, liquid brown that always made him kind of quivery, glinted slightly in the multicolored glow as she peered up at him, and Han Solo fell in love all over again, as he did pretty much at least once a week. He'd been lucky to have found such an amazing woman. Life would never, ever be dull with her.

"I had a very happy, stable childhood," Leia continued. "Two parents who were very much in love with each other. I was raised on politics, but it never harmed the family. Resisting the Empire never seemed to conflict with storytime, or trips together as a family, or . . ."

Her brown eyes bored into his. Han knew that the reason for the conversation was about to be made manifest, and he braced himself.

"Or wonderful, sunlit afternoons spent riding my thranta."

Han waited. But apparently that was it.

"I don't get it. I must be too sleepy to be having this conversation," Han said.

"The Coruscant Livestock Exchange and Exhibition just started. We have the credits and the property to buy Allana something special. Something she can spend wonderful, sunlit afternoons riding."

Han's own eyes widened. "You're not serious."

"Oh, very, I'm afraid."

"You want to go to the Livestock Exchange and Exhibition."

She nodded. Rivers of dark brown hair shot with gray that only made her look more gorgeous gleamed with the movement. Han frowned. It wasn't fair, sometimes.

"Let's get her a thranta just like the one you had and we'll call it good," Han said. "I think Lando had a couple on Bespin. Bet he could find us a nice one."

"Han . . . thrantas can't live on Coruscant. There's too much pollution for them here."

Han groaned quietly. "Livestock Exchange. I bet you're going to say we can't just send her along with Artoo and Threepio and a couple of Jedi guards."

Leia shook her head, her brown eyes crinkling at the corners as she smiled. "We need to go with her." She reached out a small hand and cupped his cheek. "Sweetheart, that's what is going to make it special to her when she remembers the day years from now. Not that she got to go, not that she found a mount, a pet—but that we took her."

"Yeah. We took her . . . to the smelliest place on the planet. Don't you think that little button nose of hers will have enough after the first three minutes? *Mine* will."

"You don't mind things like that when you're her age. I certainly didn't. My thranta was one of the smelliest creatures I've ever met, and I adored her. To Allana, it's all part of the fun and excitement."

Han thought about the various creatures he'd had to ride during the course of his life. Grondas, rontos, banthas, and, most memorably, tauntauns. Even now, years later, his nose wrinkled at the memory of the stench of the creature's entrails, spilling out steaming onto the snow as he cut the fallen beast open with Luke's lightsaber in a desperate bid to save the young Jedi's life.

Leia squeezed his arm. "Come on, it'll be fun. And educational. A day out, looking at all the exotic animals, not having to worry about Seff or . . . Allana will be beside herself with delight."

Han grumbled to himself. The thought of his little granddaughter, her eyes shining, laughing and clapping her hands, with no shadow of fear upon her bright little life for a change—yeah, it was a pretty appealing image.

"On one condition."

Leia snuggled closer. "What's that?"

"No tauntauns. Those things *stink*."

Chapter Thirteen

ABOARD THE *JADE SHADOW*

THEY DROPPED OUT OF HYPERSPACE, THE STARS ONCE AGAIN becoming white, glowing, stationary dots in the blackness of space instead of streaking white lights. But Ben had no interest in white dots. Who would, when one of the most beautiful spatial phenomena he'd ever seen was suddenly right before his eyes?

Ben literally felt his breath being taken away for an instant before he recovered himself. The tiny hologram of the area that Luke had displayed did not do the Kathol Rift any kind of justice and had done little to prepare him for the spectacle he now saw. He'd seen nebulae before and, like most humans, found them pretty. But this—

It was every color he'd ever seen and some he hadn't, this glowing, swirling cloud that filled most of the screen. It seemed to shift and pulse like a living thing, its colors constantly changing. He wanted to sit and watch it for a long time, mesmerized by its dance.

"That really is beautiful," said Luke, his voice holding just a hint of awe. Ben felt a little better about his own reaction if his dad, too, was similarly impressed. "But I'm sure it won't be so beautiful once we get inside it."

Ben nodded. He thought about the journals Luke had had him read, of those who had hallucinations in the

Rift, and wondered if part of the reason was that the mind had difficulty transitioning from beauty to danger so quickly. With a final admiring glance at the spectacle, he let his gaze fall to his copilot's console.

Luke thumbed a button that would send a signal to Cilghal's comlink. When the Mon Calamari did not respond, he caught Ben's eye, shrugged, and began to record a message.

"Cilghal, this is Luke. Ben and I are preparing to enter the Kathol Rift. Considering the nature of the Rift and the amount of electromagnetic radiation we're looking at, I expect that any communication attempts are going to be spotty at best, and more likely simply nonexistent. Please attempt to continue to contact us with any updates on the situation with the Jedi. We'll do the same with anything we learn, on the off chance that something might get through. Otherwise, we'll contact you when our mission here is accomplished."

He hesitated, then added, "May the Force be with us all."

That more than anything Ben had yet learned sobered him like a bucket of cold water. The gravitas of the situation finally settled on his shoulders. It told him that his father wasn't at all certain they'd come back from this mission.

That was all right. Ben was sixteen, but he'd endured more than most people three times his age. He'd been on missions where he was very unsure as to whether he'd survive—some where he was pretty darn sure he wouldn't. Returning from the mission was never the point. Succeeding at it was.

Luke turned to see his son looking at him and gave a little smile. "How was lunch?"

Ben was puzzled. They'd eaten an hour ago. "Uh—fine. Why?"

"Because it just might come back up again."

Ben snorted, offended. "Not likely."

Luke chuckled. His hands flew over the controls, and Ben's eyes were drawn inexorably back to the Rift.

Somewhere in there was the homeworld of the Aing-Tii. It was not impossible to find—Jacen had done so. Ben wished his cousin had been a little more forthcoming in the notes he had left in the Archives about his time there. All Jacen had contributed to Jedi knowledge about the Aing-Tii amounted to little more than a few pages, and even that shed no new light on them, their abilities, their world, or how to find it.

But even with the sketchy knowledge they had, he and Luke had been able to narrow their search, at least a bit. First, and most important, the world had to have an environment that would support humans, because Jacen had made no mention of needing special equipment in order to survive. Nor had Jorj Car'das. Ben was glad of that; he'd gotten awfully tired of constantly having to wear the breath mask—and its accompanying backpack rig laden with canisters—back on Dorin.

The planet had to be protected in some fashion from the radiation of the Rift, or else the Aing-Tii would not have been able to evolve as highly as they had. So it would be in one of the "corridors" and not in the denser parts of the Rift itself.

And . . . that was about it.

The rest was up to them, their skills, the Force, and sheer luck.

Luke calculated their first jump. Ben raised an eyebrow at how short a distance it was. Luke glanced at Ben and smiled. "Ready?"

Ben shrugged. "I guess so."

They jumped.

Ben was used to the sight of stars streaking past him, appearing as white lines. But when he couldn't see the stars, it looked as though nothing at all had happened.

The beautiful cloud that was the Rift looked exactly the same during their brief transit, and when they materialized in the first corridor, it looked just as if—

The *Jade Shadow* shook violently. Lights in all colors flashed wildly about them. Ben tried to stabilize the ship, but it was like trying to ride a spooked ronto—it was all he could do to hang on, let alone try to get it under control. He suddenly thought that Luke might have been right about his lunch.

Luke, however, seemed to sit as still as if he had been glued to his chair. In the back of his mind, Ben guessed that it was another way to use telekinesis—if you could hurl yourself across a room, it made sense that you could stay still even when your ship was tossing you about. And then he had no thought for how his father was managing this, because he suddenly jerked his hands back from the console, hissing in pain.

What looked like Force lightning danced across the console and then scurried across every surface of the *Jade Shadow*. Ben turned to his father to shout out that they were just short-circuited, but then he realized that his father was causing it. The blue, jagged, flashing lines were coming from Luke's hands on the console. Ben suddenly understood what was going on.

Luke was utilizing the *hassat-durr* technique.

The Baran Do Sages had taught it to Jacen, and then they had taught it to Luke. The lightning-rod technique suffused the user's body with a very low level of electromagnetic radiation; an inexperienced practitioner performing it in a storm would attract lightning. From what he could see, while trying to stay in his seat and still keep the ship steady, Ben guessed that Luke was turning the *Jade Shadow* into a reverse lightning rod.

And after a couple of moments that seemed like hours, he realized that the *hassat-durr* was working. The ship calmed down, and the crackling cloud that enveloped them no longer posed a danger.

". . . handy," Ben gasped. He ran a hand through his hair and wondered how many bruises he'd gotten in the last few minutes.

Luke opened his eyes. "Very. That should last while we assess what damage we took and plot the next jump."

"Great. Just—next time, let me know when you're going to do that, okay?"

As they made their way from jump to jump, they developed a routine. It was immediately apparent that both could not sleep at the same time—not when their situation was constantly changing. But neither did they need a full eight hours of sleep apiece every twenty-four. Both of them were familiar with healing trances, which in a pinch could substitute for a good night's sleep. Ben figured that the Kathol Rift definitely qualified as a pinch.

"So," Ben said, with exaggerated nonchalance. "We're going to go see the Aing-Tii."

"Yes . . . we are." Luke's voice held a question.

"We're going because Jysella Horn flow-walked, and you suspect that Caedus might have used flow-walking to kick off the whole Jedi-going-crazy thing in the first place."

"Right again. Perhaps you'll tell me my name next, or who my sister is?" Luke's voice held no irritation, just mild amusement. He was trying to figure out what Ben was getting at. Ben continued.

"So . . . I'm thinking that the best way to understand something is to learn about it."

"Ah. Now I see where you're going with this."

"Well, you wanted to master the *hassat-durr,* even when the Baran Do Sages were leery of teaching you,"

Ben offered. "Even when they thought it might turn you into another Caedus."

"True enough."

Ben waited, but Luke offered nothing further. He waited longer, patiently, but still no more words came. So he tried again.

"It's not a dark side ability per se," Ben said. "Not exclusively. It isn't inherently a harmful thing, like Force lightning or Force grip. I mean—you can't even really change anything substantial, from what I understand. And Jedi already are able to look into the future a little bit—that's why our reflexes are so sharp and fast."

"We use the Force to do that."

"And don't you use the Force to flow-walk?"

"True, but . . . Ben, it's not what you are imagining it to be like."

"You don't know what I'm imagining."

"I bet I've got a good idea, because believe it or not, I was once sixteen, and I know what I would think it was like," Luke said, a smile softening what was starting to develop into an argument.

"But you were a very *young* sixteen," Ben said with a slight touch of arrogance.

"Also true," Luke admitted readily, chuckling softly. "Even so, some things are universal. I don't think I want you learning flow-walking, Ben." He held up a hand as Ben opened his mouth to protest. "No, wait, hear me out. It's not because I don't think you are strong enough to use it wisely, but because—" He stopped suddenly.

Ben inhaled swiftly, his green eyes flying wide open.

They were *everywhere*.

Dozens—no, hundreds of them. They emerged from every nook and cranny on the suddenly ominously dark vessel, squeezing up from hairline cracks, flooding out from under chairs and consoles. Their legs were waving frantically, and they moved with astonishing speed up the chair, across his boots, up the legs of his pants—

"I see them, too," Luke said. His voice was completely calm. "Nothing but hallucinations, Ben. Remember what we talked about."

Ben did remember, but it was difficult to focus on remembering that these were simple mind tricks when he could *feel* the vaping things crawling up his legs and arms. He closed his eyes and took a deep breath, falling back on logic when his mind kept feeling those myriad tiny little legs scurrying across his skin.

For one thing, such a profusion of arachnids would have been noticed immediately during the preflight check. And even if somehow this many living things got missed both by technology and human eyes, he would be able to sense them in the Force now—and he couldn't. For another, the ship couldn't even contain them all. All logic concluded that the spiders did not exist.

The thoughts, calming and settling, flitted across his brain in less than a second. He opened his eyes and, of course, saw nothing. He turned and met his father's approving gaze.

"Good job, son. What did you see?"

"Spiders," Ben said.

"Me too."

The adrenaline was fading now. The meditation, even as brief as it had been, had sent calming endorphins through Ben's system. "It seems kind of odd that the hallucinations are so universal, you know? Why not something more specifically tailored to the individual? I mean, there are a lot of things that rattle me more than a bunch of spiders."

As he spoke, he thought back to the several nights he had spent on Ziost a few years earlier; of the voices, first in dreams and then when he was awake, telling him to do horrible things . . . leading him to want to do them.

He also thought of the torture that his cousin had put him through, attempting to temper him like a piece of metal.

Oh, yes—there were a lot of things scarier than a ship full of bugs.

"I'm not sure. We'd have to study the type of radiation we're being bombarded with, and the effects it has on human chemistry. It's possible that it simply activates a basic, primal fear center. Spider bites could be deadly on a primitive world. Strange creatures hovering around us could be, too. Fear is a logical reaction."

"But . . . *bugs*, Dad. Squish. End of problem."

Luke gave his son a glance. "Still scared you at first, though, didn't it?"

Ben felt his face grow hot. Not for the first time, he cursed the pale, freckled skin he had inherited from his mother.

"I was just—surprised, that's all. Now that I know what to expect, I won't be."

Luke shrugged. "We know the spiders and the mysterious beings are typical hallucinations. They might not be the only ones. We should be cautious. Anything distressing, out of the ordinary—we shouldn't automatically assume it's real."

"Agreed."

Ben decided not to try to pick up where they had been interrupted on the conversation about flow-walking. He did not think he was in a strong position to argue that he was ready to learn such a discipline when he'd just been taken aback—even momentarily—by an illusionary bunch of spiders.

They continued on for several hours, carefully planning short jumps. Luke's *hassat-durr* technique proved consistently useful, although it did seem to drain him. Ben started to get a sense for navigating the corridors, extending himself in the Force to assist his father in determining which way felt right in a place where everything was constantly changing.

The series of short jumps that sometimes felt like one step forward, two steps back, eventually led them to planets. The concentration of corridors was greatest here; it was what permitted life to evolve at all. But each planet proved to be a disappointment. What life there was was primitive and stunted. And a sick suspicion rose in Ben.

He was reluctant to voice it, but he knew he had to. "Dad," he ventured at one point, "what if we're completely wrong?"

"I'm always prepared to entertain that suggestion," Luke said. "The universe is nothing if not humbling. What do you think we might be wrong about?"

"Well—everything we have says that the Aing-Tii live inside the Kathol Rift. But what if they don't? What if everyone is just assuming that?"

"Good question. But you taught me the importance of following the evidence, remember? If everything points to them being here, clearly this is the first place we should look."

"Well, yeah, under normal circumstances," said Ben. "But 'looking around' here is not good for the *Jade Shadow* or her crew."

Luke eyed him. "That's true. Do you have a better suggestion?"

". . . uh. No." Ben was inordinately pleased that Luke freely admitted that he, Ben, had taught him something. He was less pleased that he hadn't been able to come up with a better idea. "I guess we follow the evidence."

Luke grinned. "Then let's be about it. It'll take as long as it takes. After all, Ben, we've got a decade to kill."

Ben grimaced.

This time Luke let him plot the jump, checking to make sure Ben had calculated properly. The planet they found, though, could be almost immediately ruled out. Ben took a break to eat and drop into a healing meditation for about twenty minutes, then he and his father traded off.

Luke rose from the pilot's seat and Ben slipped into it. His dad patted his shoulder as he headed back to the galley to get a bite to eat.

Ben didn't like to admit it, but he was starting to get bored. He refocused his attention on what he was doing, because he was wise enough to know that when you got bored, you got careless, and when you got careless Bad Things often happened. He was refreshed, fed, and alert, and his mind wasn't wandering, but he really, really wished they'd hurry up and find the Aing-Tii. Despite Luke's quip earlier, and despite the beauty of the Rift, he didn't want to spend the next several years hopping from corridor to corridor.

Suddenly there came a harsh beeping sound. The lights on the console began chasing one another around like lampflies in summer. The vessel began to shake, but there was no storm—

"What the—" yelped Ben. He stabbed at the controls, damping down a quick spike of fear and harnessing the adrenaline to sharpen his reflexes instead. But his reflexes suddenly didn't matter.

He was staring at readings that told him that he was not inside the Kathol Rift, but in orbit around Coruscant. A blink of an eye later, the readings insisted that the ship was in imminent danger of tearing itself apart. Then they were picking up signs of a ship that wasn't there.

Another illusion. Ben almost smiled to himself. Maybe this was what happened in the Rift—the hallucinations started out as generic and became more and more specific. Although the whole Coruscant thing was kind of stupid, because Ben knew good and well that—

Luke came racing back from the galley, dropped into the copilot's seat, and began, swiftly but with control, to bring the *Jade Shadow* back in line. Ben felt him extend his senses in the Force, and the ship seemed to quiet, almost like a living animal responding to the calmness of its master.

"Oh," Ben said. "That . . . wasn't a hallucination."

"No," Luke said, his blue eyes narrowing as he gazed at the readings. "Although I can see how you thought it was." On the screen was a "reading" of Tatooine.

Then there was that ship.

There was a sudden bright flash, and the ship that had appeared on the readings was right in front of them.

It was huge, it had come out of nowhere, it was discordant, and it was directly on top of them. For an instant Ben was reminded of the Yuuzhan Vong ships, but if their vessels were organic in a plant-based fashion, this was living stone. It was a sphere, sort of, but nothing so precise. Strange projections jutted out—exhaust ports? thruster ports?—seemingly at random. It was covered with thick hull plates that were etched with some kind of writing or symbols. And it was moving steadily toward them.

"Well, Ben, looks like we can stop searching. The Aing-Tii have found *us*."

It had to be. The Sanhedrim ships could move from one place to another in the blink of an eye. And clearly, they had the ability to affect or confuse readings. As he started to think more clearly, Ben realized that what he'd seen had been stored images and information on the planets, not actual live readings.

"When you can't trust your eyes," Luke said, and Ben finished for him, "Trust the Force."

Ben softened his gaze and dropped into a receptive state, extending his feelings and senses out into the

Force that had once so frightened him and was now such a source of strength, knowledge, and even comfort.

It took awhile, and he kept part of his attention on the enormous ship in front of them. It made no attempt to contact or fire upon them, but neither did it move away. Ben was certain that the Aing-Tii were watching them as surely as he and Luke were watching their ship.

And then Ben felt them.

They were like no other energy he had ever encountered in the Force. They felt—shifting, weaving in and out of the Force—like they were not really a part of it, although Ben knew that all living things were part of the Force. They were there, and they were not, and they managed both at the same time, and holding that contradiction in his mind was starting to give Ben a headache.

He felt his father reaching out, a strong, clear, bright, calm presence in the Force. There were no words, but Luke was open and inviting. Luke was still as stone, his eyes, like Ben's, open, seeing and also focusing inward.

The response all but took the wind out of him, so powerful was it.

There was a definite sense of—not hostility, but notwanting. They were not welcome, but neither were they being repulsed. Yet.

They were to be tested. They must prove themselves. There was a hint of softening, and Ben realized that somehow the Aing-Tii knew why they had come, and would at least give them the chance to speak. The softening suddenly turned hard, cold. Ben knew that if they failed the test, they would be refused . . . and he got a definite sense that that "refusal" would not be anything pleasant.

He felt his father agree, and then Luke took a deep breath. Ben felt him withdraw from the Force as a conscious presence. He still sensed Luke—he would always be able to sense him, unless Luke himself deliberately chose otherwise. Just as Ben sometimes chose not to be present in the Force. He, too, withdrew, and ground a palm into his tired eyes.

"You agreed to their test," he said.

"I don't really think there was a choice, Ben."

"I don't either. But how do—"

Their screen blinked. Coordinates suddenly appeared on it.

"Never mind," Luke said. "Let's go."

Chapter Fourteen

AFTER ALL THE STRUGGLING, GUESSWORK, AND SHEER teeth-rattling endurance Ben and Luke had suffered through over the last several days, their current situation had a definite air of relief about it.

Soon after Luke had conveyed his agreement to the Aing-Tii's proposal, coordinates had begun scrolling across the screen. It was a series of jumps that proved to be shockingly easy. On the third jump, Ben said, "You know, we should have been able to figure these out on our own."

Luke replied mildly, "Seems to me that we've spent several days attempting to do precisely that, and that the jumps we're now executing had not occurred to either of us. Besides, we had no specific direction—we were simply trying to cast our net as wide as possible."

Ben sighed. "I know . . . I just feel a little foolish. It's so obvious, now that I look at it."

"Things are usually obvious when you're on the other side of them," Luke replied. "Also, if we had arrived unexpectedly in orbit around the Aing-Tii homeworld, we might well have been attacked and killed before we could even present our case properly."

Ben threw up his hands in surrender, laughing. "You

win. I don't know why you needed to hire Nawara Ven. You argue a case well enough on your own."

Both fell silent, though, when after the final jump they found themselves orbiting not a planet full of sentient beings but a small, uninhabited moon.

"Dad," Ben said slowly, "do you think we just walked into a trap?"

Luke shook his blond head. "No. If they had wanted to kill us, they had a perfect opportunity to do so earlier. I'd hoped that the test would be conducted on their homeworld, but apparently this is the site they've selected."

Ben touched the controls. The moon was rocky and inhospitable. "It has an oxygen-nitrogen atmosphere, which is good, although the oxygen is a bit lower than ideal. And we're not entirely protected from the EMR of the Rift, but the *hassat-durr* technique should keep us safe enough," he said with just a touch of uncertainty.

"Will we need breath masks?"

"No." Thank goodness. "We should be all right outside the *Shadow* for a few hours. And there's a single life-form. Mammalian."

"Our welcoming party," said Luke, "who will no doubt be the one administering the challenge."

The surface was as rocky as it had appeared from space. As they maneuvered the *Shadow* in for a landing, still following the extremely precise coordinates they had been given, they saw the Aing-Tii vessel. The ship was clearly of the same make as the Sanhedrim ship that had confronted them earlier, but on a smaller, more personal scale. It still looked unsettlingly organic to Ben. There were similar protrusions extending from its ovoid, but he could see no doors or ramps. Nor was there any sign of the Aing-Tii representative they had anticipated would greet them. Ben and Luke exchanged glances.

"Maybe it will disembark once we show good faith," Luke suggested.

"I hope so. This is all feeling pretty weird."

"I'm afraid I have to agree."

Luke settled the *Shadow* on the rocky soil, near but not too close to their host's vessel. Ben reached for his cloak—after all that time spent on Dorin lugging around a breath mask and assorted canisters, he wanted to take only the minimum he'd need.

"Leave the lightsaber," Luke said, already unfastening his own. "We're not coming anticipating a fight."

"What if they give us one?"

"The Force will give us enough to rely on if we have to defend ourselves. But Ben—this is the species that Yoda sent a man to for healing. I don't think this challenge is to the death."

Ben wasn't so sure. "Yeah, and they sometimes appear out of nowhere and ram ships, too." But he left his lightsaber behind as his father wished.

Ben felt slightly light-headed the moment they stepped down the ramp, but the sensation wasn't extreme. They approached slowly, giving the Aing-Tii plenty of time to exit his own vessel. Several large, gray rocks were clustered within a few meters of the ship. Ben wondered why the Aing-Tii had chosen such a landing site when a few hundred meters to the north there was a large area that was completely clear.

Luke slowed the pace even further the closer they drew. He frowned a little, revealing that he was as puzzled as Ben. "Perhaps this is part of the challenge," he murmured slightly.

And then one of the rocks near the ship moved.

It uncurled slowly, languidly, extending a long tail, two powerful lower limbs, two smaller forelegs, and a large head on a sinuous neck. It fixed them with large, dark, unblinking eyes as it curled its tail beneath it and

sank back on its hind legs. Ben instinctively knew that
the slow revelation of its presence was deliberate and for
their benefit. This creature could probably transform
from appearing to be a simple rock formation to a
deadly threat in a heartbeat. Even now that it was not
curled up but rather sitting, it still blended in with its environment.

It was much more imposing than the holographic
image Ben had studied. Something about its plating and
its stillness was unsettling. Ben glanced at his father.

Luke bowed politely and Ben followed suit. "I am Jedi
Luke Skywalker. This is my son, Ben. Thank you for
being willing to meet with us. We have come as requested to accept your challenge."

Ben and Luke waited. The being did not move. Ben
took in the geometric designs on certain pieces of the
jointed plating that covered its body. He recognized a
few of them as being the same as some of those he had
seen on the Sanhedrim ship. This close to the creature,
he could see now that the patterns were not simply
painted on but were etched into the Aing-Tii's shell and
then stained. Ben wondered if it had hurt, or if, as it appeared, the plating was more like armor or some kind of
exoskeleton than like skin.

"I don't think he understands Basic, Dad," Ben said
quietly after a few minutes.

"Doesn't look like it, no."

Ben glanced at the vessel. "They seem to be highly advanced technologically. And we know that they've been
able to communicate with humans before. So why is he
not making use of his equipment? How's he supposed to
tell us what our challenge is?"

Luke smiled slightly. "Because I'm willing to bet that
our challenge is to figure out a way to communicate
with him without the use of technology. Which is going
to be a fine challenge indeed, as the Aing-Tii communi-

cate among themselves by tasting, smelling, and touching one another with their tongues," he added.

As if it had heard and completely understood everything that had been said, the stone-still creature suddenly opened its mouth. Six thin, bright green tendrils shot out and flickered about wildly.

"Oh gross," said Ben.

Then he wondered if the Aing-Tii actually *had* been able to understand everything they had said, and he blushed a little.

The Aing-Tii withdrew its glistening green tongues and was as still as if it had never moved at all.

"How are we supposed to learn that kind of language?" Ben asked, his voice slightly sharp. He would have died before admitting it, but the sudden movement of the previously motionless being—particularly when that movement involved green tongues—had startled him.

"We don't," Luke said quietly. His gaze was locked with the dark, shiny, fist-sized orbs of the Aing-Tii. "We don't learn his language, and he doesn't learn ours."

"But we have to communi—" Ben blinked. "Wait a minute. How do you know it's a he?"

"The same way I intend to communicate with him," Luke replied. His voice was softer, slightly deeper, and although he was still regarding the Aing-Tii, Ben realized that his father wasn't really seeing the being. Luke took several steps forward, closing the space between himself and the Aing-Tii, and then eased himself to the rocky ground to sit facing it. Him.

And then Ben got it.

Without another word, he followed his father's example, moving to sit cross-legged beside Luke, turning his face up—for even seated, the Aing-Tii was taller than they—to the alien. He let his gaze soften but did not close his eyes, and slowed his breathing despite the thinness of the atmosphere.

He felt a touch on his hand, and turned it so that his father and he were clasping hands. Luke needed physical contact if he was to extend the *hassat-durr* technique to protect both himself and Ben. Ben wasn't accustomed to holding hands with his dad, but he felt a slight tingling and was grateful for the shielding Luke was offering.

He sensed his father in the Force immediately, of course. Luke Skywalker was a bright, shining presence to anyone who was Force-sensitive, and his bond with Ben enabled the youth to connect with him at once.

Ben did not sense the being before him, and wondered if the Aing-Tii knew the same technique for masking his presence in the Force as he, Ben, knew. He felt a little puzzled. He was certain his father had gotten it right. But if this being truly wanted to communicate with them in the Force, then why the—

And then suddenly he was *there,* shining as bright as Luke Skywalker but in an entirely different way. Tadar'Ro, for suddenly Ben knew his name, was a completely different type of Force-user than any Ben had ever encountered. His presence felt—splintered somehow, but not in a negative way. This was not a splintering caused by being broken, but by choice, by design. It was as if Tadar'Ro's Force self was a sort of fabric, woven of many threads, and he was now permitting the Skywalkers to see and comprehend this.

Ben had felt it when people's life essences had winked out of the Force. He was accustomed to the sickening sensation. He had been told that his namesake, Obi-Wan "Ben" Kenobi, had staggered and appeared faint when Alderaan had been blown to bits by the Death Star. So many deaths all at once had to have been traumatic.

What Ben experienced now, though, while overwhelmingly intense, was not horrifying, not at all. He realized his breathing had speeded up, and that the air that he was sucking into his lungs wasn't quite doing the trick, and the shimmering, many-stranded being that was Tadar'Ro had somehow gotten hold of him in the Force and—

He had no option. Ben abruptly withdrew from the Force and slammed the door shut.

He realized he was sweating heavily and shaking. He turned to look at his father, who had lifted a hand in a dismissive yet gentle gesture.

"Go back to the *Shadow*, Ben," Luke said. He was still gazing raptly at Tadar'Ro. "I'll be there soon."

Ben felt his face flush a second time. He hadn't been able to handle it—whatever *it* was.

He rose and walked back to the ship. As he started to ascend the ramp, he turned and looked back to see Tadar'Ro's long, thin green tongues flickering and caressing his father's upturned face.

Ben was glad to return to the more familiar, comfortable artificial atmosphere of his mother's ship. Once back on board, though, he threw himself into his studies of the Aing-Tii as a sort of penance for what he perceived as a failure, only to realize how very little specific information there actually was. He therefore amused himself with a holodrama, embarrassed that he was doing such a thing but too agitated to bestir himself to do anything else.

He was lying back in the flowform chair, going over what he had experienced with one part of his mind and observing the acting with the other, when he heard the door slide open and Luke's voice calling him.

"Ben?"

Ben turned off the holodrama quickly. "Dad . . . How did it go? What was he doing? I'm sorry I couldn't—"

"You did just fine," Luke said reassuringly. "Even I've never experienced anything like what Tadar'Ro tried to share with me."

He did look a bit drained, Ben thought. The knowledge mitigated his own feeling of falling short.

"Did you communicate with him in an acceptable way?"

Luke got a glass of water, gulped it down, refilled it, and dropped into the chair beside Ben. Ben seemed to notice, really notice, the creases in his father's face and the gray in his blond hair. The fingers that curled around the glass were strong and calloused and nicked. Luke Skywalker looked quite mortal at the moment, and Ben realized that the revelation made him uneasy. Then he thought about how wiped out he'd felt after a much shorter stay in the thin atmosphere, and convinced himself his father was just fine.

Almost.

"Yes, though it was quite exhausting."

"They're a very . . . alien species, aren't they?" Ben said.

Luke chuckled slightly and took another swig of the water. "Very. It's absolutely fascinating. I can see why Jacen was so intrigued by them. They're . . . like no other species I've ever met."

"So," Ben asked with fake casualness, "are we going to have the opportunity to meet more of them, or am I going to be stuck watching second-rate holodramas while we head on to the next possible clue?"

"Let me put it this way," Luke said. "Get used to being licked."

Chapter Fifteen

"IT'S NOT TELEPATHY, IS IT?" BEN INQUIRED AS HE PLOTTED out the jump according to the information Tadar'Ro had transmitted to the *Jade Shadow*.

"No. But there's more of an understanding of specifics than you and I are accustomed to experiencing when we touch someone through the Force," Luke said. "And it seemed to be enough for them to understand Basic."

"But how are they going to talk to us?" Ben inquired. "I mean . . . those tongues don't look like they'll operate the way ours do."

"Tadar'Ro didn't seem to think there would be any problems once we arrived," Luke said. Ben frowned a little. He knew that sometimes you simply needed to accept the way a circumstance was, but his father was sometimes so *cryptic.* Luke caught his expression and said, "Don't look at me this time. That's as much as I know, too."

The jumps were easy and precise. Tadar'Ro had given them directions as to not only where to jump, but also when. It had been calculated down to the second.

"So that's how they manage it," Ben said. "They know when it's safe to jump into one of the corridors. You think it has to do with flow-walking?" Ordinary Jedi could touch the future to a greater or lesser degree, enough to give them a slight edge in combat, but Ben was thinking about Jysella Horn knowing exactly where the hidden security droids would emerge . . . and exactly when.

"Possibly," Luke said. "I'm sure we'll find out. Right now we need to focus on making those jumps."

Ben sighed inwardly. Luke was still obviously not ready to continue their interrupted discussion on flow-walking. But he felt he was right. If Tadar'Ro thought it useful to calculate the timing of the jump so precisely, they'd be wise to follow his instructions.

They emerged from the last series of jumps to see a plain that was strikingly similar to the moon that Tadar'Ro had selected for their challenge. The atmosphere was similar, but the EMR from the Rift was slightly less and there was at least life on this world. Ben could see bodies of water and patches of green here and there amid the stretches of rock.

"Well, we're here," he said. "Now what?"

As if in immediate answer, coordinates began flowing across the screen on the console.

"Set down there and we'll find out," Luke said.

The habitations of the Aing-Tii were definitely recognizable as cities, but it was also immediately obvious that the beings they had come here to request aid from strove to be in harmony with their environment. Just as their bodies had evolved to blend in physically with the landscape, the Aing-Tii sought to have their cities do so as well. The landing site, located a short distance away from one of the smaller cities, was in a canyon, surrounded on all sides by steep, almost vertical stone walls. Luke was reminded of Tatooine as he regarded the forbidding landscape, harsh and inhospitable. The patches of green—fertile river valleys—were few and far between and, curiously, seemed not to be where the

Aing-Tii chose to dwell. It was as if these beings deliberately sought the harsher areas, as if the challenge was
something they desired. If Tatooine was a hot, desert
world, this was a colder, rockier one. But as they descended and sped over machinery and homesteads, Luke
recognized equipment that he immediately knew was
designed to farm moisture. It was not quite the same
machinery that he had grown up with, of course, but it
was sufficiently similar. He sat with the conflicting emotions of nostalgia and unease for a moment, letting both
flow through him.

He sensed them all in the Force as they settled the *Jade
Shadow* down on a rocky plateau. Accustomed as he
was to experiencing the vast, luminous variety that was
the presence of many lives, this staggered him for a moment. As he had said to Ben, there was something
unique about the Aing-Tii presence in the Force.

Tadar'Ro was waiting for them. He stood with that
inherent stillness as they lowered the ramp and disem-
barked from the *Shadow.* In each foreclaw, he held a
long, cylindrical metal object that flared to a rounded
bulb at the end. A third device, a flat circle about the size
of Luke's fist, was affixed to his chest. Small lights
blinked and chased one another around the face of the
circle.

Luke and Ben approached him, nodded acknowledgment, and stood quietly, waiting. Tadar'Ro held up one
of the strange metal wands and indicated the bulb at the
end, bringing it to his mouth, then handed it to Luke.

"It looks like a microphone of some sort," Ben said
quietly. Luke nodded, lifting the device to his mouth and
watching Tadar'Ro.

"Is this how we will be able to speak to you?" he said,
holding the instrument up to his mouth as the Aing-Tii
had indicated.

Tadar'Ro's head bobbed up and down on his long,

plated neck. It did not look like it was a natural gesture, but it was definitely a nod. He lifted his own wand to his mouth, opening his jaws and extending his tongues. Each one was capped with a small, glowing mechanism; they flickered over the end of the "microphone."

"Yes," said Tadar'Ro in a completely human, masculine voice. The sound had a slight mechanical tinge to it, like a droid's, and it issued from the circular device on his chest rather than his now closed mouth. But it was unmistakably human, and Ben and Luke exchanged glances. "We tended one of your species. His knowledge of your language enabled us to create this device, so that we might speak with you."

"I am very glad of this," Luke said, speaking into the device. He was, indeed, quite relieved. He'd wondered how they would be able to bridge that barrier.

"How does it work?" Ben asked, peering at the device.

"We communicate through pheromones," Tadar'Ro said. "It took time, but the device is able to analyze the pheromones we emit and find corresponding words in Basic for them. Now. You are expected. Follow."

He turned and began striding across the rocky ground at a brisk pace, heading for the single means of egress, a narrow tunnel through the sheer stone face. Luke and Ben broke into a trot to keep up with him. The thinner air of this planet made the short run harder than it should have been, and Luke found himself tapping into the Force to enable his body to absorb more oxygen. Beside him, Ben was panting, just a little.

As they emerged on the other side of the tunnel, Luke realized that the jagged rocks they were approaching were artificial constructs—the city he'd glimpsed from above. There was no structure to their arrangement; it appeared as random as if nature itself had created them.

But there was a long, long line of motionless Aing-Tii,

standing like the stone themselves and fixing the two strangers with their large, unblinking black eyes.

"They will say something to you. Respond with the phrase the Wounded One used," Tadar'Ro said. *"As Those Who Dwell Beyond the Veil will it."*

Luke and Ben both nodded. Luke stepped up to the first Aing-Tii in line, observing that neither this one nor, as far as he could tell, any of the others held a translation device. This one was a very large male. His plating was chipped, and the geometric patterns etched on them were obviously very old. Sensing that this was a respected elder of the group, Luke bowed graciously. He waited for a name to come into his head, but it did not. Apparently, Tadar'Ro was the only one willing—so far—to disclose such information.

Luke stood still as the Aing-Tii's tongues flickered over his face. It wasn't an unpleasant sensation; the tongues were not particularly wet, and the touch was light and gentle. Without the translation device, Luke had no idea what the being was saying, but he did not sense hostility, only the caution that an elder of a group would be wise to display.

The elder retracted his tongues and stood waiting for Luke's reply. "As Those Who Dwell Beyond the Veil will it," Luke said, bowing slightly. He moved on to the next. Also an elder, this one was female, and Luke got a very strong hint that she was not at all happy he was here. Beside him, out of the corner of his eye, he saw Ben flinch infinitesimally as the first elder's tongues danced across his features. Poor Ben. Luke wouldn't have appreciated the gesture when he was that age, either, and he was proud of Ben, who endured it with only the vaguest ripple of discomfort in the Force.

The touch from the female elder's tongues was strangely cold—not physically, but in the Force. No, she was definitely not pleased that he and Ben were here.

Nonetheless, he repeated the phrase with all the respect and courtesy he could summon, bowed, and moved on.

It took a long time, but at last Ben and Luke had officially introduced themselves to their new hosts. Some of them were welcoming, some hostile, some entirely neutral in their attitudes. Luke wondered uneasily what he and Ben might have stumbled into, but he kept that thought carefully shuttered. When the last Aing-Tii had finished with Ben, the two Jedi turned to Tadar'Ro.

Tadar'Ro beckoned them to follow him. Like the nod he had given the two Jedi previously, this seemed to be a forced gesture on his part, but one that was easily understood. They obeyed, following him as he took them around a large, jutting rock outcropping.

Luke was surprised by what he saw on the other side. He hadn't been sure what to expect, but it wasn't this. Rather than another one of the rock-shaped dwellings, it was a small, single-story house, with four straight walls, a roof, and a door. While clearly constructed with materials native to the planet—also obviously designed for human aesthetics.

"Jorj Car'das," Ben said, then realized he hadn't spoken into the translation mechanism. Taking it from Luke, he inquired, "This was Jorj Car'das's home during the years he spent here, wasn't it?"

Again the nod. "Yes," said Tadar'Ro. "We used what we learned of human needs and comforts, and created this dwelling to accommodate him."

Luke pushed open the door.

It was surprisingly cozy inside. A small mattress, lumpy looking but not uninviting, was nestled in a corner. A rug, woven of colorful dried fronds of some sort of plant, covered and insulated the floor. There were two tables, and one wall was filled with shelves. The floor, tables, and shelves were pleasantly cluttered with knick-knacks so familiar that Luke felt an unexpected tug on his heart: repair parts for an astromech, spare parts for a blaster, datapads. Mixed in with these were colorful stones and carved wooden statuettes of various vaguely recognizable images—a small bantha, an astromech, and one he suspected was intended to be Tadar'Ro. It had obviously been a hobby rather than a true artistic calling for Jorj Car'das, whom Luke suspected of having many empty hours to while away.

"Jedi may stay here, if they wish."

"Thank you, we would like to visit here, and perhaps stay here during the day. At night, though, we will return to our ship. Your atmosphere, while tolerable, is not ideal for us."

"So Jorj Car'das told us as well," Tadar'Ro said. "Such is acceptable." He indicated the mattress. "Sit. We will speak of why you have come . . . and what it is you expect to find here."

Luke and Ben sat on the mattress. As Luke had expected, it was fairly comfortable, if a little awkward to settle into.

"You know why we have come," Luke said. He'd been scrupulously polite, enduring all the face-licking and mystery. But now it was time for him to learn something from Tadar'Ro, rather than the other way around. "I sense that not everyone here is as welcoming as you, Tadar'Ro. Can you tell me why?"

The being considered, then gave the forced nod. "It is best that you know. You are less likely to give offense."

Ben made a soft snorting noise, but—thankfully, Luke thought—did not speak. Tadar'Ro continued.

"You have said you studied what Jorj Car'das brought back of our people. Then you will know that for long and long, the Aing-Tii have believed that certain things are a certain way. We deeply respect the Force, but do not use it. Not the way others do. To us, it is a thing to be respected and experienced. It is not a tool, a weapon, for us to use to make the universe what we wish it.

"We believe we are being guided. Events are not predetermined, but they flow, gently, to a certain place, in a certain manner."

He was sitting back on his haunches, his tail tucked under him like a built-in chair. As he spoke, he moved his short forearms in a surprisingly graceful manner, the claws seeming to trace patterns in the air, and his eyes were half closed. Luke felt him even more strongly in the Force, and again wondered at these strange beings' relationship with it.

Tadar'Ro opened his eyes and his hands stilled, then lowered again to his chest. "So we have believed for long and long. But over the last few years, a Prophet arose and spoke many things."

"Do you believe in him?" Luke asked. "Do you think he prophesies truly?"

"It is such a strange concept, to prophesy," Tadar'Ro replied, his voice, unnaturally created as it was, nonetheless conveying his confusion. "To think that events are so firm. Like stone, rather than like wind and water and thought. And yet—he has seen things, and they have come to pass."

"Coincidence, or misinterpretation," Ben said at once. "People hear what they want to hear. Keep it vague enough, and a prophecy or prediction'll fit pretty much anything."

"The young one speaks wisdom. And yet these are very specific. It could be, as you say, coincidence. Or it could be foreknowledge. The future is not unknown to my people."

No, it wouldn't be, not to flow-walkers, thought Luke. "Could it be that the Prophet simply has had good luck, or good judgment, in determining which of the possible futures will come to pass?"

"All these things you say, we have thought of already," said Tadar'Ro. "And yet, it is hard to discount what we have seen. As I have said, the Prophet told us many things that later did come to pass. Specific, accurate things. In fact, everything he said . . . happened. Except for one final prophecy. He foretold the coming of Those Who Dwell Beyond the Veil in his lifetime."

"And that's really gotten people upset," Ben said.

"It has indeed," Tadar'Ro said. "Especially because a few weeks ago, the Prophet became one with the Force—and we have had no sign of the coming of Those Who Dwell Beyond the Veil."

Ben grimaced slightly and glanced at his father. "So it's been made apparent that he wasn't infallible, then."

Tadar'Ro made an odd, ducking motion with his head, and Luke sensed his agitation. "His death has thrown my people into an uproar. We have become divided . . . we, who never had schisms or even disagreements that were anything more than trivial. Now there is anger sown, and accusations of deception, or worse. We—are tearing ourselves apart."

The pain he felt pulsed like a raw wound in the Force. Luke felt it almost as his own, and he saw Ben wince a little, as well.

"We cannot serve in this way. Not when we are focused on our own hatred and fear and desire to be right. We must find resolution on this matter. And that, Jedi Luke Skywalker and Jedi Ben Skywalker, is the only reason we permitted you to come."

"You . . . want our help in figuring out if this Prophet was real or false?" Ben's voice conveyed his puzzlement. "We know almost nothing of your people, and the Prophet is dead. How can we possibly help you?"

"You can touch the Relics," Tadar'Ro said, his voice reverent. "We are forbidden to do so."

Luke remembered one of the bits of information they

had learned about the Aing-Tii. They traveled the Rift looking for artifacts regarding Those Who Dwell Beyond the Veil. The data didn't specify whether these were artifacts created by the deities, or if they were collected to please them.

"It is my understanding," Luke began, feeling his way cautiously, "that your faith tells you to gather these . . . Relics."

Tadar'Ro nodded. "It is our sacred calling to do this," he agreed. "We find them, and recover them, and bring them here. It is through these items that we can perhaps determine the will of Those Who Dwell Beyond the Veil."

"They are . . . of these beings?"

"We believe them to be, yes."

"And yet, you can't touch them."

Again Tadar'Ro nodded. "It is blasphemy. Only infidels may handle them freely without offending Those Who Dwell Beyond the Veil."

"That must make it difficult to study, if you can't touch them," said Ben.

"It does. We have managed, however, to keep to both sacred laws—to gather, and not to defile. We have enlisted aid from time to time."

Luke nodded, awareness dawning. "Jorj Car'das," he said. "Yoda sent him to you for healing, and you did so provided he learn everything about you."

"Once he understood us, he could aid us. He was very useful."

"You knew him?" Ben asked.

"I did. I was sad when he finally departed."

"And because of him, you were the one appointed to challenge us," Luke said. "To see if we were worthy of handling your artifacts for you, so that we could help your people decide whether to embrace so profound a change in their way of thinking."

"Yes."

"Well," Luke said, "it seems like we are in a position to help each other. Ben and I can peruse these Relics and tell you what we find out. I give you my word that we will handle them with the utmost respect."

"I know you will. I have been with you in the Force. Had I not deemed you able to behave so toward our most sacred items, you would not have survived your challenge."

Ben looked skeptical, but Luke nodded. If the Aing-Tii could flow-walk, could alter time, it would have been quite possible to—as Jysella Horn had done—anticipate movements and kill the two Jedi on the inhospitable moon. Not to mention that the giant Sanhedrim ship they had initially encountered could have destroyed the *Jade Shadow* with ease.

"In return, we would like for you to tell us everything you know about Jacen Solo. Your impressions of him, what he learned, what he did here. I'm guessing that you instructed him?"

"Yes. Because of my knowledge of humanity through my interaction with Jorj Car'das, it was thought best if I instructed Jacen Solo."

"And you will tell us of the time you spent with him then?"

"And teach me flow-walking?" Ben blurted.

Luke's head whipped around to stare at his son. Ben continued before Luke could interrupt, "I think that it's important that we learn all we can, Dad. I think if Jacen knew something, some skill, some technique—we should, too. We're trying to retrace his steps, after all. Find out if it was during this journey that he started to go dark."

Luke remained silent. He knew that Ben had not protested when Luke alone was instructed in the *hassat-durr* by the Baran Do Sages because he had not been all that interested in learning the technique. This request was purely selfish—motivated only by Ben's curiosity. He opened his mouth to speak, to gently reprimand Ben, but Tadar'Ro beat him to it.

"We will accommodate both requests," he said.

Luke looked at him, surprised. Ben tried and failed to stop a huge grin. Luke felt disquiet stir within him but did not say anything.

"We wish you to feel that our side of this agreement is fully honored," Tadar'Ro continued. "Our word is dear to us. We will not willingly violate it, for to do so shows contempt for Those Who Dwell Beyond the Veil. It is why we do not readily interact with other species. But," he added, turning to look at each of them with those deep black eyes that seemed to stare into their souls, "we hold you to the same standard. You must do your very best to comprehend our ways, our culture, our faith. And you must use that comprehension to help us find our way back to a true path—wherever it might lead us."

"We promise to help you to the very best of our ability," Luke said, choosing his words carefully. It was entirely possible—even probable—that he and Ben wouldn't be able to figure out anything useful. Luke could not promise to solve their problem, but he could vow to give it his very best effort.

Beside him, Ben nodded. "We'll do our best. And . . . thank you. For agreeing to teach me."

Tadar'Ro seemed satisfied. "It is approaching the time when we rest," he said. "Tomorrow, at first light, we will begin the sharing. Do you wish to stay here, or return to your vessel for the night?"

"We'll return to our vessel, thank you. But a question before you go?" Luke asked.

"Speak."

"There are many items here that are designed for humans. May we take them to our vessel?"

The Aing-Tii nodded. "If they will be of use to you, of course. I would ask that you not keep them, however, as they have become . . ." He floundered a little. "They are part of who we are now."

Luke inclined his head. "I'm pleased that one of my species is well thought of among the Aing-Tii. We will return everything we take. You have my word."

After Tadar'Ro had departed, Luke turned to Ben. His son held up a hand. "I know what you're going to say, Dad. But he said it was all right."

"I didn't."

"I know, and thanks for not putting your foot down."

Luke sighed and shook his head. "You know how I feel about this, Ben, but I won't stop you from learning this if you really feel you must."

Ben shifted uneasily on the makeshift mattress. "I . . . I kinda feel like I do need to, Dad. I can't explain it better than that."

Luke didn't want to think that the Force was prompting Ben to do this, but it was beginning to seem that way. He knew that there were times when a parent had to let his children make their own choices—and their own mistakes. Ben had made his choice, and the Aing-Tii had agreed to instruct him. It was out of Luke's hands now, and he chose to let it go.

"I noticed there were a lot of datapads around here, as well as droid and ship parts," Luke said, rising and changing the subject. "Let's see if we can learn anything from them."

They felt eyes upon them as they emerged from Car'das's house and headed back through the passageway to the *Jade Shadow*. Now that Luke knew what the situation was, the division of those who had regarded them with favor, or at least neutrality, and those who resented him made sense. It was unfortunate and awkward, but it was the situation. Luke only hoped that he and Ben would be able to find some sort of answers for them.

When they returned to the *Shadow,* Luke began sorting through the datapads and other items they had brought with them while Ben prepared dinner.

"These . . . these are journals," he said. "It looks as though what Car'das was permitted to bring back with him was just the barest fraction of what he learned."

"Maybe," Ben said. "Or maybe it's just filled with ramblings along the lines of *Get me away from the rock creatures with the tongues.*"

Luke chuckled despite himself. "One way to find out," he said. He hooked up one of the pads to the holoreceiver, and an image appeared. It was a human male, with dark hair and a short, neatly trimmed beard. He seemed hale and fit, and wore a shirt, pants, and boots.

"If you're watching this, then presumably you, too, are a guest of the Aing-Tii," he said, smiling. The voice was deep, pleasant—and very familiar.

"That's Tadar'Ro's voice!" Ben said as he came back with a tray of spiceloaf sandwiches.

"No," Luke said, "Tadar'Ro got his voice from Jorj Car'das." He snagged a sandwich. "Let's listen to what he's got to say."

Chapter Sixteen

KESH
TWO YEARS EARLIER

VESTARA'S HANDS WERE TIGHT ON THE REINS AS TIKK FLEW toward the Temple. He cawed and bobbed his head. Vestara turned her attention toward the beast who bore her and, sensing his discomfort, immediately relaxed her grip. Her thoughts had been so crowded that she had become distracted. She felt bad. Just like weapons and slaves, transport animals were valuable property, and the wise Sith did not abuse them without good reason. Too, Tikk was more to her than an ordinary mount. She had bent him to her will, causing him to imprint upon her within moments of hatching, and she was fond of him.

She shivered a little. At this altitude, she was paying the price for her choice of clothing in which to attend the Council meeting. The delicate, almost flimsy material of her lovely green dress, while beautiful, offered no protection against the cold air and the wind that was starting to whip up. She didn't even have anything to put her hair up with, and it blew about wildly. Vestara placed a hand on Tikk's shoulder, right in front of the saddle, and sent calm through the Force. She then let the reins hang loosely about his sinuous neck and quickly began to braid her long, light brown tresses. She could do nothing about the dress.

Some things would be sent to her from her home, she knew. As a Sith Saber himself, her father would decide what was necessary and appropriate. Everything else would be provided at the Temple: clothing, bedding, food, weapons. She would sleep in a dormitory with all the other apprentices, and very little would be truly hers alone.

Once she had successfully completed her training and had become a full Saber, she would be permitted to have a private room, and a blind eye would be turned on whatever luxuries she chose to fill it with. She would have earned the right to whatever vanities and indulgences she liked. Until then, though, Vestara would live a simple existence. The Tribe did not scorn material goods, but first they needed to know that every Saber could live without them.

She was not overly concerned with what would and would not be sent. At the moment, all she could think about was what she would learn.

Vestara took up the reins again, gently directing Tikk toward the dark stone spires that she could now distinguish from the rock out of which they had been carved. It was late afternoon, and the shade of the mountain's steep side fell heavily on the Temple. There were no glow rods lit to gleam from the colorful glass windows, and even the white statuary in the courtyard seemed dim to her.

She felt Ship before she saw him, swathed in purple shadows as he was; felt the now familiar and welcome probing, the soft swell of dark side energy emanating from him, distinguishable and unique even when surrounded by the energy coming from the Temple itself. Vestara felt her lips curve in a smile and sent what she hoped was a respectful greeting.

Using the pressure of her legs and adjusting the reins slightly, she guided Tikk in toward the courtyard. Tikk descended and landed with only a slight thump. Vestara slipped off, patting the uvak absently.

No less a figure than Lady Rhea herself stepped forward to take the reins. Vestara, horrified, looked around. There were several other apprentices, but none made as if to intercept the Sith Lord.

"As I take the reins of your beast, so I take the reins of your life, my apprentice," said Lady Rhea. She gave Vestara a cool smile. "There will be a formal ceremony later, but for now, we begin here."

Vestara calmed her thoughts. She disliked being taken unawares, and she suspected that this was exactly why Lady Rhea had made this gesture. She bowed deeply, respectfully, in control.

"Of course, Lady Rhea. I submit myself to your guidance." She met her Master's eyes evenly, demonstrating her poise and confidence, honoring her teacher by indicating that Lady Rhea had accepted a strong young woman for her apprentice. Lady Rhea held her gaze. By sheer will, Vestara forced herself not to shiver as a particularly cold wind gusted across the courtyard, slicing through the pathetically thin material of her dress.

"Good. As you should." Now Lady Rhea nodded and another apprentice hurried forward to take Tikk. As the uvak lumbered off, wings folded against his sides, Vestara felt a sudden lurch. Would she be permitted to ride Tikk at all, or was he now property of the Temple? Would he even be returned to her when she completed her training?

"Attachments are nothing to avoid in and of themselves." Of course, Lady Rhea had noticed. "Indeed, passion is what drives us. But you must let go of the need to possess, Vestara. Anything that you have can be taken away from you. You come from a wealthy family, and you are used to having. Perhaps one of your lessons needs to be in not-having."

She nodded to the apprentice leading Tikk. The youth paused, drew Tikk's head down, activated his lightsaber, and lifted it high.

Tikk!

Vestara bit down on her tongue so hard she tasted blood. She kept her arms locked at her sides, swallowing the cry that ached to be uttered. Her eyes were enormous, and she did not tear them away from the scene before her.

"Very good," Lady Rhea said in a voice that was almost a purr. Another barely perceptible nod of her white-gold head and the apprentice deactivated his weapon. Tugging gently on the reins, he led Tikk down a ramp. The uvak, blissfully unaware of just how close he had come to decapitation by lightsaber, followed compliantly.

"Had you protested, your uvak would be dead now." Lady Rhea's hand dropped to Vestara's shoulder. "Go ahead and be fond of him, my dear. And of your pets, and family, and lovers you may take one day. Enjoy to the fullest all the trappings that power gives you, for you will have earned them. Want everything you wish— hunger, burn for it, if that fuels you. But never love anyone or anything so much that you cannot bear to lose it."

For just a moment, Vestara was angry at the display and the brutal casualness of it all. And then she realized that Lady Rhea was right. Completely right. With that realization, the anger bled out of her and she inhaled a hitching breath. Lady Rhea was watching her closely.

"My lady is correct, of course. I apologize for my reaction."

"Your reaction was better than most, my dear. I expected nothing less. Come."

*   *   *

The dormitory hall was cavernous and cold. No attempt had been made to beautify or soften the black stone from which the room had been hewn. The floors were smooth and even, but the walls were still rough. Only one side had windows, and those were high, round, and small. The little pools of light they cast on the ebony floor seemed feeble.

There were other lights, though. Two large fires roared in hearths large enough for Vestara to stand upright in, and each bed had a candle on the small table beside it. The beds themselves were simple cots with sheets, blankets, and a single pillow. Vestara thought of her lavish, canopied bed at home, piled so high with comfortable pillows that one could sink into sleep surrounded by them, and could not suppress a brief sigh.

One day, she would have such a bed again. Until then, she was certain that by the time she was permitted to return to this simple, crude, uncomfortable-looking cot, she would be so exhausted she would fall asleep the moment she crawled between the sheets.

They were alone in the vast hall at the moment, and Vestara followed Lady Rhea as she walked down between the rows of beds.

"This one is yours," Lady Rhea said, stopping before one of the beds. Indeed, Vestara recognized the small, neat pile of clothing as the simplest of her own. Folded on top of the pile was her black robe—the one in which she had been training when Ship had first arrived. It had been sweaty and sandy when she had discarded it; now it was clean and folded, ready to wear. Tucked beneath the cot were exactly two pairs of shoes—both boots.

On the table was a handful of personal grooming items. And that was it. That was all Vestara Khai would be permitted from her old life.

"You will soon realize that this is all you will need," Lady Rhea said.

"Of course," Vestara said automatically.

"Go ahead and change into your robe."

Vestara hesitated. Belatedly she realized that there was no privacy at all in the vast room. Was there even a refresher or would she have to utilize a pot of some sort and bathe from the mountain streams?

"There is no place to change," she said.

"No," Lady Rhea said, her perfect mouth curving in a smile. "There isn't. Nor will a room miraculously appear. You will quickly discover that no one here cares, Vestara. All are equal as apprentices. You will learn to change quickly and effectively. How clever you are about it is up to you. Some apprentices have no modesty at all; others have mastered the art of changing clothing without revealing anything unseemly. And yes, there is a refresher."

At Vestara's look, Lady Rhea laughed in her lovely, husky voice. "I cannot read minds, Vestara, but I have trained many an apprentice in my day, and every single one of them has reacted as you have. You are doubtless wondering why we utilize such primitive forms of heating and lighting," she continued. Vestara hesitated for a moment longer, then sat down on the bed—it was just as lumpy and uncomfortable as it had looked—and began to unlace her sandals.

"The reasons are twofold. First, we wish to purge apprentices of anything that smacks of luxury. There will be time for such things later, but now, we will pare you down to the very bone. Artificial light and heat are technological gifts. As Sith, you must learn to be at home anywhere. The entire galaxy is ours. Some of that galaxy is rich and comfortable. Some of it is bare and harsh. When your training is complete, you will be able to sleep anywhere, know how to make a fire, and be at peace whatever your surroundings."

Vestara slipped the dress over her head. For a moment, she was pale and naked and vulnerable in the dark, dim room. Then she slipped the heavy black robe over her head and was immediately comforted by its familiarity and tradition.

"The other reason"—and again Lady Rhea smiled—"is simpler. It's more practical this way."

Vestara, bent over lacing her boots, smiled, too. She rose, fastened her lightsaber onto her belt, and took a deep breath.

"I know you are familiar with some areas, but now much more is accessible to you. And yes," Lady Rhea added, anticipating the question, "you will be permitted to set foot in the historic vessel that brought us to this world. It is all part of your training."

"And . . . Ship?"

"Patience," chided Lady Rhea. "It is only your first day. You have years of training ahead of you. Come. I will let you familiarize yourself with the Temple."

It was a few hours later, when they were having something to eat in the dining room, that Vestara felt the summons at the back of her mind; a cool, probing touch that sent shivers down her spine.

Ship.

She had been eating a simple meal of barrat stew and oro bread. It was not a sophisticated dish, but the apprentices who had prepared it had a knack for seasonings, and she was hungry. Now, though, the bite of bread seemed dry and tasteless in her mouth. She glanced up at Lady Rhea, mutely asking if she, too, had felt it.

"Yes," Lady Rhea said. She rose immediately, leaving her half-eaten meal on the table. "It wants us."

They went.

Apparently, Ship wanted many people. As Lady Rhea and Vestara hastened at a brisk trot out into the courtyard, Vestara saw that several had already gathered and more were emerging. It looked as though everyone in the Temple had been summoned, and when Vestara had threaded her way through the crowd to the front, as was her right as Lady Rhea's apprentice, she glanced up and saw that several others were approaching on uvak-back. Even, she realized with surprise, Lord Vol. He landed and dismounted stiffly, waving off offers to assist and walking proudly, if slowly, to stand beside the strange, orange-red vessel.

Apparently, when Ship called, one came.

Ship seemed to have patience. After that one summons, Vestara sensed nothing further from him. He seemed to have shuttered himself off from them, still and quiet. Vestara stood rigidly at attention as the minutes ticked past, resisting the urge to shift her weight or otherwise betray any emotion other than stoic patience. At least she was somewhat warm now in her heavy Sith robes. At one point, Lady Rhea placed her hand on Vestara's shoulder.

And then, with no hint, he was there, in her mind again. All around her, she felt her fellow Sith coming sharply to attention.

You are needed.

Vestara nodded. Twilight had come fully, and the temperature had dropped. Her breath misted softly on the evening air.

Long have you dwelled here. But you are needed now.

Of course they were needed. They were Sith of the purest stock. Members of the Tribe could trace their origins back in an unbroken line for over two hundred generations. Doubtless they were truest to what it meant to be Sith than any others out there. Five millennia past, the *Omen* had crashed on Kesh, exiling the Tribe from their Sith brethren. But there had been no doubt in the minds of any Sith on that vessel that their brethren would succeed in the ultimate Sith goal. And there was no doubt now, that across the galaxy, the Sith ruled world upon world, as they did Kesh. That—

No.

The statement was flat and brooked no argument. Vestara was confused. *No what?*

The Sith have been hunted. Pushed back. Almost destroyed. Only a handful remain. I have seen them, the so-called One Sith, and found them wanting. Jedi are on many worlds. They do not rule, but their numbers are great and growing.

The shock in the Force from those assembled buffeted Vestara, and her stomach clenched. She tasted bile and had to fight the urge to vomit. Beside her, even Lady Rhea was stunned. Her hand on Vestara's shoulder suddenly gripped painfully, the nails digging in even through the thick cloth layer of the black robe.

How could this be? Ship would not lie to them. They would have sensed it. Besides, it was designed to serve them. Its blunt statement had shattered five thousand years of complacency, of smug satisfaction. Everything they had believed, for all this time, was untrue.

She felt Lord Vol's powerful presence in the Force. He, too, could not quite hide his shock, but his resolution to remain strong in the face even of this disastrous news was like a lifeline. Vestara—indeed, she suspected, everyone present—clung to it as such.

"We are Sith," he said. His voice carried clearly; he was obviously using the Force to augment it. "Even if every other Sith on every other world has died . . . we are still here! Our traditions, our beliefs—they still endure. We have thrived on this world. And perhaps this is why we were here—so that in this time of need, we, the Tribe, can restore the Sith!"

Vestara listened raptly. The idea that they could simply leave Kesh and rejoin the rest of the Sith had been exciting enough when everyone believed that the galaxy was under their sway. To think now that they might be the greatest surviving number of their kind—to think that they might wrest control of the galaxy from the hated Jedi—it was almost too much to hold.

Ship assured them this was why he had searched his data banks and sought them out. He could teach them. He could teach all of them.

"Now is the moment of our destiny!" Vol lifted his fist and shook it defiantly. "And we will not shirk it. This Ship will serve us. It will teach us about this universe as it is now, not as we thought it was in our naïveté, shunted away to this unknown world. We will emerge from our rest and conquer. It is in our blood. It is in our bones. We are Sith, and we will not falter!"

The crowd was cheering now. Even so, Vestara could still sense their worry in the Force, a hint of cold fear: *What if we fail?*

But they would not fail. It was not an option. They had a task laid before them. They would plan, and learn, and mount an attack on the Jedi who had defeated their forefathers five thousand years past.

The Sith would rise, completely unexpected, and claim what was theirs.

After all, they were Sith, were they not?

Chapter Seventeen

"WOW, THIS PLACE STINKS," JAINA SAID WITHOUT PREAMBLE.

Han gave Leia a meaningful glance. "Hey, this was your mother's idea."

Leia sighed and forced herself not to cover her own nose as they passed the nerf corral.

The Coruscant Livestock Exchange and Exhibition had been under way for several days by the time arrangements had been made for the Solo family to attend. But as it lasted for a full month, they still had plenty of time. Many creatures had already gone home with their new owners, to be displayed, ridden, petted, or eaten, as said new owners saw fit. But the reek of animal excrement of all varieties that made the daily pollution level of Coruscant seem nonexistent was testimony to the fact that there were still plenty of things that walked, crawled, slithered, hopped, and/or flew to be seen.

Escorting the Solos were two Jedi Knights, Natua Wan, a Falleen, and Radd Minker, a Brubb. Han and Leia had tried to get Yaqeel and Barv for the assignment, as Allana knew and liked both of them, especially Barv, but they were offworld at the moment.

Natua and Radd, being there on official duty, were dressed in the traditional white and brown robes of their order. Leia and Jaina wore comfortable street clothes. All four Jedi carried lightsabers, though Leia and Jaina had theirs in roomy bags slung over their shoulders. All six of them strolled along leisurely, and Allana certainly had enough entertainment to keep her giggling happily for hours.

And the littlest Solo was, as Leia had predicted, immune to the stench. They had not even entered the main exhibition area yet and already Allana's eyes were wide. Leia stroked her short hair, dyed dark to disguise its too-recognizable natural red, and smiled. Allana rewarded her with a grin and pointed at the large, furry animals with four horns, thick shaggy coats, and a cloud of flies hovering over them.

"I know them, don't tell me!" Allana said. She had indeed been a diligent student over the past few days. Leia had said there would be a test afterward. What she hadn't told the girl was that the reward for passing the test—and both Leia and Han were sure Allana would pass with ease; she was an extremely intelligent little girl—would be the riding animal she most gravitated toward.

"Even a tauntaun, if that's what she wants," Leia had said.

"Hey, we had a deal," Han had protested, but only halfheartedly.

"Those are nerfs," Allana said proudly. "Jaina has a very pretty coat made from their hide, and we all like the steaks." The animals grazed, placid for the moment. Allana pointed to another corral. "And the rams are separated because it's mating season. They can become very aggressive and fight each other, as well as trample their young."

Leia wasn't sure, but she could have sworn she saw Han blush a little as his granddaughter cheerfully rattled off the words *mating season*. She smothered a grin.

"That's right, sweetheart," Leia said. "Nerfs aren't the nicest animals in the world."

"But they're dewicious," Allana said. She had outgrown most of the slight lisp she'd had as a younger child, but now and then it crept back on certain words. "Can we have nerfburgers for lunch? With hubba chips?"

"If they're available at the cafeteria," Leia said. She expected they would be, along with more exotic foodstuffs. After all, if she were a breeder or seller of livestock, she'd make sure everyone had a chance to find out how "dewicious" said creatures were.

"And those are banthas," Allana said, hurrying down the entrance walkway to the next open-air corral. Natua Wan quickened her pace slightly, unobtrusively closing the gap between the child and her, keeping a close eye on Allana while maintaining the illusion to anyone who was watching that this was nothing more than a normal family and their Jedi friends on a social outing. Radd brought up the rear. Brubb were a social people, and his present cheerful demeanor was completely unforced. He was enjoying himself.

"They are a highly adaptable species and live on many worlds," Allana said. "And those are—oh, those are rontos! I've never seen a live one before!" She started to run, but a strong hand gently caught hers.

"Be careful, Amelia," Natua Wan said kindly, the blue beads woven into her long black hair clacking with her movement. "There's a reason you haven't seen one. They're good animals, very loyal and fond of their masters, but they spook very easily. You don't want to be running up and scaring them."

Allana nodded seriously. "You're right, Jedi Wan." She dropped down to a measured pace, unconsciously straightening.

"Any way you can break her of that?" Jaina murmured to Leia as they walked side by side. The secret of Allana's identity was a closely guarded one, but Leia shared Jaina's fear. The girl was intelligent enough to not deliberately give herself away, but she had the movement and bearing of one bred to royalty, even at age seven. It would be a significant clue if anyone understood what they were looking at.

"I figure that everyone knows she's a ward of a former Princess and Senator," Leia replied, pitching her voice equally soft. "It would make sense."

Jaina snorted. "*I* didn't move and stand like that."

"Well, you are your father's daughter. There wasn't much I could do with you in that area."

Han had moved ahead and swept Allana up onto his broad shoulders as she giggled delightedly. Mindful not to startle the rontos, Allana, now much closer to their eye level, slowly extended a hand. One of the great creatures perused her, then stretched out its long neck to sniff the hand curiously.

"Gentle as they come," said a voice right next to Leia. A heavyset human with a single brow, tanned skin, and a name tag that declared him to be TEVAR SHAN, OWNER, RONTO-RAMA FARMS, TATOOINE, grinned down at her. "If you have any heavy loads to move, rontos'll do the job for you. And as you can see, they're even good with younglings."

"Thanks," Leia said, "but we're not in the market for something that large."

"For the girl, eh?" The man's grin widened. "How about an eopie? I'm also part owner of Eopies Extraordinaire. We specialize in the dwarf variety, perfect for a little one." He pointed across the flood of people to a corral that housed the pale, long-snouted, humpback creatures.

"Throw in a dewback and Uncle Luke would feel right at home," Jaina said.

"Thanks, but I think we'll keep looking," Leia said, giving the man her best smile. A few paces ahead, Allana seemed more than content to stay on Han's shoulders, and Han seemed delighted to have her there. Leia nodded to herself. This had been a good idea—not just for Allana, but for all of them. So much had been going on. A little break, to look at animals and walk around for a bit, was just what they all needed.

"How is he, by the way?" Jaina continued.

"Luke? I've felt him in the Force now and then, but I haven't had a lot of contact. Especially not recently."

Jaina nodded. "Me either. Enough to know he and Ben are all right, though. Cilghal says she's been keeping him up to date. More than that we probably shouldn't know."

Something about the way she said it caused Leia to give her a searching look, but Jaina offered nothing further. Following her instincts, Leia said, "How are things with you and Jag?"

Jaina graced her mother with a smile of rare sweetness. "Good," she said. "Be nice to be able to have a date without making a mission out of it, but good."

"Comes with the territory, I'm afraid. Javis Tyrr again?"

"Mostly him, some others, but mostly him. We got him good, though." In a conspiratorial tone, Jaina told her mother about how they had tricked Tyrr at the restaurant.

"Well done. Just hope he doesn't catch you at something. He might not enjoy the idea of us laughing at him. Something about him—maybe the hair—makes me think he doesn't have a sense of humor when it comes to himself."

Jaina shrugged her narrow shoulders. "He's just a journalist. This family has survived being smeared before. What can he do? He's not even an official observer."

"But he is observing right now," came Radd's voice. He jerked his head to the left. Jaina looked in the direction indicated and groaned slightly. "Shall I go over and have a word with him?"

"No," Jaina said quickly. "Any attention will only encourage him. Let's head inside to the main halls and see if we can ditch him."

Leia agreed, and the family picked up their pace. Leia spoke to her husband and Natua, and the Falleen smoothly navigated them through the river of people, threading her way while Radd, watching out for Tyrr, brought up the rear. Right before they stepped inside the large exhibition center proper, Leia caught movement from the corner of her eye.

She turned her head to see several small, brown-pelted, horned creatures milling about in a pen. They stood upright on muscular, hooved hind legs, their smaller forelegs tucked close to their chests, and she was reminded of Han's loathed tauntauns.

But these were much prettier creatures, graceful and gentle with long bushy tails. As she watched, one of them leapt and ran for a few paces, and Leia smiled, watching it until the last instant when the press of people blocked them from her sight.

Kybucks. Too small to be used as mounts . . . by adult humans at least. Yoda had ridden one, she remembered hearing. And they were the perfect size for a seven-year-old girl. Kybucks originated on Kashyyyk, the home-world of her husband's best friend, the much-loved, late Chewbacca.

It fit perfectly. She would contrive for Allana and Han to see it before they left. If the girl took to the kybuck as Leia suspected she would, then she and Han would return tomorrow and secretly purchase one. Pleased, Leia turned her attention to the sights, sounds, and, unfortunately, smells of the enclosed exhibition hall.

The main hall was filled with displays, banners, and all manner of advertising. In the center was an elaborate scale display of some of the more standard animals to be seen at the exhibition, along with a sign that announced MAIN EXHIBITION HALL, in case anyone couldn't figure that out.

Off to the left was the SMALL ANIMAL HALL, whose smaller rooms held the cages or pens of the smaller creatures such as gizkas, twirrls, voorpaks, and the still-popular, though not all the rage anymore, chitliks. To the right was a large WARNING: DANGEROUS ANIMALS sign, with a great deal of smaller print below the bold statement: "The animals on display in this section of the exhibition hall have been known to exhibit violent behavior. All security measures have been taken to ensure the safety of our valued patrons. Attendees of the Coruscant Livestock Exchange and Exhibition should be aware, however, that they proceed at their own risk, and that the exhibition hall management assumes no responsibility for any injuries incurred."

"Nice," Jaina said. "I'll remember that when I've got a rancor nibbling at my ankle. Oh wait, I've already got Javis Tyrr. Where is he anyway?"

"I think we lost him," Natua said, her narrowed eyes scanning the crowd.

"Good," Leia said. She was anxious to tell Han about the kybucks she'd spotted, but Allana seemed glued to her grandfather. She was off his shoulders now but clinging to his hand, tugging him along in the direction of—

"Honey," Han was saying to her, glancing at Leia with a slightly desperate glint in his dark eyes, "don't you want to go see the cute little critters in the Small Animal Hall?"

"No," Allana said, not rudely, but clearly. "I want to go see *those*." She pointed at the WARNING sign.

Leia shrugged at her husband. "She's a Solo," she said, and he was forced to nod in understanding.

It was, of course, perfectly safe. Leia half suspected that the overly large, garishly colored WARNING sign was more advertisement than caution, especially as gaining entrance to this area required a separate and not insubstantial admission fee. Regardless of the lurid warning and the steep price, the area was crowded.

Only a small portion of those waiting patiently in line were permitted in at a time. Patrons stood single-file in a winding line for admittance to the turbolift that would take them to an area beneath the exhibition hall. Han, Leia, Allana, Jaina, Radd, and Natua crowded in with about fifteen other beings as the turbolift slowly descended.

Allana did not like the close press in there. It had been rare that anyone other than her mother or servants even came into her presence, let alone touched her or stood so very close. She stood with her back pressed against Han and his arms folded protectively around her. Leia could feel her nervousness in the Force and sent her calm.

"We can always ride right back up, honey," Han said to his granddaughter.

"No," Allana said stubbornly. "I want to see the animals here."

Leia met Han's eyes and shrugged.

The turbolift doors opened and everyone surged out, almost getting stuck in the doors. Jaina was the first out from their group, having been the last one to wedge herself in when the turbolift doors were closing, and Leia heard her daughter's annoyed voice carrying over the murmur of the crowd.

"Oh, for the love of . . ."

Leia actually laughed when they emerged. The décor,

the lighting, the ambient noise—a dull heartbeat with a barely audible, tension-inducing sound from some wind instrument in the background—all conspired to set the scene for anticipation of something dreadful. It was so over-the-top it was positively ludicrous.

The lighting was slightly tinged with red, casting a slightly bloody hue on everything they would see. The walkway that stretched before them was bare metal, and their feet clanged ominously as they moved forward. The ramp was narrow, forcing everyone to proceed single-file. It did have banisters, and cross sections so that patrons could either linger at a particular pen or move steadily across the entire viewing area. A quick perusal proved that everything was quite solidly built.

But below—protected by force fields, thick transparisteel so cleverly lit it was all but invisible, and security measures that would have given the designers of a third Death Star pause—were creatures that, despite the precautions, would have unsettled any viewer. The designers of the area had not needed the silly mood-setting tricks to get the desired result.

Leia felt a sense of unease as the crowd moved steadily toward the first viewing pen and wondered if they hadn't made a mistake in bringing Allana to this part of the exhibition. Not because the creatures themselves were alarming to behold, although they were, but because of why they were here. These were animals that had been captured or bred as a display of their owner's power, and none was trained to win the title of Most Placid in Show. They would likely be kept in uncomfortable conditions during their short lives, their innate tendencies toward aggression fostered. They would probably be mistreated and die painfully in gladiatorial combat on worlds where such entertainment was legal. Of course the owners would sign contracts assuring that their new purchases would never be used in such a fashion; Leia knew better than to assume any of those promises would be honored.

She wasn't looking forward to explaining to Allana how sick and cruel some beings could be to animals.

They were almost over the first viewing pen now. While the ceilings over the animals were transparisteel, the partitions between pens were thick duracrete. No one wanted to take any chances with one species getting into another's pen. The placard hovering in the air announced that this was a reek. Leia braced herself for the inevitable bad pun from Han about the creature's name, but it didn't come. And from that alone she realized her husband shared her concerns. His big hands were on Allana's shoulders, letting her move where she wanted, but protectively there.

Allana stood up on tiptoe, the banister being sufficiently tall that she couldn't otherwise see over it, and peered down at the animal. It was large, with mottled red skin on its head, neck, and chest. Two horns curved out on either side of its massive jawbone and a single huge central horn jutted from between its eyes. The solitary animal paced for a bit, then, grunting, pawed at the grassy matter it had been given to sleep on. It looked up at the throng gazing down on it, opened its mouth—it had jaws strong enough to snap a humanoid limb in a casual bite—and bellowed at them, then moved to one of the rocks in the pen to sharpen its cheek tusks.

"Why aren't the reeks out in the riding animal pens?" Allana asked. "They're bred to be pack animals, aren't they? And I thought their skin was supposed to be brown. Is this one hurt?"

Leia and Jaina exchanged pained glances. Jaina spoke first. "Well, yes they are pack animals. And they're usually fed plants. But sometimes people feed them a diet of meat, which enhances their aggression. They want to use them to fight other animals."

A frown marred Allana's sweet face, but it wasn't shock and horror. It was righteous anger. "I have heard of such things," she said quietly, "and I think it's very wrong of people to do that."

Of course. Protected as she had been as Chume'da, Allana was in many ways not nearly as innocent as children born to more ordinary parents. There were certain harsh realities that she would not have been shielded from.

"You're right, honey," Jaina said, a bit loudly so that those nearby—presumably those considering buying the beasts for such a purpose—could hear. "It *is* very wrong of people to do that."

They moved slowly past the reek to the next pen, which housed a beast that had a special significance to the Solo family—a rancor. Leia's lips thinned in recollection of a time, many years past now, when she had been a slave of Jabba the Hutt and had been forced to watch him feed many of his enemies—and some servants who had displeased him for one reason or another—to a rancor. It was always a one-sided affair, until the time Luke Skywalker had been dropped into the rancor pit.

"Queen Mother Tenel Ka has a lightsaber whose hilt is a rancor tooth," Allana said. There was a hint of wistfulness in her voice, but she had not blurted out *my mother*.

The rancor squatted in its pen, staring sullenly up at the visitors. Then without warning it leapt upward.

Allana—and half the people on the walkway—shrieked. Han had one arm around her in a heartbeat, the other hand going for the blaster that wasn't on his hip. The rancor impacted with the transparisteel and a bright flash dispelled the dull red lighting for an instant, and when Leia could see again the beast was crouched on the floor of its pen, shaking its head and twitching from the shock it had received.

"Any emergency exits?" Han asked quietly, holding Allana. "I'd just as soon get out of here."

"There's one next to every pen," Natua said. "At the end of the crosswalk."

"Then let's go. I'm ready to see something small, fluffy, and with no teeth," Han said.

"No," said Allana stubbornly. "I want to see all of them." She was struggling now, and her grandfather reluctantly put her down.

"You know, we just might trade you in for a chitlik," Han said, ruffling her hair. "They're a lot easier than little girls."

Recovering from her fright already, Allana giggled. "But not nearly as cute, right?"

"I'm supposed to be the one with the wisecracks, missy."

They moved onward, over boarwolves, tusk-cats, and other creatures, until they came to a pen that contained several animals curled up so tightly they looked like furry pillows—furry pillows whose spines were crested with large quills. One was large and tan; the others—Leia counted ten of them—were much smaller and white. At one point the larger lump of fur stirred and looked up. Leia saw four eyes and an enormous row of teeth as the creature snarled. A few of the white lumps of fur looked up, as well.

"Oh! It's a nexu—and she has cubs!" said Allana. "How cute!"

"For creatures with four eyes and a mouthful of teeth, they are rather cute," Leia admitted. Their eyes were large and liquid, and their mouths were still full of tiny milk teeth. The cubs couldn't be more than three months old, since they were still snowy white.

"They're still young enough to be bought as guard animals rather than attack animals," Radd said. "You have to find excellent trainers, though."

"Wait—you mean you can keep those as pets?" Jaina said.

"Well, yes. If you get them young enough and train them well enough. I mean, they're never going to be a little twirrl, but—"

A prickle of unease stirred at the back of Leia's neck; a brush of foreboding, like cold fingers lightly stroking her skin. Her hand dropped to her bag and reached for the lightsaber contained therein.

She caught Radd's eye and he nodded, his own hand clasping the hilt of his lightsaber. Jaina's face told Leia that she, too, sensed the sudden change in the Force. Leia turned to Natua, her mouth open to ask the other Jedi if she could take Allana to the nearest emergency exit.

Natua was nowhere to be seen.

All the lights went out. And the screaming started.

It had happened so fast Natua couldn't believe it.

"Any emergency exits?" Han had asked, holding on to the frightened Allana. "I'd just as soon get out of here."

"There's one next to every pen," Natua said. "At the end of the crosswalk." Her eyes flickered to the exit, judging how long it would take for them to make their way through the crowds to it, and then back to Amelia.

No. Not Amelia.

An imposter.

All along, Valin, Jysella, Seff—they had been right.

Her hand dropped to her lightsaber and she looked quickly at Jedi Leia Organa Solo, at her husband, her daughter.

"You know, we just might trade you in for a chitlik," Not-Han said. "They're a lot easier than little girls."

Natua stared as the false Amelia giggled. A child?

How could they—whoever they were—impersonate a child? And why? "But not nearly as cute, right?"

All imposters. All of them, even Radd. She scanned the crowd. Was every being here one? How deep did it go? All the way through the Masters, through the GA?

Natua dropped back, letting her pheromones activate, exuding a feeling of calm toward those crowd members close to her, and began to think about how she was going to get out—and find those who were still their true selves. What had been done with the real Leia, Han, Amelia, Jaina?

It was her duty as a Jedi Knight to find out—and stop the imposters any way she could. Her gaze fell to the pens below her and the creatures they contained. It was a desperate, dark measure, but it was one she was willing to take. The imposters' voices floated back to her as she moved toward the exits she herself had pointed out.

The fake Han's quip was lost in the murmur of the crowd as Natua opened the door and slipped through.

This area was bare-bones utilitarian in contrast with the theatrical décor in the pen area. She could see ducts, wiring, and unpainted duracrete as she glanced around. Next to the door was a uniformed human male with his feet on his desk, reading a holozine. He did a double take at her, the feet came down, and he hurried toward her.

"Good afternoon, ma'am, I hope our exhibition of dangerous animals wasn't too intense for you. Are you in need of medical attention? Feeling faint perhaps?"

Natua would have rolled her eyes had the situation not been so dire. They kept up the charade even in the back areas, it would seem.

Something was wrong with him, too. She could not put her finger on it, but even though she had never met him before, she knew that he, like the others, was not who he pretended to be. She wanted to simply Force-hurl him against the wall, but she needed him. She stepped forward, her skin reddening as she exuded pheromones and moved two fingers very gently.

"Jedi. There's an emergency. You have to take me to the control room immediately. Lives are at stake!"

His skin, too, reddened as he blushed slightly in reaction. "I—lives are at stake out there. Come with me at once! I'll take you to the control room."

Leia activated her lightsaber at almost exactly the same instant as Radd. The pale blue glow of her weapon gave her enough light to see the panic on their faces that she could already hear in the screaming voices. Allana's, right beside her, was the loudest. The only other illumination came from several tiny rows of light below them that outlined each pen and marked where the force fields were erected. The crowd, already unnerved by the sudden leap of the rancor, was now pressing toward the exit doors.

"They're locked!" someone yelled.

"Blast it," Leia murmured under her breath, then, more loudly, using the Force to augment her voice, she shouted, "Everyone remain calm! I'm certain it's just a glitch and will be remedied soon. We're in no danger."

She caught Radd's eye and jerked her head in the direction of the nearest exit. He nodded and began to push his way through the crowds.

"I'll get the one over by the rancor pen," Jaina said. She suited action to word, Force-leaping over the crowd and running lightly on the banister on her way to the exit.

"Radd," Leia continued, "Jaina and I are going to begin cutting exits through the doors to get everyone out as soon as possible. Hopefully the lights will have come back on by then and—"

There was a clanking, grinding noise from below

them. Leia glanced down quickly. Behind her, Han swore very colorfully and Allana's frightened wails increased.

The transparisteel ceilings that formed a physical barrier between the patrons and the hungry, tormented, hostile creatures that milled below them were slowly, methodically retracting into the wall. The creatures looked upward eagerly. At the same moment, Leia watched as the tiny lights that so comfortingly announced that the force fields were active . . . winked out.

Something wet and solid dropped down on her, catching her shoulder heavily. A quick glance down revealed a large amount of blood—but not her own. At once Leia understood what was going on.

The animals, carnivores all, were being fed.

It was a smart plan from a safety perspective. At feeding time, the transparisteel ceilings would be retracted, the force fields would be deactivated, and instead of risking lives by asking the animal caretakers to physically carry in the raw meat, it was simply dropped from compartments in the ceiling.

Except it wasn't feeding time, and lots and lots of beings were in the way. Even as Leia tried to again shout out calm to the crowd, she thought it was poor design that the ramps would be so positioned. The food was dropping right down on them, as well as into the pens.

And then she realized what must inevitably come.

"Protect Amelia!" she cried to Han. She felt Jaina through their Force-bond, and sent her daughter a fresh sense of urgency. Force-leaping upward to land lightly on the narrow banister, Leia ran along it as Jaina had, concentrating hard to keep her balance, toward Radd and the hole he was cutting through the door. The danger made gentleness go right out the air lock, and Leia had to Force-push several screaming crowd members back from herself and Radd.

"How close are you?" she cried, extending a hand to keep the mob from descending upon the Brubb as he worked frantically.

"A few more minutes," he replied, dragging his lightsaber through the heavy metal of the door.

"We may not have that," Leia told him, turning around to lend her lightsaber to his.

"Why not?"

"Because it's suddenly become feeding time," she said, pulling the blade through her side of the circle with all her strength. "The force fields are deactivated, the ceilings are pulled back, and any minute now the walkways will be—"

The metal upon which they stood trembled and began to move, pulling them closer to the wall.

"—retracted," Leia said.

Chapter Eighteen

NATUA NODDED IN SATISFACTION AT THE SCREAMING THAT could be heard even through the thick walls. She took no pleasure in the noise, but she had done what was necessary. Every person in that room was an imposter, and while she would not willingly kill them on general principle, those who had somehow managed to spirit away Leia, Han, and Radd were obviously very powerful . . . whatever they were. Their motives could not possibly be benign. The pretenders wearing the faces of friends—who, likely, had probably murdered said friends—had to be contained and stopped.

Now they would be.

She glanced back at the two unconscious guards. The first one had taken her to the control room; the second had tried to stop her. She had Force-hurled both against the walls upon entering. Bloody smears trailed from the point of impact to where their heads lolled against the wall. It had been easy for a Jedi to override the security systems in the Dangerous Animal Hall. She was sorry to discover, however, that this room did not control all security throughout the exhibition. She'd have to do the rest on her own.

The Falleen Jedi raced through the back corridors, keeping her eyes peeled for security cams and shorting them out every time she passed one. She slammed into a door marked EXIT and emerged in the main hall. Had it been only half an hour or so since she had been there, her greatest concern a nosy journalist spying on them? Her heart lurched in pain. She had been ignorant then, had thought her fellow Jedi now encased in carbonite to be insane. She knew better now.

Natua glanced around. She eyed the Small Animal Hall for a moment, then shook her head. It would be annoying for dozens of little creatures to be milling about underfoot, but nothing more. She wouldn't waste her time there. The distraction—the chaos, the damage she needed in order to both ensure her escape and cause as much harm to the doppelgängers as possible—would be found outside.

The screaming was nearly deafening, and now the crowd began to stampede in earnest. Leia whirled, lifting her lightsaber, desperately hoping she wouldn't have to use it but prepared to if necessary. On the other side of the door would likely be the emergency controls to stop the ramps from retracting. She gripped her blade with one hand, holding out the other, fingers splayed hard, to keep the press of beings from jostling Radd in his urgent task. She hoped that Jaina was making better progress than the Brubb.

She wished heartily she weren't so short and craned her neck to see into the center of the room. Those on the ends of the ramp would be frantic, trying to retreat to the safety of the walls as the surface beneath their feet inexorably disappeared a centimeter at a time. And yet Leia was trying to hold them back, to give Radd room to work.

A sudden shrill cry soared over the other screams, and Leia felt a sharp stab of terror in the Force. Without pausing to ascertain what was going on with her five physical senses, Leia leapt upward, landed on the banister again, and then jumped down toward the source of the fear.

A little boy, about Allana's age, had landed hard on the duracrete floor of the boarwolf pen. His pain shot through Leia, red-hot and urgent—the boy had suffered broken bones at the very least—but his terror was even more overpowering than the physical pain. Leia dropped beside him, bending her knees to absorb the impact, then put her own body between the boy and the snarling predators.

One of them lunged forward, teeth bared. Leia brought the weapon across her body in a sweeping motion and the creature fell in two still-wriggling pieces. Two others lunged at her in tandem. She darted forward, impaling the first one right through its opened mouth and slicing upward. She extended a hand and Force-hurled the second one back into a fourth animal that was charging. The boarwolf struck its packmate heavily, and both beasts went sprawling. Leia sensed a fifth one coming behind her and whirled. She decapitated it immediately. The little boy screamed, covering his head as blood rained down upon him. Leia was sorry for the trauma she'd caused him, but at least he'd be alive to deal with it. She looked around, clutching the lightsaber in preparation for another attack. One of the bodies spasmed in its death throes, but then lay still. She had killed them all.

She turned back to the boy, crouching beside the hysterically sobbing child. She touched his shoulder lightly, exuding comfort and reassurance.

"It's okay," she said. "You're going to be fine." She had just started to gather him in her arms, intending to Force-leap upward to the ramp and return him to his no-doubt terrified parents, when out of the corner of her eye she caught motion.

She glanced up. Above her she saw a blur of tawny fur and realized that the mother nexu had leapt clear out of her cage and was now scrabbling for purchase on the ramp. Her two front paws were hooked into the small holes in the metal plating, and one of her hind legs had almost managed to get a solid grip. Her naked rodent-like tail thrashed and wound about the banister. The nexu opened her horrifically wide mouth in a savage snarl, her head looking almost like it would split in two with the gesture.

Leia left the boy where he was. He would be safer in the pen with the five dead boarwolves. Switching the lightsaber to her left hand, she leapt upward. She caught the banister with her right hand about a meter from where the nexu was still struggling to climb atop the ramp and started to pull herself up. A strong hand shot out of nowhere, grabbed her arm, and hauled her up the rest of the way. She turned to see Han, his other arm wrapped tightly about Allana's small waist as he pressed the girl to him like a package he was carrying on his hip.

There was no time to thank him, or reassure Allana. Leia spun to face the nexu. Even as she whirled, she saw the creature lash out with one of its forepaws as both hind legs came up and gripped the retreating end of the ramp. It caught the leg of an Ithorian. The unfortunate being cried out in pain in the unique, twin-mouthed fashion of his people, his utterance of agony sounding incongruously beautiful and hauntingly musical. He fell backward, his long fingers clutching at the ramp, his left leg caught in the huge jaws of the nexu.

Leia dived forward, lifting the lightsaber in both hands high over her head and bringing it down in a sharp stabbing motion. The energy blade impaled the nexu at the back of its neck, continuing the downward momentum until it was partway through the ramp. Exactly as Leia had intended.

"Get him! Get him!" she cried over her shoulder. The lifeless body of the nexu swung limply now, but its jaws remained clenched in death's rictus. Some of the beings were jolted from their mindless horror and moved forward, prying open the beast's mouth and pulling the still-wailing Ithorian back from the edge of the ramp. Leia deactivated her lightsaber, and the huge feline—no longer pinned like an insectoid specimen to a flimsiboard display—tumbled limply into the pen. The cubs scampered to their mother's corpse and mewed piteously.

The ramp had been retracting slowly but inexorably, and now all the ramps were only halfway extended. Crowded to begin with, now the beings were pressed tightly together. Leia was surprised that no one had snapped and begun hurling bodies down at random, but she knew enough to simply be grateful for the fact. Maybe it was the calm she had been pouring into the Force this whole time.

And then with an unexpected jolt the ramp suddenly stopped. Leia looked up to see a large, smoking, circular hole cut in the door. Radd stuck his head through and gave her a grin. He'd done it. Then his eyes widened and he ducked back quickly as the patrons began to pour through the hole.

An arm snaked around Leia and she was suddenly crushed to her husband's chest. The immediate danger was over for the moment, and so she allowed herself to be held for a heartbeat, slipping one arm around Han and the other reaching to touch her now sniffling granddaughter.

"Leia!"

It was Natua's voice. Leia whirled, activating the lightsaber, searching for the other Jedi in the crowded ramps that still jutted precariously over the animal pens.

"I know what you are—imposter!"

Leia narrowed her brown eyes. She had realized what

must have happened the minute she had been unable to find Wan. Even so, to hear it—

"You want me, Leia? Come find me."

No, Natua was not present in the crowd. She had to be speaking over a comm, and that meant she had captured the control room. Leia would find her there. Why the Falleen had issued the challenge, she did not know, but she was glad the fight would be contained. Enough innocents had been terrorized and made to suffer this day at what should have been a pleasant, safe outing.

"Take Amelia and get out of here," she told Han.

"I'll have Radd take her back home and then I'll—"

"Radd and Jaina need to stay here and help take care of these people, and you and Amelia need to get to safety." Leia's voice was clipped and cool, and Han scowled.

"I'll get her to safety, Your Worship," Han promised. "But then I'm coming back. With as many blasters as I can strap to my body."

With any other man, it would be simply a turn of phrase. Leia knew better than to assume such a thing where Han Solo was concerned and for a wild, inappropriately amusing instant, wondered just how many blasters Han *could* strap to his body. Without another word, she pushed her way through the crowds trying to squeeze out through the hole Radd had cut with his saber, gently Force-turning them aside. She reached out for Jaina in the Force. Her daughter's presence was steely and calm, but with a fiery rage burning hot underneath it.

Leia had intended to wait, to let the patrons get to safety, but with the taunt from Natua Wan still echoing in her ears, she knew the rogue Jedi had to be stopped as soon as possible.

*   *   *

Han held Allana tightly to him as he eased his way through the hole, careful not to touch the red-hot metal or let it touch Allana. She clung to him, as silent now as she had been vocal before, little arms and legs wrapped tightly around his torso. Guards were coming up, grim-faced and worried, helping people through, taking those with injuries aside. Han waved away help and concentrated on finding his way back to the main hall and then getting the frip *out*.

Jaina raced up beside him. "Dad! Where's Mom?"

"I think Natua Wan cracked up," Han said. "Called your mother out. She's gone to find and stop her."

Jaina nodded. "That's what I figured, too. Just what we need—another crazy Jedi. You know Tyrr is going to make the most of this."

Allana whimpered and tightened her grip. "We can't catch a break," Han muttered. "*It'll be fun,* she said. *Educational,* she said. *A day out.* Right."

"This way," Jaina said. Not slowing her pace, Jaina turned so her shoulder slammed the door open. They spilled out into more chaos.

"What the—"

The central area, which an hour earlier had been filled with calm patrons, bored sales representatives, and lines to get into the two halls, was now pandemonium. Four rontos were rearing in terror, their massive legs coming down on anyone or anything unfortunate enough not to get out the way. A nerf bull bellowed, lowering its head to charge. It had already impaled one victim, judging by the blood glistening on its horns. Other herd animals were milling about—banthas, tauntauns, dewbacks—all terrified, all *loose*.

"*Stang!*" Jaina yelped. "She opened the corrals!"

Han swore. "The corrals surround the main building."

Jaina nodded, her eyes darting back and forth. "Too

dangerous for you to try to go outside now. Stay here and wait for me."

"Like chubba I—"

"Dad! You have to keep Amelia safe! I'll go fight my way through, grab a speeder or a speeder bike or something, and come back for you. That display—climb on top of it. Most of the herd animals can't climb, and the only ones tall enough to get to you would be the rontos, and they're trying to get out, not attack."

Han glanced where his daughter pointed. It was the large display of representational animals they'd seen when they first entered, located in the middle of the hall. His strength wasn't quite what it used to be, but he thought he could get on top of the life-sized model of the bantha. Allana would have to hang on tight, though.

"Okay," he said. "But if you're not back in here in fifteen minutes with a way out for us, I'll ground you. I don't care how old you are."

Jaina couldn't help but snort with amusement. This was one of the things she loved best about her father. No matter how dire the moment, he could make her laugh—and when she laughed, her mind cleared.

"Bet I'll be back in ten," she said, then turned and charged for the crazed nerf bull, lightsaber lit.

Leia skidded to a halt in front of the control room. The door was wide open, and she felt a pang at the sight of the two bodies inside. Natua had been here but was nowhere to be seen. Leia dropped to her knees beside one of the guards and felt for a pulse. Faint, but there. She checked the other—he was alive, too.

"Leia!"

Leia was on her feet. "Natua! This isn't what you think it is! You know it isn't! Let me help you. You are a Jedi, you don't want all these deaths on your hands!" She glanced around quickly at the console, thumbed a switch, and said, "This is the control room for the Dangerous Animal Hall. Get a medical team to the control room now! We have injured!"

"Injured? Who is this?" came a suspicious voice.

"Just get here." Leia did not have time for further conversation. She needed to find and stop Natua before she injured—or killed—any more.

The voice came from just around the corner. Natua was taunting her. "Oh, of course it isn't. You're Leia Organa, Jedi Knight, Princess and former Senator, loving mother." Scorn, anger, and a dreadful sense of betrayal laced the words.

Leia moved carefully toward the sound of the voice. Natua was most assuredly not in her right mind. Further conversation was not going to convince her, not if the way Seff, Valin, and Jysella had behaved was any indication. The best thing to do would be to incapacitate the Falleen as quickly and painlessly as possible.

She extended her senses but could not pick up on Natua's presence in the Force. Could Natua, too, hide herself from detection in the Force? If so, it was becoming altogether too common an ability and far too annoying for Leia.

"You're not an imposter who's stolen the real Leia away." The voice dripped sarcasm. "And Amelia? A child? How could you do it?"

The voice was coming from right around the corner. Leia turned the corner and, lightsaber lit, sprang—on nothing.

Jaina realized she was going to be late in picking up her father and niece. She was going to be late because she was a Jedi, and people were in trouble, and she could stop it, and so she would.

Security was now coming into the main hall and firing on the loose creatures. Jaina winced as the hall was filled with the sounds of blasterfire and animals in pain on top of the screaming of the terrified patrons. It was grimly necessary; there were far too many animals running free, and the lives of sentient beings were at stake. But there were some that she could help.

Jaina closed her eyes for an instant, calming and centering herself. This was a challenge for her at the best of times, and now it was almost impossible, but she managed it. Opening her eyes, she stretched out each hand toward the nearest frightened beasts. One was a dewback, agitated at the press of people. The other was a kybuck, leaping about frantically.

It's all right. You don't need to be afraid. No one will hurt you. Come back to the safety of the corral. Follow me.

The dewback bellowed, but after a few moments trundled toward Jaina. The kybuck came even more swiftly, and Jaina patted its soft flank. When the dewback lowered its head to her, Jaina smiled at it and stroked it as well. She leapt onto its back and reached out again, and again, until there was a small cluster of animals pressed close to her.

Jaina planted suggestions in the milling throng right in front of her. Some were stronger-willed than others, but they were all looking for direction and guidance, and in the end they parted for her and her little parade. Jaina burned to go faster, but that would agitate the animals, and it was more important that they stay calm than that they get to the pen two minutes faster. After what seemed an eternity, they came to one of the corrals. Its elaborate security system had been shorted out, but there was still a basic gate with a bar that fell down into place, and that would suffice. Jaina herded the beasts through, gave them one final thought of *You're calm, go ahead and sleep,* and turned around.

Right into a familiar and disliked face.

"You!" Jaina shrieked, pointing at Javis Tyrr. The sleemo was filming her! She marched up to him, placed her hand over the cam droid's lens, and pushed her face into his.

"Jaina Solo, can you verify that Jedi Natua Wan has succumbed to the same mental illness that—"

Jaina reached out with her other hand and gripped his shirt. "You saw her? Where?"

Faced with the prospect of imminent bodily harm, the calm, professional journalistic demeanor bled away. "Just a minute ago. She was opening up all the corrals. I have it all recorded."

"Where did she go?"

He pointed to the side of the exhibition hall. The corrals went all the way around. Natua, it would seem, was bent on opening them all.

Jaina shoved Tyrr away, simultaneously sending a pulse to short out the hovering cam droid and reaching for her comlink. "Mom, Natua was just out here about a minute ago. She's heading around the north side of the exhibition hall."

"That explains something," Leia said in a dry voice. "Looks like I've been chasing shadows. I'm on my way."

"How about an exclusive interview since my information proved useful?" Tyrr said.

"How about I don't punch you in the nose?" Jaina retorted. She was already turned around and running toward the exhibition hall, comming Radd as she went.

She found the Falleen at the bordok pen. Jaina didn't slow her speed, didn't cry out as she charged, merely dived toward the other Jedi. Natua, however, sensed her approach, and right as Jaina leapt toward her she opened the pen and the maddened animals stampeded out. Unable to move aside in time, Jaina simply Force-leapt upward, ran lightly across the backs of the creatures, and sprang toward Natua.

The other Jedi had her lightsaber up and the two blades clashed, sizzling. Jaina gritted her teeth and hissed over the noise, "I don't want to hurt you!"

"But *I* want to hurt *you*. The real Jaina will thank me." Natua broke the lock and pushed. Jaina fell back a pace and dropped into a defense position.

Stang, she really *didn't* want to hurt Natua. The other Jedi was troubled, and needed to be taken care of. She was—

"Oh, now the gloves come off," Jaina hissed angrily, realizing that Natua was trying to influence her with pheromones.

"Nice trick, Natua," came Leia's voice. "You led me on a merry chase there for a little bit. Jacen was able to throw his voice like that, too. Don't suppose you'd care to tell me how you did it?"

Jaina didn't take her eyes off Natua, but said, "About time you got here."

"Sorry," Leia said. "Natua did a pretty good job of misdirecting me."

"Surrender," Radd said, hurrying up. "You're outnumbered three to one, Natua. You know we are only concerned about your—"

Natua lunged at Jaina, snarling. Both Solos brought their blades down on hers in perfect tandem, as if they'd rehearsed it. The sheer physical pressure of two crossed blades on her single one forced Natua's blade toward the ground and she stumbled, caught off-balance. It was then that Radd sprang on her. There was no grace, no finesse, no skilled usage of the Force in his attack. He simply jumped on her from behind and rammed his hard skull into hers.

Natua crumpled, unconscious, to the ground. Jaina and Leia blinked at Radd. He shrugged, a little embarrassed.

"Hey," Jaina said. "It did the trick." She wiped a hand

across her forehead and sniffed. "Whew. Is that me? I need a sanisteam."

She glanced up to see a familiar figure striding toward her. "Looks like I missed all the fun—again," Han said. Allana was walking at his side, her hand held tightly in his. She looked pale and frightened still, but was clearly recovering.

Leia looked sorrowfully at the unconscious Falleen and sighed. "This keeps getting harder to witness," she said. "Valin, Seff, Jysella, and now Natua. All so young to have something like this happen."

"Guess they don't make Jedi like they used to," said Han.

"Dad, I'm *right here.*"

Chapter Nineteen

THE DAYS PASSED, AND LUKE AND BEN LEARNED.

They learned primarily from Tadar'Ro, whom they grew increasingly to like. Even though he was Aing-Tii, and therefore would in part always be incomprehensible to them, he was clearly comfortable in his dealings with the two Jedi and seemed to like them after a fashion. He answered their questions as best he could, which sometimes was very well indeed and sometimes hardly at all. He was clearly trying.

"You are the third and fourth humans I have met," Tadar'Ro said one day as they sat in what was clearly the Aing-Tii's favorite spot. It seemed as rocky and barren as any other place, but the stones had been worn down by time. They held the warmth of the sun when it was cool and moved into shade from the taller standing stones when the day grew warmer. Ben even caught glimpses of small animals now and then. There was a calmness, a serenity about the place that both he and Luke could sense.

Luke even commented on it one afternoon. Tadar'Ro radiated pleasure and warmth into the Force as he responded.

"This is a teaching site," he said. "Many of the young gather here to learn. So, too, did Jacen Solo and Jorj

Car'das." Always the Aing-Tii used the full names of those he referred to.

"A . . . school, then?" Ben asked.

"Yes, that will do. A school. For centuries have open and willing minds been taught in this place. We find joy in learning and in sharing knowledge. The energy of so many minds, so much learning and enlightenment—that is what you feel here."

Ben nodded slowly.

"You taught Jacen here," Luke said. "How good a student was he?"

"He was only the second human I had ever met, and the first Jedi," Tadar'Ro replied. "He seemed very eager for knowledge, but it was . . . not as joyful to him as to others. Is this a human trait?"

Luke and Ben exchanged glances. "Not universally. Everyone is a unique individual. How long ago was Jacen here?"

"There was a newness, an expectancy about him," Tadar'Ro said in typical cryptic Aing-Tii fashion. By now, though, Luke and Ben were starting to be able to "translate."

"He was just starting on the five-year journey," Luke said to Ben, who nodded.

"You said he seemed eager for knowledge, but it wasn't a joyful experience," Ben continued. "Can you elaborate?"

Tadar'Ro sat back on his haunches, his tongues flickering in and out, but no words came forth. Clearly thinking and speaking were sometimes one and the same for the Aing-Tii. Ben stifled an inappropriate laugh as he realized that sometimes, thinking and speaking were one for members of his family, as well.

"It was a task, rather than a delight. As if—it was something to be accomplished, so one would not need to worry about it anymore. Something to get, to have."

"That sounds like Jacen," Ben said quietly. "So even then his feet were set on this path. At least somewhat."

"Path?"

Luke sighed and turned to Tadar'Ro. "Your people use the Force, but it is my understanding that you don't believe in a light or dark side."

They had learned this from Jorj Car'das's journals. At the beginning, Car'das had seemed to be very much like them: He had not been at all certain of what to make of the Aing-Tii initially.

"I didn't really understand what it was Yoda had done for me until I frittered the gift away," the small image of Car'das had said. "I wasn't, and am not, and probably never will be, a Force-sensitive individual. And frankly, before I came here, I really didn't care that much about it. But the Aing-Tii do—and yet they barely use it. Never have I seen a people so fascinated with something they respect enough not to use like a common household implement."

"We don't do that," Ben had said as they watched over dinner one night.

"No," Luke had replied. "That denotes a lack of respect, I think."

"Most of my understanding about the Force, which is admittedly limited, points to it having only two aspects—light and dark," Car'das had said. "The Jedi work with the light side of the Force, and the Sith and Dark Jedi with, obviously, the dark. That's nice and simple and clear, and maybe we humans like our philosophies that way. But the Aing-Tii have a much more complicated view of it. They view it as—"

The image of Jorj Car'das had paused and his hands moved, as if he could physically grasp the words he wanted. "As having variations. Gradations. Like light, when put through a prism. Kind of—a rainbow."

Ben thought of this image as Tadar'Ro nodded. "It is

true. We do use the Force. It is sacred. It is of Those Who Dwell Beyond the Veil. Such a thing is much more complex than light or dark, wrong or right. Jacen Solo seemed to understand this."

Luke and Ben exchanged glances. Ben knew that look; they'd talk about this more when they were alone.

Tadar'Ro continued, "We do use the Force to power our vessels, so that we may move beyond this world and search for any objects that might have belonged to Those Who Dwell Beyond the Veil. We will send you on such pilgrimages, as well. You will be able to aid us greatly."

"Of course," said Luke carefully. "We will be happy to do so while we are here. You shared with Jacen your understanding of the Force—of this rainbow aspect as Car'das called it. What else did you teach him?"

"Jacen Solo was very strong in the Force, which is why we agreed to instruct him. We believe that he had been sent to us to learn, just as Jorj Car'das was, just as you were. We taught him that one does not need to be Force-sensitive to use the Force. We taught him the understanding of how our vessels move instantly from place to place—how even as simple a thing as a rock or a tool can be moved so."

He extended a clawed hand and pointed at a small stone. There was a clap of displaced air, and suddenly the rock was at Luke's feet. Both Ben and Luke started.

"Perception is all, if it is powerful enough," Tadar'Ro said. "I saw the rock here, and not there, and here it is. It is difficult to convince the mind that it is so, but once you have mastered and understood that—it is supremely simple."

This, Ben thought to himself, was totally astral. He bent and picked up the rock. It was just that, a rock; not smoking, not unnaturally warm or cool, just a rock that had been there a minute ago but was now here, resting in his palm.

"Jacen Solo was able to learn this quickly," Tadar'Ro continued. "I will teach this to the both of you. Hopefully your minds will grasp it as quickly as Jacen Solo did."

"And flow-walking?" Ben said. "How did he take to that?"

"Easily as well," Tadar'Ro replied. "It is tied in with how we view the Force, and how . . ." The Aing-Tii ducked his head in an odd gesture. Consternation emanated from him. "How until the coming of this Prophet, we viewed destiny and fate. We believe the Force guides us, and we do not try to direct it in any particular manner. It is the same with flow-walking. One must surrender one's emotions to the Force; center oneself in its flow." He turned his head and fixed Ben with one great, liquid black eye. "Perhaps you will be like your cousin, and learn it very quickly."

"Perhaps," Ben said, uncomfortable with the notion that he might be like Jacen in any way. And still . . . he couldn't suppress a twinge of excitement at being able to go back into the past, or into the future—even an uncertain, not-really-sure-it's-going-to-happen future. Out of the corner of his eye, as if his father could read his thoughts, Ben saw Luke frown.

They listened to more of Car'das's holographic recording over dinner that night.

"They use the Force to power their vessels somehow—to make those crazy jumps that seem as much luck as anything else," the little hologram continued. "And they discuss it endlessly. At least Tadar'Ro seems to want to discuss it with me."

And Tadar'Ro wanted to discuss it with Luke and Ben, and presumably Jacen as well. It was odd. They were the most secretive people imaginable—even hostile about it—yet once they had accepted one into their ranks, as it were, they wanted to share everything.

"The Force as a rainbow," Ben said. "I gotta say, it's a nice image."

"It is," Luke agreed. "I don't like to think of myself as closed-minded, Ben, or intolerant. And I am fully prepared to admit that viewing the Force this way seems to work for the Aing-Tii."

Ben thought about the time he had spent on Ziost. At that point in his life, he had been solidly Jacen's creature, although a few doubts had begun to creep in around the edges. He had believed that the Force was a tool, like a lightsaber or a blaster. That it was what you did with it, how you manipulated it, that was important. That there was no real dark or light side, only a neutral side. Gray, if you will.

Or rainbow.

And yet—even as he first saw the planet, he had felt something malevolent about it. As if it was watching him, the way he was watching it. He remembered the voices, which spoke first in his dreams and then in his head, urging him to abandon the young girl who was accompanying him. To kill her, to—to *eat* her, in order to grow strong. And when those thoughts were on him, the girl, Kiara, recoiled from him. From the dark side growing within him.

And it was at that moment that Ben had wondered about his belief in the Force's neutrality. The malevolence he had sensed had come from nothing alive. It was the imprint of the Sith who had been there for so long; the echoes of their presence, their energy, even though they had long since physically left the world.

He realized that it was the dark side. And although it had taken him a long time to process that revelation, he had.

"I used to think of it like a tool, a weapon," he said. "A blaster isn't inherently evil. It can shoot a friend to betray him or an enemy to save a life. I thought of the Force that way. As neither good or evil, just kind of—gray."

Luke nodded. "I remember when I entered the cave on Dagobah. I sensed something wrong at once, even before I went in. It was so cold, so unsettling. I was—" He laughed slightly. "I was setting myself up for failure, is what I was doing. Yoda told me I wouldn't need my weapons, but I took them anyway. He warned me that a Jedi uses the Force for knowledge and defense, never attack, but when the image of Vader approached—I activated my lightsaber first. That's not what Jedi do. We protect and defend those who can't defend themselves. So I failed my first test on the whole light side–dark side thing pretty miserably."

Ben chuckled. "You know, it gives me hope that you screwed up so badly and so consistently as a kid, Dad."

"Watch it, son." Luke grinned.

"I—I think Jacen wanted it to be gray," Ben said slowly, speaking as he worked things out in his head.

"What do you mean?"

Ben suspected that Luke knew exactly what he meant, but wanted to hear him say it. He continued. "Jacen wanted a safe galaxy. That's something all right-thinking people want—a safe place to raise their kids, pursue their art or their passions. It's not a bad ideal."

"No, it's not."

"But—Jacen wanted it too badly. Badly enough to do really evil things to get it. Badly enough to become Sith in order to get the power to make it happen."

"It's the classic example of the end justifying the means," Luke said quietly. "You want something—even something that everyone agrees is a good thing—too desperately. And so you start eliminating obstacles to your success. And then in order to keep going, you've got to harden yourself to doing more and more things that are at odds with your core beliefs of what is right and wrong. Make it so that your goal is so important, you have to lie or betray or kill for it."

Luke paused. "I once asked Yoda if the dark side was stronger. He said no, but it was easier, more—"

". . . *seductive,*" said Ben in his smoothest Lando Calrissian impression as he waggled his eyebrows suggestively.

Luke laughed. "You know the story. But the lesson—which I failed miserably—was that you really do find only what you take with you. The dark side can't corrupt you unless you let it, let it use the anger, hatred, and aggression you already have."

"Or your wants," Ben said quietly, the humor fading. "That's what Jacen did."

"For a Jedi, there is no place for a rainbow Force," Luke said quietly. "There's no room for compromise. We walk the path of the light side, or we fall to the darkness. There's no gray area, Ben."

Ben sighed. "It sounds like a nice idea, but . . . yeah. I saw what happened to Jacen, up close and personal. And I've felt the dark side on Ziost, just like you did on Dagobah. But Yoda was wrong about one thing."

"Oh? What's that?"

"It *didn't* dominate Vader's destiny. You pulled him back from the dark side, and when he died, he was one with the Force. And you pulled Mom back from it, too."

Luke smiled gently. "And Leia pulled me back, when I got too close. I think you did the same thing for Tahiri, Ben. You didn't just abandon her, even when she had done all the things she did to you."

Ben struck a heroic pose as best he could in the flow-form chair. "Jedi Skywalkers," he said melodramatically. "Practicing a fine family tradition of rescuing people from the dark side."

"Hey, there are worse family traditions."

"Like Aunt Leia's spiceloaf."

"You think the dark side is scary, you say that to her."

"I won't. I like my body intact, thank you very much."

The journeys upon which the Aing-Tii sent Luke and Ben were fascinating. The Aing-Tii sometimes knew the precise location where an artifact would be. Other times, Luke and Ben were sent on missions based only on a "sensing" that something "might" be there. Traveling was much easier now that they had the Aing-Tii to help them plot jumps. Ben once asked if they could learn how to make the *Jade Shadow* jump the way the Sanhedrim vessels did, as they were now on a pilgrimage on behalf of the Aing-Tii.

Tadar'Ro shook his head. "Your vessel is without the Force," he said. "Ours . . . are not."

"Are they organic, then?" Luke asked, thinking of the Yuuzhan Vong.

Tadar'Ro cocked his head, considering. "Yes and no," he said finally. "They are of the Force, but they are not organic, not as you understand the word."

"More rainbow philosophy?" asked Ben.

"Indeed," said Tadar'Ro. The question could have been perceived as flippant, but Luke and apparently Tadar'Ro both knew that it wasn't intended as such. "Things are not just one thing or another. Not with us."

The artifacts they were sent to find were of all varieties. Sometimes they seemed to Luke and Ben to simply be exceptionally beautiful stones, crystals, or other natural formations. Other times they carefully brought back what was clearly a piece of advanced alien technology. Each time, the item was received in the same manner: with reverence. And most of the time, Luke and Ben, the ones who managed to obtain the item, were treated with gratitude and courtesy.

Most of the time. Increasingly, though, Luke began to sense resentment from the Aing-Tii. He asked Tadar'Ro about it one afternoon.

Tadar'Ro seemed agitated. "It is not directed at you," he said finally. "The schism between the two factions— those who believe the Force guides us, while not directly shaping things, and those who believe the Prophet was a voice for Those Who Dwell Beyond the Veil—increases each day. More and more, each side swells with those who step from neutrality, from being comfortable with the not-knowing, to a firm stance. Fewer and fewer are staying open to all possibilities, as I am. We need to heal this rift, and soon."

"What can we do to help?" Luke asked.

"When you are ready, we will take you to the Embrace," Tadar'Ro said.

Beside Luke, Ben started violently at the word. Luke reached to squeeze his arm reassuringly. For Ben, for a long while yet, the word *Embrace* would be followed by *of Pain*, and would produce an instant and visceral reaction. Tadar'Ro of course picked up on it.

"It is nothing of harm," he said reassuringly. "It is simply our term for the site that contains the Relics. That . . . embraces them lovingly, holds them safely."

Ben was calming down and nodded. "Sorry," he said. "So why can't Dad and I go to this . . . Embrace . . . and try to answer that question for you?"

"You are not yet ready to do such a thing," Tadar'Ro replied. "There are still things you must learn; things you must understand about us. Things that Jacen Solo and Jorj Car'das learned and understood, at least to some degree. Then I will lead you into the Embrace."

Luke knew what Tadar'Ro was talking about. He was

not at all happy that Ben had asked to learn flow-walking, or that Tadar'Ro had agreed to teach it. For beings who had a multifaceted approach to the Force, even to physics itself, flow-walking was probably not that big a deal.

But for humans, it was something else entirely. Still, the situation was what it was.

"I know Ben is anxious to learn flow-walking from you, so I will leave you two to it," he said, rising and nodding respectfully at Tadar'Ro. Ben didn't meet his father's eyes, instead gazed straight at the Aing-Tii. He was still looking intently at him as Luke turned and walked back to the *Jade Shadow.*

The shadows of evening were stretching out when Ben finally came back. He was excited by what he had learned, but was doing what he could to conceal that excitement. He was silent as he rattled around in the galley for a bit, finally emerging with a plate piled high with food.

"I'm a little later than usual," he said. "I figured you'd already eaten."

Luke nodded and turned to pause the holographic journal entry he'd been perusing. "I did. How is it going?"

Ben filled his mouth with food so he wouldn't have to reply instantly.

"Okay," he said finally, then took another large bite.

Luke sighed. "Care to elaborate?"

"Not really. I mean, I know you don't like it, Dad, so what's the point?"

"I think it'd be interesting to hear how it is being taught from the original source," Luke said, keeping his voice mild.

Ben shrugged. "Kind of what you'd expect from the Aing-Tii. All rainbowy."

Luke felt a pang of sorrow at the new wariness his son displayed. He knew that it was a direct consequence of his disapproval, but what was he to do? What was any father to do when he saw his son doing something that was unnecessary and perhaps very dangerous? He couldn't just pretend that it was all fine, and Ben knew it, and for the first time on this journey together, Luke could feel the old rift between them opening again.

He took a deep breath. "Ben . . . do you understand why I don't approve of this?"

"Of course I do," Ben said, snapping a little. "You believe it's dangerous, that it'll hurt me somehow. That it's wrong to try to meddle with the past or future."

"I do believe it will hurt you, but not the way you think," Luke said, searching for the words.

Ben eyed him, still wary but also curious. Luke took a moment to gather the words, hoping they were the right ones.

"It's an empty promise, Ben. Full of hopes and wishes, but in the end, it's just ashes and disillusionment. Yes, you can see those who have died, but you can't change what happens to them. And yes, you can see the future—even alter it to a small degree if you're skilled enough—but you can't be sure you're doing the right thing. The very wanting that is prompting you to do this is what's started many down the path to the dark side."

"What do you know about what I want?" Ben snapped. "You never even *asked* why I wanted to do it!"

Luke blinked, realizing his son was right. "I'm sorry," he said. "I assumed—"

"You shouldn't."

"You're right. I shouldn't make assumptions. I thought you wanted to go back in time to see Mom again . . . or to find out when Jacen started to go wrong. So that you might be able to change things."

A sudden bright flush on his son's cheeks told Luke

that he had hit the mark. The silence that suddenly descended was painfully awkward. Luke waited a moment, but Ben said nothing, didn't even continue to eat.

"Ben . . . I'm just a father wanting to spare his son pain, that's all. And I knew that's why you wanted to learn the technique because—well, because it's what I would have wanted to do at your age."

"I'm sick of being my age," Ben said coldly. He shoved the food away from him with a sharp, violent gesture and rose. "I guess I'm not hungry after all."

Luke watched him stalk off toward his cabin, his heart aching. Everything he had said was true, but in the state Ben was in, he couldn't or wouldn't listen. He would have to figure all this out on his own.

And Luke would be there when he did.

Chapter Twenty

DESHA LOR GASPED AND HER HAND FLEW TO HER MOUTH.

Wynn Dorvan stood, hands loosely clasped behind his back, his face inscrutable as he, Desha, and Daala watched the shocking events unfolding on the holonews. They were in Daala's office, the décor of which was crisply white and scrupulously clean. Daala was a meticulous and precise woman, and of the Empire, and both these attributes of hers were on display here to anyone who cared to look.

"It's madness, absolute chaos," Javis Tyrr was saying, peering earnestly into the cam. "Whereas only a short while ago the Coruscant Livestock Exchange and Exhibition was a safe, fun-filled way to while away an afternoon, now it has become a site of carnage and terror."

Daala's face was strained, her green eyes fastened on the unfolding events. This was not the first time news had revolved around something as seemingly innocuous as the Exchange and Exhibition. Plenty of times in the past a creature or two—or three or four—had broken loose to stampede about for a while before it was brought down by crack security teams. Or sometimes the less-than-savory dealings unofficially conducted in back rooms went awry. But even Dorvan was surprised to see this.

"I received the call a few moments ago and took the liberty of sending out some special teams from the GA," he said to Daala, who nodded absently, her gaze still riveted.

The cam pulled back to show the main floor as Tyrr continued to narrate. "What you're seeing are empty corrals that should be filled with herd animals. Someone has deliberately sabotaged the gates and set dozens of creatures loose to stampede among the populace. The source of—"

The cam moved so suddenly, Dorvan felt a hint of nausea. And then he saw why. A Falleen, her skin reddened as she exuded hormones, was bringing a lightsaber down upon another gate, this one containing rontos. The animals, skittish in urban areas under the best of circumstances, were terrified, rearing and snorting. As they dived for freedom, the Jedi, for it could only be a Jedi, leapt clear, then darted away.

"A Jedi?" said Desha, disbelieving. "But a Jedi would never put civilians in harm's way like this!"

"These days they would," Daala said grimly, her lips pressed together in a thin, furious line. "And have."

"It's a Jedi!" Javis Tyrr was crying, echoing their words. "Another Jedi, sworn to protect, has clearly gone insane! Who knows how many innocents will die here, terrorized, trampled, or gored to death? When will this stop?"

The cam swung around to a close-up of the back of a woman's head. Her hair was long, dark, and pulled back in a ponytail. Suddenly the woman turned.

"You!"

"That's Jaina Solo," Desha Lor said, her eyes wide as the Jedi strode up to the cam and covered it with her hand. "What's she doing there?"

"She, her parents, and her niece were attending the exhibition," Dorvan said. When Desha stared at him, he answered her unspoken question. "While we do not exactly follow her or other notable personages around, the GA does take care to know exactly where such personages are at all times. You'll soon learn about this. And I'll be putting you in charge of such operations." The Twi'lek looked uncomfortable with the idea, but said nothing.

Meanwhile, despite the vibroblades Jaina was metaphorically shooting at him, Tyrr wasn't giving up. He continued to speak. "Jaina Solo, can you verify that Jedi Natua Wan—"

Dorvan tuned out the rest, instead listening to a message from his earpiece comlink. He turned to Daala. "Admiral, there's worse going on in the Dangerous Animal Hall. I have reports of injuries and a possible fatality."

"Oh, no!" Desha looked stunned and shocked, and again Dorvan wondered if anyone could really be this innocent.

Dorvan directed his gaze back to the holonews. Javis Tyrr had moved away from covering the current crisis; apparently he had switched to a second holocam; the image was not as clear as before. Dorvan was willing to bet a month's wages that Jaina had damaged it somehow. The fact that Tyrr had a backup cam indicated that this sort of thing must happen a lot to a holojournalist.

". . . exclusive footage," Tyrr was saying. "Natua Wan's murderous rampage is not the first example of a Jedi harming the public. Nor is it likely to be the last. And yet the Jedi continue to operate without restrictions. While Valin and Jysella Horn are safely encased in carbonite, Natua Wan is still on the loose. And so, we thought, was another rogue Jedi—Seff Hellin."

What he saw next shocked even Wynn Dorvan.

It was Seff Hellin, captured, raging at nothing, and then collapsing on a comfortable-looking flowform couch. The cam pulled back to reveal what looked like a pleasant apartment complete with tables and chairs and what appeared to be a state-of-the-art holographic center.

"What you're seeing is footage from deep inside the Jedi Temple," Tyrr's voice said. "Seff Hellin, murderer, has apparently been captured by the Jedi and held in a prison that looks like a luxury apartment."

"Admiral, did you know about—" Dorvan turned. Daala was livid. Her face was white with anger, a vein pulsed in her forehead, and she looked as if she were about to snap the datapad in half. It was obvious she was exercising every ounce of her formidable control.

"I take it you didn't," he said mildly, turning back to the news broadcast. Another figure had come into view, blocking the cam for a moment. Then it moved out of the way, and turned to look back at Hellin.

Jaina Solo.

The scene cut back to Javis Tyrr, looking directly into the cam as if into the viewer's eyes. "When I encountered Jedi Solo a few moments ago, I gave her an opportunity to explain the situation with Hellin, but she refused to grant me an interview. I can only conclude that everything surrounding this criminal has been done on the sly. Shame on you, Jaina Solo. Shame on the Jedi. You have done nothing to redeem yourself in the eyes of the public with this action.

"And Admiral Natasi Daala," Tyrr said intently, "you are the leader of the Galactic Alliance. You were appointed such with every hope that you would keep us safe. And yet right under your nose, the Jedi are smuggling prisoners to safety and lying about it to you. Or . . . *are* they lying to you? Admiral, you owe us an explanation for your abandonment of—"

Daala shut it off.

"Admiral, my advice would be for you not to be overly hasty. Reports do indicate that Leia and Jaina Solo were able to—"

"Shut up, Dorvan. Prep Security Team Alpha. And get me Kenth Hamner. Now."

MASTERS' COUNCIL, JEDI TEMPLE, CORUSCANT

The emergency meeting of the Jedi Masters was in an uproar.

Only a few had been able to attend in person. Most were simply appearing via hologram. The result was that often one party was unaware another was attempting to speak and they stepped on one another's words.

". . . is absolutely what Jedi should be doing," Corran Horn was saying. "Daala's snatched every other one from us without so much as a by-your-leave and stuck them in carbonite. It's about time we had one of our own, and if Han, Leia, and Jaina can get Wan to us, we'll have another."

"While I admit that I'm glad we have Hellin and hopefully now Wan—not least because that means they're no longer in a place where they can harm innocents—we should have been informed of his capture," Kyle Katarn chimed in. "Who knew about this?"

Hamner rubbed his temples. "Obviously Jedi Solo," he said drily. "Who else?"

"I did, though not until after the fact," said Cilghal. Hamner shot her a startled glance.

"Master Cilghal," he said, "why did you not bring this to the Masters' Council?"

The Mon Calamari did not seem in the least abashed. "Your job is a difficult one at present, and no one wished to add further complications to it. You are an honorable man, Master Hamner. No one wished for you to have to choose between supporting your Order and lying to Admiral Daala. It was simply easier this way."

Hamner closed his eyes briefly. He'd expected that Jaina would take the words he had spoken to her exactly as she had. He'd expected that she would understand his tacit instruction—*Go ahead and do what you need to do, but leave the Order officially out of it.*

Wasn't this, as Horn had said, exactly what Jedi were supposed to do? How could they figure out what was wrong with these young Jedi if they weren't allowed to study and interact with them? The Order was responsible for Jedi actions; they should be permitted to retain the Jedi who had exhibited such distressing behavior.

"It was certainly easier when none of this was public," he said acerbically. "Now I'm afraid this incident with that reporter has forced my hand. Daala has already contacted my offices. I have delayed speaking with her, but my sources tell me there is a security team en route to demand the release of both Seff Hellin and, when she arrives, Natua Wan. I can't see how I can refuse the Chief of State."

The shouting began in earnest. No one wanted to hand over Hellin or Wan. Some took up Hamner's position, perhaps feeling a slight sting at not having been included in the "plotting." Others insisted that it was time for the Jedi to stand firm against the bullying the GA had been imposing.

Hamner's comlink beeped. It was Jedi Leia Solo. He flicked it on and listened while the uproar raged about and without him.

"Sir, request permission to speak with you immediately. I'd like to bring Jaina, as well. I know the situation is . . . challenging, but with your permission, I'd like to run a possible solution by you."

"Jedi Solo," Hamner said quietly, "if you have anything in the neighborhood of a solution to this dilemma, I will most happily listen to it."

"Thank you, sir. We're just arriving with Jedi Wan. Once we get her safely into the medcenter we'll meet you in the Room of a Thousand Fountains."

"I would welcome the serenity," he said, and clicked off the comlink.

Daala had contacted Javis Tyrr and every other reporter she could think of. By the time she, Dorvan, and her security team had arrived at the Temple, there was quite a throng of press crowding the steps.

She had taken a few moments to get her anger under control. While ultimately her desire was to be able to, finally, completely control the Jedi, she had always thought she'd played fair with them. To find out about this deception was insulting and infuriating. She wanted more than simply having the two rogue Jedi handed over to her. She wanted to see the Jedi humiliated, as they had humiliated her. Javis Tyrr's "special report" stung.

"You shouldn't let him get to you like that, ma'am," said Dorvan as they drove up.

"If anyone else had said that to me, Dorvan," Daala said quietly, "firing would be the least of their worries."

He absently petted Pocket. "I'm well aware of that, ma'am. I am also aware that you know I'm right."

Daala gave a noncommittal grunt but continued to compose herself. A free press had its advantages and disadvantages, and she intended to make use of this particular weapon. Hamner had asked to meet with her in private; she had refused, instead insisting on a public meeting at the very top of the steps of the Temple. Eventually they would retire somewhere and speak, of course, but before then she wanted to shake up the Jedi just a bit more.

The night-blue personnel transport speeder she had arranged for was already there, and upon her vehicle's arrival the sides of the transport, large swing-out doors, opened wide. Two full squadrons of men and women in the instantly recognizable blue of Galactic Security— well, blue except for their black riot body armor— poured out. Each was armed with a blaster rifle, but thus far the weapons were not lifted. The threat was all Daala wanted.

They marched in solid formation up the steps. The beings standing there were equally solemn in their stance. Kenth Hamner, calm, tall, not a hair out of place; Cilghal, standing quietly; Octa Ramis; Saba Sebatyne, her eyes unnervingly unblinking.

And three people Daala did not expect to see: what was left of the Solo family.

Han, as was to be expected in situations like this, looked like he wanted to blast someone or something. Leia—a master politician, and one Daala could not help but respect—looked calm and composed. Jaina, her father's daughter, looked more like Han than Leia right now. Bright spots of color were in her cheeks, but she stood straight without fidgeting. Daala took her time ascending the steps, then nodded to each of them in turn and briefly introduced Dorvan.

"I'd really hoped there would be no need for this sort of thing again," she said, knowing that every word was being recorded.

"I share that sentiment, Admiral," said Hamner. "Shall we retire to discuss the situation?"

"Lead the way."

Chapter Twenty-one

DAALA WAS VAGUELY AMUSED THAT THE MEETING TOOK place in the gardens of the Tower of Reconciliation. Despite the short notice, somehow a small table had been prepared and delicacies and caf provided. The air was redolent with pleasing, calming scents, and quiet music was being played somewhere. It was all rather transparent; if the Jedi expected to move her by such pleasantries, they were sorely mistaken.

She and Dorvan sat down. Daala refused sweetcakes but accepted caf. Once it was poured and the attendants had left them in private, she got right to the point.

"You can't tell me, Master Hamner, that you didn't know about this," Daala said.

"I can, and what is more, it is the truth," Hamner replied calmly. "I was unaware of anything any of the Jedi Knights or the Masters were doing along these lines. Admiral, you yourself specifically requested that I step in during Master Skywalker's absence. That is because you knew you could trust me to not deceive you. And that, I have not done."

"I will admit that I, and a few others, have," Leia said quietly. "I believed and still believe it is in the best interests of everyone involved—in the interests of the Jedi, those poor unfortunates who are suffering from this

malady, and in the interests of the Galactic Alliance—
that the Jedi who have exhibited this behavior be kept
conscious and studied by others like them. With all due
respect, we can sense things that your doctors cannot.
We—"

"This is exactly the issue I raised with Skywalker,"
Daala retorted. "Judge, jury, executioner—Jedi. The rest
of us just have to *trust* that you have our best interests at
heart. Leia—beings are getting seriously harmed, even
killed by this . . . *malady,* as you so delicately put it. And
I can't simply rely on the Jedi to police themselves."

"Actually, you can," put in Jaina, and Leia winced,
just a little. "Because I did. Master Hamner is completely innocent in this. He knew nothing. I made sure
he didn't. I acted on my own initiative."

"Alone?" said Daala sarcastically. "That would be
quite the trick, even for the Sword of the Jedi."

Jaina scowled. She, too, was thinking of the news coverage. "Obviously not."

"Then name your accomplices." Daala took a sip of
caf. It was delicious, robust and hot. The Jedi obviously
didn't skimp.

"I can't do that."

Daala sighed, placed the caf down, leaned back in her
chair, and folded her arms. "Then we're back to square
one. I demand the release of Natua Wan and Seff Hellin,
as criminals against the Galactic Alliance. You will hand
them over to me and—"

"You have two, they have two," Han said. He didn't
use *we.* He was not a Jedi, and the word choice was very
clear. "You may not like it, Daala, and frankly much of
the time I don't like it, either. I've had to live with it for
over forty years, that extra sensing thing they have. But
it's saved my life more than once, and I've learned to
trust it."

"You trust it because you trust the individuals," Daala said. "I've got no reason to trust you. Less now."

Jaina blew a lock of hair out of her eyes. Her mother spoke before she could. "We are all acutely aware of that. And that's one thing that Master Hamner, Han, Jaina, and I have discussed."

"Jaina Solo knew that what she was doing was contrary to what I had instructed the Order," Hamner said. "I have not been able to extract from her the name of her compatriots, only her assurance—which I believe—that none of them other than Jedi Solo, Master Cilghal, and one other are from the Order. Jaina understands that she is to be reprimanded for what she chose to do."

Daala bit back a retort and instead lifted an eyebrow. "I'm listening," she said. Beside her, Dorvan entered data quietly. His caf cooled, untouched, in front of him.

"She will be confined to the Temple for a period of two weeks. The same punishment will be enacted upon the other Jedi. Even Master Cilghal will be subjected to this, for her decision not to come forward immediately."

"I'm impressed," Daala said, and she was. This was a step toward the humiliation she desired to see them experience. "Will this be made public?"

Jaina winced.

"Yes," said Hamner. "And I'm prepared to talk with any reporters of your choosing."

"As am I and Jaina," said Leia.

"And you'll hand over Hellin and Wan," said Daala.

"No," said Leia, quietly but firmly. "As we said before . . . we have ways of helping them, of understanding them, that you don't have access to. And as Han rather bluntly but aptly put it . . . you have two, we have two."

"I can have you arrested," Daala said.

"Yeah, you can do that. But you know, it's gonna start looking uncomfortably like the old Empire if you do," said Han. "First Luke, then Kenth, whom you asked for by name—and isn't that the kind of thing that got you so ticked with Jacen?"

Daala's lips pressed together so tightly they almost disappeared. She took another sip of the caf, buying time to compose her thoughts. She would not lose control. Finally she set her cup down and looked at them all evenly in turn.

"Here is what will happen. My people will have access to the prisoners at any hour, day or night. All your findings will be turned over to them. The other mysterious Jedi involved *will* be named. Immediately after this meeting, Hamner, Leia, Jaina, Cilghal, and said Jedi to be named will be interviewed by Javis Tyrr. Live. Unedited. With the Jedi Temple in the background. You will all formally apologize for the actions you have taken, or," she said, eyeing Hamner, "the actions you let slip by on your watch."

"I don't think—" Jaina began.

"Obviously," snapped Daala. "Let me put it this way. If you do not agree to all of these stipulations *to the letter*, then I have no qualms about conjuring up images of the old Empire and taking the prisoners who rightfully should be incarcerated right out of your Temple. And there are more GA Security members than there are Jedi."

Leia, Han, Hamner, and Jaina exchanged glances.

"Agreed," said Hamner quietly, and he held out his hand.

"What?" yelped Jaina as soon as Daala had exited. "You want me to sit for an interview with that bottom-feeder, you want me to turn in—"

"Jedi Solo," said Hamner, his voice and face both hard as ice. "Whatever tacit approval you had or thought you had from me before you started this little adventure, you knew full well that you would be forced to take responsibility for your actions if they ever came to light."

"We have Wan and we have Seff," Leia said, reaching across the table to squeeze her daughter's hand. "That's what you performed the mission in order to accomplish. Daala's letting us keep them—if not our pride."

Han muttered something and Leia elbowed him. "Your mom's right. We won this round and Daala knows it."

Hamner rubbed his eyes tiredly. "I could wish that no one involved was thinking about *winning rounds* at all. What's important is that we find a way to help these poor Jedi and keep them and others safe."

"Say that to Javis Tyrr just as you said it here, and you'll have a chance to make Daala's so-called punishment work for us," Leia said. "And I, too, wish we weren't on sides. But we are for right now, and we simply have to deal with it the best that we can."

"Ma'am," said Dorvan as they were escorted out of the room and walked the long, imposing hallway toward the entrance where the reporters hovered, "I've taken the liberty of drafting a statement for you to read. There's a way you can turn this all to the GA's advantage."

Daala threw him a disbelieving glance, but quickly skimmed the statement on his datapad. She was impressed. All the facts were there, but the word choice, the order in which they were presented, and the conclusion that would be drawn from it all certainly gave the impression that all was right in the Galactic Alliance.

"Wynn, what would I do without you?"

"I rather think you'd miss Pocket."

Still, Daala mused as she stepped out in the throng of reporters and now gawkers, she had not gotten what she wanted. The Jedi had wriggled out from under this, yet again. A thought began to form in the back of her mind.

If she couldn't have the Jedi where she wanted them, she might settle for the next best thing.

She smiled, stepped up to the makeshift podium, and began to speak.

MOFF LECERSEN'S PRIVATE RESIDENCE,
CORUSCANT

"Vansyn," said Lecersen, speaking into his comm, "are you watching HNE?"

"I am, and I must say, it's absolutely riveting programming."

It was, without a doubt, Javis Tyrr's day. First the coverage of the "Insane Jedi Rampage," then the exposé of the fact that the Jedi had another crazed Knight stashed away in the bowels of their Temple. And now, the coup de grâce, an exclusive interview with no lesser personages than Acting Grand Master Kenth Hamner, Master Cilghal, a Chadra-Fan Jedi named Tekli, and both living Jedi Solos.

"I understand he has his own show now," Vansyn continued. "I wouldn't be surprised if it gets bumped to prime time after this."

"Indeed," said Lecersen. Leia Solo was speaking now, looking directly and sincerely into the holocam, doing her best to smooth over the bluntness of her offspring. "He is a resourceful one, isn't he? He could prove very useful."

JAINA SOLO'S QUARTERS, JEDI TEMPLE,
CORUSCANT

The reporters finally drifted away at twilight, after the interviews had all been conducted and the Temple had resumed what looked to them like its normal, boring routine. The curious onlookers had begun to drift away in search of other distractions.

Jaina was exhausted and furious. What part of her day had not been spent swallowing her pride had passed in basic hard labor. All part of Kenth's punishment for doing something he had known kriffing good and well she—

Jaina stuffed that emotion down. He'd been right. Once this came to light, she'd known she'd be forced to own her actions and take the proper punishment for disobedience. So she had not uttered a word of complaint as she helped out in the laundry and the cafeteria along with apprentices and staff members.

Now all she wanted to do was get to her quarters and fall into the blessed unconsciousness of sleep.

She was therefore surprised to open the door to her room and find Jag Fel waiting for her. The room's lighting was dim, and the table that was normally covered with datapads, flimsi, and various assorted knickknacks had been cleared. Two plates with something lavish and complicated looking on them were flanked by gleaming silverware, along with a bottle of something sitting in a bucket of ice.

"I've been swallowing my pride all day," Jaina muttered. "I'm not hungry."

Jag shrugged. "Well, I am. Do you know what time it is?"

"I've been a bit busy."

"I know. That's why I thought you might want something to eat. You tend to forget to fuel yourself when you're in full-on-charge mode." He rose from the bed where he'd been lying, went to her, gently pressed her into a chair, and tugged off her boots. She was so distressed by the events of the day, she let him.

"Come on. Eat something and tell me what happened.

I saw the holonews, of course, but something tells me that Javis Tyrr might not be reporting the entire story."

Despite her disgruntlement, the aroma of the roba steak was appetizing, and Jaina found herself digging in as she told him about what had happened. Jag listened quietly, his eyes intent on her, offering silent support.

"I never mentioned you, Tahiri, Winter, or Mirax," she said. "I was forced to reveal Tekli, but I honestly think that was a good thing. You know how agitated she can get. I think it was kind of a relief for her."

"I agree. And thank you. I knew you wouldn't."

She gave him a fleeting smile that turned into a real one, reached across the table, and laid a hand on his. He squeezed it tightly.

"Everyone who matters knows exactly what the situation is," he told her. "Up to and including Master Hamner. I'd go so far as to say even Daala understands, but it's contrary to what she wants and frankly what I think she believes to be a positive thing. Your actions helped the Jedi retain two very valuable study subjects, and that might be what solves the whole problem."

"Hey, you think my double could stand in for me here?" Jaina said, making a feeble and somewhat wistful joke.

"She's good, but her mouth is all wrong. I don't think she'd fool Jedi," Jag said, looking completely serious.

Jaina actually laughed. They finished the meal in good spirits and shared a deliciously gooey dessert. Jag leaned back and lifted the sparkling wine from the ice.

"And now to celebrate," he said.

"This day?" Jaina wrinkled her nose. "I think it needs to be buried, not celebrated."

"So far, I would agree with you. But I have something to suggest that will, I certainly hope, let this hitherto horrible day end on a very positive note." He poured the wine into two fluted glasses. Jaina accepted, looking at the amber liquid with the small bubbles for a moment, then turning her attention to Jag.

"This better not be about the Moffs, the GA, or the Empire," she said.

"Well, then I must disappoint. Because this is most assuredly about the Empire. Specifically about the head of said Empire and a joint venture he is suggesting. I think that a formal alliance between two key factions would be a wise idea at this juncture. Both parties would benefit." He turned to her expectantly.

Jaina peered at him. She couldn't fathom what in the galaxy he was talking about. He had a very odd look on his face, too, though he was trying hard to keep his expression composed.

"Have you been in negotiations with some world I've not heard about? Or are you trying to push that whole rival Jedi school thing on me again?"

He blinked. A smile curved his lips, then became a chuckle. "Jaina Solo," he said, warmth lacing his voice, "I'm asking you to marry me."

Her mouth dropped open. "I—what—you—how would this possibly work?"

It was not a romantic response, but it was from her heart, and Jag knew her well enough to know that.

Still holding the celebratory wine, of which neither had yet partaken, Jag replied, "You'll continue exactly as you have, of course . . . and so will I. Eventually I am certain the Jedi will determine exactly what's going on with Valin, Jysella, and the others. Once a treatment is found, Daala will be severely defanged. Luke will still be gone, but this whole rather grotesque sideshow will be over. I am also certain that Luke will return sooner rather than later with enough information on what happened with Jacen to get his sentence turned over. Once he accomplishes that, public sentiment will swing back toward the Jedi. As for the Moffs," he said, frowning a little, "they may think I'm a fool for love, but I actually have some very solid leads on who the troublemakers behind the scenes are."

He leaned forward, looking into her eyes. "Jaina, I love you for who you are. I have for a long time. I have absolutely no desire to curtail, impede, cripple, modify, or thwart you in any way. There is my detailed argument for this formal union. What do you think of the proposition?"

Jaina was still reeling. It was all so well thought out, so precise, so . . . *Jag*.

But beneath the military bearing and the clipped, logical, formal presentation of a proposal of marriage, she knew that Jagged Fel was deeply in love with her. He was even nervous, she knew, as he waited on her reply.

So she gave it to him.

She sprang into his arms with such vigor that the chair fell over, but neither of them particularly seemed to mind.

Chapter Twenty-two

LUKE HAD BEEN ENCOURAGED BY HOW WELL HE AND BEN had been getting along through most of this odyssey they had embarked upon. There had been some friction, and some arguing, but by and large they had been growing closer.

Now, as he had feared ever since Cilghal had suggested they travel to the Aing-Tii, the issue of flow-walking had divided them. Luke had to struggle against the desire to protest, to try to stop Ben, every time he went off with Tadar'Ro. He had hoped that by biting his tongue he would encourage Ben to volunteer information about how the training went, but Ben remained silent, almost angry.

So it was no surprise initially when Luke's dreams were chaotic and oppressive—as if he were coming under physical attack.

And then a fraction of an instant later he realized it was no dream.

Luke sprang up, fully awake immediately, executing a somersault over the length of the bed as he summoned his lightsaber to him. By its light he saw his attacker strike where he had been sleeping with a strange metal rod, then whirl angrily to charge.

He couldn't sense anything from the Aing-Tii who

was so bent on causing him harm. It was as if the being were still a dream—as if it didn't exist in the Force at all. The Aing-Tii was startlingly fast for someone who appeared to be carved out of stone, and Luke's lightsaber was a blur as he blocked the attacks from the metal stick. Then, before he realized what was happening, the intruder was gone.

He ran out the open hatch, lightsaber aglow, but there was no sign of his attacker. Ben ran to join him, his lightsaber lit, too, his hair mussed but his face alert and calm.

"Who *was* that? How'd they get in? And why were they attacking us?"

Luke shook his head. "I don't know who it was. He or she was completely absent in the Force. And I haven't spent enough time with any Aing-Tii other than Tadar'Ro to distinguish individual differences in such a brief encounter. As for how they got in—they are masterful Force-users, though they seldom do so unless they feel it serves Those Who Dwell Beyond the Veil," he said, deactivating his lightsaber. Ben followed suit. Luke scanned the area with more than his physical senses before jerking his head in the direction of the ship and moving back up the ramp. Ben followed, casting a last glance over his shoulder. "Jedi can get past all kinds of locking mechanisms. It wouldn't surprise me to learn that the Aing-Tii can, too."

Ben nodded as he closed the door and activated the lock. "Yeah. Or maybe it just hopped right on in like the Sanhedrim ships do."

"Caf?" Luke asked. Ben nodded. Luke got some brewing. "We know that Tadar'Ro said that tensions between the two factions were increasing. I think we can safely say that our mysterious midnight caller was from a side that's hostile to our presence here."

Ben yawned and scratched his head as the caf finished.

"It's almost dawn. I'm going to just go ahead and stay up. Practice—" He paused in midsentence.

Practice flow-walking, of course. Luke turned and busied himself with pouring the caf. "There's no point in heading back to bed," he agreed, smoothing over the uncomfortable pause. "I'll be in my room meditating."

"Okay. Tadar'Ro should be here in an hour or so anyway. Be interesting to see what he has to say about all this." Ben poured himself a cup of caf and turned away without another word. Pained but resigned, Luke let him go.

Tadar'Ro was horrified to hear of the attack. "A *Vor'cha* stun stick," he explained. "That was the weapon the intruder was attempting to use. It is very powerful, and a mere touch of it would have rendered you unconscious for some time."

"I don't understand," said Ben. "Why break in and attack us just to knock us out?"

Tadar'Ro's agitation in the Force was painful. "I do not know. Perhaps to simply frighten you. Perhaps to incapacitate you for transportation elsewhere."

"Or to kill us when we couldn't fight back," said Ben. Luke didn't contradict him. The Aing-Tii had been known to attack with lethal intent before.

"I deeply regret that this has happened," Tadar'Ro said. "To so ignore the fact that we have offered you hospitality, that you are attempting to help us . . . it is proof of how dangerous this rift is to our people, our culture."

"And any guests," Ben grumbled.

"I had hoped for more time, but . . ." Tadar'Ro's tongues flickered for a moment; Luke guessed it the equivalent of a resigned sigh. "Ben Skywalker's training is progressing well, and it is becoming tragically clear to me that we no longer have the luxury of time. Luke Skywalker, Ben Skywalker . . . the moment has come for you to go on your pilgrimage and receive the Embrace."

The two Skywalkers exchanged glances. "Very well, if you think we are ready."

"I think we cannot wait until you are. Besides, only Those Who Dwell Beyond the Veil know who is ready and who is not. I am sure that They will guide you."

"Very well," Luke said. "Is the Embrace far?"

"Many kilometers."

"We'll prep the *Shadow* for—"

"You must travel on foot. To approach the Embrace in a vehicle is to give great offense."

Luke nodded. "All right. I could use a little physical exercise."

Two days later, he was regretting the quip.

The thinner atmosphere was starting to take its toll. They had packed water, but it was becoming obvious that they should have packed more. Even though they were Jedi, they could not move as fast as they had expected. The Force could only augment so much for so long.

Tadar'Ro accompanied them, but as soon as he had taken his first formal step on the journey, he refused to speak to them. Luke and Ben, their relationship already strained, found themselves imitating him. For Luke, at least, it made the journey feel that much more difficult.

They were heading east from the Aing-Tii city toward a mountain range that ran from north to south. Over the course of three days of hard hiking, they reached their destination—a nondescript aperture in what appeared to be a sheer wall face.

Ben trudged to a halt, sweaty, his fair skin sunburned. He stared. He said nothing, perhaps because he was out of breath, but Luke could read his expression: *Is this it?*

After keeping utter silence for the entire trek, Tadar'Ro

finally spoke. "This is the passageway," he said reverently. "Inside, you will find all the artifacts we have painstakingly gathered over many thousands of years. Tread carefully, for this is sacred ground to us. Go to the relics. Be with them. Please . . . find answers for us that we cannot, so that we might heal this terrible rift that wounds us as a people so very deeply."

Luke was moved by the request. He placed his hand on Tadar'Ro's shoulder and respectfully moved his face toward the Aing-Tii's, knowing that Tadar'Ro would read his intention in the Force. Gently, like a blessing, Tadar'Ro's long tongues danced over Luke's face. After a moment of looking uncomfortable, Ben imitated his father.

"I hope with all my heart that we are able to do as you request," Luke said.

"May Those Who Dwell Beyond the Veil grant you insight, and may the Force be with you," said Tadar'Ro.

Luke turned to Ben, caught his eye, and nodded. Then he turned to face the aperture and, with Ben right behind him, stepped through.

A small path wound downward. It had been worn by many feet over thousands of years, so they were able to move forward with relative ease. It grew darker as they left the sunlight of the outside behind, until at last they were almost in complete darkness.

"Lightsabers or glow rods?" Ben asked as they continued to descend, feeling their way with hands, feet, and the Force. They had discussed bringing their lightsabers with Tadar'Ro, who had agreed. If a wall caved in or some other disaster occurred, they would need to be able to cut their way out. Also, as Ben had just illustrated, the illumination would be useful if the glow rods failed for any reason.

Luke paused, frowning in the dark. "Neither, I think," he said slowly.

"Huh?"

"Come on." They moved forward, their eyes blind, for another few steps. Then, sure enough, the darkness began to lighten. It was only a faint glow at first, so faint as to appear almost a trick of eyes that desperately wanted to see. Then the radiance increased, soft and soothing, but illuminating. There was a luminescence in the Force as well, a comforting, reassuring warmth that bathed Luke's spirit as the light began to bathe his face and hands. He felt refreshed, even though he was physically weary from the pilgrimage, and excitement and anticipation quickened in him.

They turned a corner, and beheld beauty.

The light came not from artificial lighting brought here by the Aing-Tii, nor from the relics that had been carried into the cave for so many millennia. Instead it emanated from glowing stones of all hues—red, yellow, green, blue, purple, white, and all shades and gradations in between. On the floor from stalagmites; from the stalactites that hung above them like lightsabers; on each wall, they glowed.

"Rainbows," Ben said quietly, and Luke nodded. This was a place where the Force was extremely strong. It was not purely energy from the light side, but it was most certainly not a hollow of dark-side energy such as Luke had encountered on Dagobah during the trial he had so miserably failed. He could not tell for certain, but he wondered, as Ben spoke, if this was the reason the Aing-Tii had developed their rainbow theory of the nature of the Force. Standing here, embraced indeed by its power, Luke could understand why they felt so.

He took a deep breath, pulled himself back from the awe the place inspired, and said, "We're here for a purpose. Let's be about it."

Ben literally shook his head to clear it, then nodded.

They moved forward, through this antechamber crowded with Force-imbued stones, to a second cavern.

It was much larger than the first, a rectangular space about twenty by thirty meters. While this cavern, too, was illuminated by the Force, that was not the primary reason for Ben's quick inhalation.

Everywhere the eye looked were relics. They were stacked three or four deep, in haphazard piles that looked as though they'd been simply tossed down.

"If these things are so precious to them, why do the Aing-Tii treat them so carelessly?" Ben asked, nudging a round, apparently seamless object gently with a foot.

"Because they can't touch them," Luke said. "They can't organize or arrange or catalog them in any way. They just have to bring them in here somehow—wrapped in something perhaps—and set them down."

"And we have to sort through all this?" Ben said, his voice cracking slightly. Luke couldn't blame him. Such a task was not just daunting but bordering on the impossible.

"We don't have to compile data and analyze each one," Luke said. "But . . . from what Tadar'Ro seemed to think, we'll find answers as we handle them. Insight. Knowledge that we can pass along to the Aing-Tii about what direction they should go."

Ben looked slightly less pained, but still very dubious. "How long do you think it'll take?"

"Well," Luke said, "I do have nine years and a few months left to fill . . ."

"That's not funny."

Chapter Twenty-three

THE PROCESS WAS HARDLY A SWIFT ONE, BUT IT WENT fairly quickly. After a few moments of paralyzing indecision at the vastness of the task, Luke and Ben started the simplest way possible—they picked up the first item they encountered as they entered the cavern, and began there.

Everything they touched had the imprint of the Force on it in some way, shape, or form. Some were fairly powerful to handle; others only had a faint residue. Most of what they picked up, examined in the Force, and then discarded was clearly technological, although some items were fossils or stones or other organic materials.

"If only we could take all these things to the Temple," Luke said wistfully. It was impossible, of course. The relics belonged to the Aing-Tii, and they would never part with even the least of them. "So much knowledge here. So much we could learn, about other cultures, about the history of the galaxy, perhaps about the Force itself. You and I don't have the skills or the tools to properly examine even the smallest fragment of what we're seeing. All this wisdom, collected here by beings who are forbidden even to handle them, let alone study them. I respect other beings' religions, but I have to confess . . . this strikes me as a tragic waste."

"I know," Ben said. "I'm really curious about some of these things." He paused, looking up at his father as a long, twining piece of what seemed to be metallic rope twisted slowly of its own accord in his hand. "So . . . what are we looking for?"

"Guidance," Luke said. "A . . . hit, a bit of insight. You'll know it if it happens."

"There are times," Ben said drily, "when I empathize with those who express frustration with the vagueness of the Force."

After the first few hours, when they had made only a little headway and stopped for a food and water break, Luke found himself agreeing with Ben's comment.

"They're all powerful items," Ben was saying as he chewed on a stick of something greenish brown and intended to be more nutritious than tasty. "I mean, I get that. But I'm not getting any hits. Nothing that's shouting out, *Do This, Aing-Tii!*"

"Neither am I," Luke admitted.

"Dad . . . do you think we're going to find anything to help Tadar'Ro and his people?"

Luke hesitated. "It's completely possible that there isn't anything in here to find. But there are still an awful lot of artifacts," he pointed out. "It may be that there's one particular thing that will turn out to be useful, and we'll just have to find it."

Ben groaned slightly.

The hours seemed to stretch on with no sense of time passing, although their chronos were working just fine. Sometimes Luke would think hours had passed when it had just been twenty minutes. Other times, he was shocked to realize he'd spent three hours without realizing it.

What had at first been an intriguing, if laborious, undertaking had become almost mind-numbingly rote. Luke forced himself to stay open to the Force and not let his mind drift from the task at hand. He couldn't afford to miss anything, no matter how subtle. But so far, they had found nothing that could give the Aing-Tii any sort of guidance.

Luke straightened and stretched, eyeing the next round of artifacts. His eye fell on something shiny, catching the light of the glowing Force stones.

It was a small pyramid of gleaming metal. While some of the other artifacts had shown signs of age and wear and tear—some of them seemingly so fragile that Luke and Ben had been reluctant to touch them—this item looked almost newly minted. Luke extended a hand, grasped it—and gasped.

THE OUTER RIM
PRESENT DAY

Vestara had always hoped that one day, if her path toward Sith mastery unfolded as she had dreamed, she would be permitted aboard the *Omen,* the Ship of Destiny, to learn its secrets and that of her own history. She had never in her wildest dreams imagined that another Ship might descend from the skies, looking like a red, winged eye, to summon and teach her.

But the ways of Fate are strange indeed, and Vestara seized the challenge eagerly.

Shortly after the devastating news that the Sith, far from ruling the galaxy as the Tribe had ignorantly assumed, were facing extinction, Vestara had been called to enter Ship itself. She was not the first, she knew; Lord Vol, the Grand Lords, and the Masters had all preceded her. But she was the first among the apprentices, and had stood quietly before it.

The spherical vessel was bizarre almost beyond her imagining. Where a moment earlier had been a seamless, red, pebbly, curved surface, there was now an open

hatch. Before her eyes, a line formed beneath the glowing yellow, eye-like viewport. A ramp extended in welcome. Vestara did not hesitate; indeed, she had to stop
herself from racing upward. She felt the vessel's pleasure
as she first placed her boot upon the ramp. It was almost
like—a sigh of relief. She forced herself not to grin.

Steadily she walked upward, into the heart of the vessel. She was not certain at all what to expect, and so simply observed. The interior was smaller than the exterior
would indicate. It was a single chamber, four meters
across and two and a half high. The curving walls inside
looked exactly like those outside, and before she could
think, Vestara extended a hand and ran her fingers
lightly along the pebbly orange surface. She could have
sworn she felt the vessel quiver, like a pet muut being caressed. The wall was warm to the touch as well and
seemed to pulse slightly, like a living thing.

There were no sets of controls, no chairs, nothing she
had been led to find inside of a ship or indeed any mechanical construct. Ship wasn't going to give her any
clues, either. What was expected of her, then?

Vestara frowned, then knelt down in the center of the
empty, warm chamber. She closed her eyes and reached
out in the Force to the vessel.

Command me, Ship told her.

A smile tugged at the scarred corner of her mouth.

Fly, then.

She didn't really expect it to obey so simple an instruction, and when suddenly the door was sealed over, like a
wound closing, and the ship instantly vertically rose,
Vestara tasted fear.

Only for a moment, though. She did not blindly trust
the ship, but she knew what he was designed for, and she
knew she had the will to direct him if she didn't panic. She
moved forward on the strange surface to where she could
see out the viewport to the Temple that had receded, the

faces of the Sith watching in the courtyard rapidly becoming tiny dots. She was as high as she had ever been on Tikk, and then suddenly she was higher still, and looking down on her home planet with eyes wide in astonishment.

It was beautiful, green and brown and blue with wisps of white clouds here and there, and Vestara suddenly wasn't sure she wanted to leave it.

You wish to be a Sith Master, do you not?

You know I do.

Then leave this world behind, so that you may conquer others.

Slowly, her palms moist, Vestara had nodded. *We will need more than you, Ship, if we are to conquer worlds in the name of the Sith.*

I will teach you. I will teach all of you.

And so he had. Every apprentice, every Sith Knight, every Master and Lord learned how to navigate the vessel. He knew more about the *Omen* than they did, and they eagerly drank in the knowledge he shared. And then he took them to the stars.

They began with the conquest of a single vessel, alone and unprotected, no match for Ship. They harried it, dancing and fighting with weapons that Ship manifested into physical form with a thought, forcing the vessel to crash-land on an uninhabited world. What crew did not die in the accident met death by Sith lightsabers, shikkar, or glass parang—a bladed weapon originally used for clearing undergrowth that had new value as a weapon that could be thrown and then return to the thrower. The Sith aboard Ship scavenged this, their first kill, and with the vessel's parts were able to make strides toward reconstructing *Omen*.

And they returned to space. Isolated and distant from the rest of the galaxy they might have been until now, but no longer. Ship knew where to take them, how to get there, and they would hunt and take their prizes and return with no one left to reveal the location of their hidden world. So they did, again and again, until *Omen* was completed and spaceworthy. Five thousand years old it might be, but it was Sith, and with repairs, it again dominated the skies.

Two ships, now. One a Sith training vessel, the other a Sith battle cruiser. More vessels fell beneath the determined Sith attacks; more vessels that would be pressed into service to the dark side of the Force. Vestara was permitted to be part of the crew of one of the very first craft so commandeered. It had been given to Lady Rhea to command and renamed *Eternal Crusader.* Vestara learned as all of them had—by a few practice drills and by jumping with both feet into full-on space battles.

These new, spacefaring Tribe members had even adopted new garb for the purpose. Loose, flowing robes were a hindrance in scrambling aboard downed vessels and fighting in tight quarters. Instead, Vestara and the other crew members of the various vessels in the new Sith armada wore tight-fitting pants, shirts that permitted air to circulate and cool overheated bodies, comfortable boots for running and climbing, and weapons that were small, deadly, and clipped neatly to a belt, such as vibroblades, shotos, shikkars, and parangs, as well as the traditional lightsaber. Vestara's light brown hair, which she still kept long, was almost always tightly braided now. She could not afford any distractions.

Two years had passed so, and they had been the fastest of Vestara's young life. Sixteen now, she had transformed from a girl who yearned to become a Sith Master to a highly respected apprentice; from an innocent who had never taken a life or even dealt a severe injury to an accomplished killer who had slain dozens by all methods imaginable. She had once dreamed of being allowed even the most fleeting of glimpses inside *Omen;* now she served on a vessel even larger and more powerful than that ancient, respected warship.

They were returning home after a particularly satisfying attack: six Sith ships against two bulk freighters, which now were being towed back to Kesh to be repaired, refurbished, renamed, and integrated into the increasingly powerful Sith armada. They had nearly a dozen vessels now. Vestara was happy in her current assignment, though she would have preferred to stay with Ship. He had accompanied them on this battle, and she could feel his contentment in the Force at their progress.

And then she felt . . . something else.

She couldn't figure out what it was—a jolt, an unsettling in the Force, like a stone being thrown into a pond. It was nothing negative, but—very powerful.

Lady Rhea gasped, her fingers digging into the arm of her command chair. Her face had gone white, and her eyes were enormous and unseeing. Vestara glanced at her in concern, then left her station to go to her Master and kneel beside her.

"Lady Rhea—what it is?"

For another moment, Lady Rhea simply stared, wide-eyed, at nothing. Then she blinked and seemed to come to her senses.

"I—felt someone very powerful in the Force," she said, her voice slightly shaky and laced with an uncertainty that Vestara had never before heard from her. It made her stomach clench. "Strong in the power of the light side. A Jedi . . . a great Master."

And Vestara felt a surge from Ship and a name was placed in her head: *Skywalker.*

"Dad?"

Ben's voice seemed to come to Luke from far away, floating to reach him. It was only his son's touch on his arm that finally brought Luke out of his Force-induced reverie.

"What just happened? You all right?"

Luke shook his head, staring at the item in his hand, and then gently placed it back down on the pile. Once he had ceased to be in physical contact with it, the strange tingling in the Force ceased.

"I—yes. I'm all right."

"What was that?" Ben looked warily at the object, clearly deeply reluctant to touch it himself.

"It's called the Codex," Luke said, knowing this was true but not remembering getting the knowledge. "It seemed to . . . enhance my Force powers. Augment them, make them much stronger."

Ben lifted an eyebrow and looked with new respect and curiosity at the item.

"That's kinda astral. What is it?"

"I don't know. It's old . . . it's powerful. And—" Luke hesitated. "It felt . . ."

Ben frowned. "Dark? Is it dark-side technology?"

"No, no." Luke shook his head. "But it . . . while it enhanced my Force abilities, it also—" He groped for words, unused to being unable to articulate what he needed to convey. "I felt vulnerable. As if my ability to resist the temptations of the dark side was being tested. But it's not dark-side technology in and of itself, it's just . . . there's a price for that kind of power."

Ben nodded slowly.

"And there's something else. I sensed a disturbance in the Force."

"That's . . . hardly ever a good thing," Ben said.

"Agreed. But it wasn't violent, or tragic. Just . . . there was a kind of wrongness out there. Something's amiss. Out of harmony."

"Could you tell where? Or who it affects?"

Luke turned to Ben and looked at him searchingly. "It's coming from the Maw."

Chapter Twenty-four

THE AING-TII HOMEWORLD

TADAR'RO WAS WAITING FOR LUKE AND BEN WHEN THEY finally emerged, blinking slightly at the change from the comforting dimness of the Force stones to the harsh sunlight of the Aing-Tii homeworld.

Luke was willing to bet that Tadar'Ro had not moved at all during the entire time he and Ben had been inside, testing all the artifacts. The Aing-Tii teacher had curled up like a boulder, and now as they emerged he slowly uncurled and stood to face them. His tongues flickered, and his yearning flooded the Force.

"Do you have an answer for us from Those Who Dwell Beyond the Veil?"

Luke and Ben exchanged glances. Luke nodded. "I do. But I feel strongly that what I have to say should be told to all the Aing-Tii together."

Tadar'Ro was disappointed, but he also understood. He nodded, the gesture seeming to come to him more naturally now. "Very well. But let us make all haste now to return to them. I am sure that they are as anxious as I to discover what Those Who Dwell Beyond the Veil wish for us."

Tadar'Ro was indeed anxious, if the pace he set was any indication. Luke and Ben found themselves using the Force to keep up with him. They could, of course, simply have asked Tadar'Ro to slow down, but knowing what he did, Luke understood the Aing-Tii's driving need. And he, too, wanted to share what he had learned as quickly as possible.

Force-sensitives all apparently, the Aing-Tii knew they were returning. By the time Luke, Ben, and Tadar'Ro reached the *Jade Shadow,* dozens of Aing-Tii were waiting for them.

Still as stone they were, as ever, sitting on their haunches as if they had been carved so. Luke almost felt buffeted by their emotions in the Force: fear, excitement, hope, anger, resentment, gratitude. A rainbow.

Luke glanced over at Ben, who nodded solemnly. Then Luke took a deep breath, calmed himself, and spoke.

"When we came here, we had many questions about Jacen Solo. Thanks to Tadar'Ro, we have learned more about him. We also learned many things we didn't expect to: about Jorj Car'das, about the Aing-Tii and how you use the Force. How you regard it. We are the richer for that knowledge.

"And in return, you asked something of us. Something that no one among you could do—consult the relics that are compiled in the Embrace and seek guidance from them. We have done so. I give you my solemn word that Ben and I have handled every single artifact in the Embrace, trying to find the answers you, our hosts, asked of us. And here is what we have learned."

Ben shifted beside him uneasily. *Here we go*, Luke thought.

"While we learned much from the relics, and while we touched the Force through them, it is with deep regret that I must tell you, we gleaned no insight from them. No direction, no guidance, nothing that we could bring to you as proof that Those Who Dwell Beyond the Veil had plans for you at this juncture. I am afraid that the

Aing-Tii are on their own. You and you alone must decide your destiny. Whether you continue to believe as you have in the past, that the Force guides everything, or what the Prophet told you—that everything is preordained—you must chart your own path."

Grief and anger poured into the Force with such violence that Ben winced, and even Luke had to steel himself against it. Out of the corner of his eye Luke saw Ben's hand twitch. Ben, sensing the hostility rampaging in the Force, desperately wanted to grab his lightsaber—but did not. Luke was very proud of him. *A Jedi uses the Force for knowledge and protection. Never attack.*

Then as quickly as it had come, the crowd's anger abated. The onslaught of enraged, disillusioned Aing-Tii did not come. Luke relaxed slightly as he watched them. They were talking; their tongues flickered wildly. But he sensed it was less of an argument than a discussion. Something had shifted. It was subtle, but present. Luke could not understand them without the translation device, but he had a good idea as to what they were thinking. He glanced at Tadar'Ro, who hesitated, then translated.

"Some of them say, this is proof that we do not need offworlder aid to decide our own issues. Others say that Those Who Dwell Beyond the Veil have turned against us—while still others say they have enough faith in us to choose what is right. And still others say that if it were not for Luke Skywalker and Ben Skywalker, we would still be hostile to one another."

Luke smiled a little. He could live with that. It was time for them to go.

The Aing-Tii began to drift away, returning to their ordinary lives and letting the "offworlders" be about their business. Luke turned to Ben.

"If you have any more questions for Tadar'Ro, you'd better ask them now."

Ben shrugged, not looking at his father. "Nah, I'm good."

Luke frowned slightly, curious. "You haven't attempted the flow-walking yet."

"I decided not to do it. Come on, let's get packing."

Tadar'Ro was confused. "But Ben Skywalker—we discussed this."

Luke's eyes narrowed. "Tadar'Ro, can you give us a minute?"

Tadar'Ro nodded. Ben and Luke strode up the ramp into the *Jade Shadow* and closed it.

"Ben," Luke said gently, smiling, "I know what you're doing."

"Again?"

"Yep." Luke's smile widened. "You're not going to flow-walk because you want to make a gesture to me. It's been uncomfortable these last several days, and it's all centered on the flow-walking. You're denying yourself this to try to smooth things over after this rough patch."

Ben nodded, not looking at him.

"I'll be honest. I'd be just as happy if you never learned this skill, never used it. Especially not to see Jacen. Because that's what this is all about. But you know what?"

Luke placed his hands on Ben's shoulders and turned his son to face him. "The Aing-Tii aren't babies who need the watchful eyes and control of Those Who Dwell Beyond the Veil. They can make their own decisions. And the same goes for you."

Ben looked up at him searchingly. Luke smiled.

"Go on, if you need to do this."

Ben hesitated for a long moment, then nodded, opened the hatch, and stepped outside. Luke watched him as he went to Tadar'Ro, and then was surprised when Ben strode off alone. Tadar'Ro turned to look at

Luke expectantly. Confused, Luke hastened down the ramp to the Aing-Tii.

"I thought you would go with him."

"He knows the technique. For what he must do, he does not need me present."

Luke felt a pang as he glanced at Ben, a small figure growing smaller in the distance. His son looked terribly alone to him, but Luke understood.

"And," Tadar'Ro continued, "there is something else I must share with you, Luke Skywalker."

Ben wondered if he should have had a sanisteam and something hot to eat before attempting what he was about to do, but it was too late now. He trudged slowly but doggedly toward the spot where he and Luke had spent so many days learning from Tadar'Ro. It all looked as it had before, the time-smoothed stones warm from the sun, the taller stones casting cool shadows. But it didn't feel the same to Ben.

Here was where Tadar'Ro had taught Luke, and Ben, and Jorj Car'das.

And here was where Tadar'Ro had taught Jacen Solo.

For a long moment, Ben stood, his heart beating too rapidly in his chest, his arms folded. Part of him wanted to just walk away. But another part of him knew he had to do this, or else he would forever wonder if he could have learned something, anything, that might make a difference.

He sat down, but not on one of the stones upon which the students sat. He was still several strides away from the teaching site, close enough to observe and hear, far enough away so that hopefully his presence would not be noticed. That was one of the things Tadar'Ro had cautioned him about. One who traveled into the past could be seen and heard—even change things. But according to the Aing-Tii, the Force would resume its natural flow. One couldn't change things in any significant way; the Force would bring things back to the way they should be.

Except . . . and Ben's heart spasmed in his chest.

The Aing-Tii said this because they believed that the Force guided them in their everyday lives. And now, they had this dreadful schism. What if they were wrong? What if both sides were wrong? What if beings weren't guided, or if things weren't preordained?

What if he could really change the future?

He began to tremble at the awesome nature of the thought. There was only one thing to do—flow-walk, and see what happened. Since his legs were threatening to buckle underneath him anyway, Ben sat down cross-legged on the rocky ground.

He began to calm his breathing, as if he were prepared to simply meditate, but he kept his eyes open. "Soft eyes with which to see," Tadar'Ro said. "Hard eyes will not see what they need to see. Closed eyes will see nothing."

Soft eyes. Unfocused, but watching. Ben understood.

His heart rate dropped and his body relaxed. With his slightly out-of-focus gaze, he regarded the flat stones upon which he and his father had sat.

"I don't understand," came a familiar voice. Ben's head whipped toward the sound, but he kept his gaze soft. Tadar'Ro was approaching the teaching area, and with him, striding briskly, wearing the brown and tan robes of a Jedi Knight, was—

"Jacen," Ben whispered.

His cousin looked younger than Ben remembered. That was to be expected, of course; this was the past after all. But there was more to it than that. Ben hadn't realized while it was all unfolding how much the war had aged Jacen. His cousin's forehead was smooth, his eyes clear and bright and warm. His movements lacked the gravitas they had assumed later, when Jacen wore all black, a shimmersilk cape swirling ominously about him. Before Ben was no Sith, no colonel. Before him was a Jedi Knight, his cousin, a man curious and determined to learn.

Jacen sat down in front of Tadar'Ro and looked at the Aing-Tii expectantly. "How can you go into the future at all, if it hasn't happened yet? Yoda once told my uncle it was always in motion."

"Yoda was correct. And yet one can still travel into it."

Jacen shook his dark head. "How can you travel into something that is not there?"

"When you flow-walk, things become solid beneath you. Your presence brings them into being. And yet, once you depart, they return to what they were. What you see is a future, but not necessarily *the* future. It is real, and it is not, and it is."

Jacen shook his head, laughing with genuine warmth. "That explains everything," he said wryly.

He was so . . . open. So unguarded. Ben tried to remember seeing Jacen that way and found he couldn't. Was it because he was here, learning with someone like Tadar'Ro? Or had the final shell of hardness, of implacability, simply not folded around him yet?

"I'm glad you're willing to teach me. I want to learn everything I can. This galaxy . . ." Jacen looked off, his expression detached, but not with the iciness that Ben remembered. "It needs order. Healing. Help. Jedi have abilities that other people don't have. We need to do everything we can to help that process."

Help. This man had killed innocents. Had tortured a woman to death. All in the name of helping the galaxy. How had he justified it, this man who sat there with concern obviously filling his whole being?

Jacen . . . oh Jacen . . .

Ben couldn't take it anymore. With a roar he jumped

to his feet, and the images disappeared as if they had never been. The stones were empty.

Like the paradox of traveling into the future, Ben realized that Jacen had been at once firmly set on the path to the dark side, and yet not walking it. He had not become Sith, had not really even considered the option seriously. The man Ben had just seen was a Jedi, and an uncorrupted one. He was no wide-eyed innocent—too much had been done to Jacen Solo for that. But for all the pain he had endured, he was not dark. And yet the shadow was already upon him, in his questions, in his attitude; not in the seeking of knowledge, nor even in the way he would use that knowledge, but in the drive to seek it.

Ben wanted to leap up, grab his cousin by the front of his robes, and shake him, screaming, *Don't do this! Please don't do this!*

But he knew that even if he had done so, even if he had been able to tell Jacen about all the atrocities he would eventually commit, it wouldn't have made a difference. The brokenness was already in Jacen. The progression from Jacen Solo to Darth Caedus was inevitable and unstoppable, and that knowing broke Ben Skywalker's heart.

He stumbled away several steps before leaning against one of the standing stones. He let it support him, clutching it like a lifeline. Luke had been right. There was no healing here, no closure. No chance of "saving Jacen." Just a horrible racking inevitability, a feeling of helplessness, and the sensation of picking at a wound that should have healed long ago.

Ben rested his head against the stone and sobbed.

Both Tadar'Ro and Luke were waiting outside for him when he returned. He knew they knew he'd been crying and he didn't care, didn't attempt to hide his feelings in the Force. Luke looked at him compassionately as he approached.

"You were right, Dad," Ben said without preamble. "It was a horrible feeling. I don't think I've ever felt as helpless in my life. The only thing I can do now is move forward, and . . . and try to be more aware next time of the warning signs." He met his father's gaze evenly. "I couldn't save Jacen. But maybe . . . maybe there are others I can help."

He squared his shoulders and turned to Tadar'Ro. "I thank you for teaching me this technique. And I hope you won't be offended, but . . . I have to tell you, I don't intend to do it again. Ever. I—I think for me, it's better to just live in the present."

Luke remained silent, but Ben felt his father's pride wash over him like a warm, comforting wave. He blinked hard, not wanting to cry again.

"There is no offense," Tadar'Ro reassured him. "The ways of the Aing-Tii are not for all. You wished to learn; we teach those who ask. It was the same with Jorj Car'das. In answer to his questions, we only asked him to learn about us, not become like us."

Briefly Ben wondered what *the ways of the Aing-Tii* were, now that they had to decide such things for themselves. But it was not his concern, nor should it be.

"While you were . . . gone," Luke said, "Tadar'Ro and I had a very interesting conversation. It turns out that you and I were not the only humans to have handled the Codex."

Ben felt a jolt, then gently pushed it down. Despite what he had witnessed through flow-walking, he knew that sooner or later he'd have to learn to not wince when someone talked about Jacen. "Jacen did, too?"

Luke nodded. "I told Tadar'Ro what we experienced, and apparently Jacen felt the same thing happen when he touched the Codex."

"The whole augmenting-your-powers thing?"

"Well, yes, that. But more importantly, he had the sensation of something wrong in the Maw that I did. He told Tadar'Ro that when he left, he was going to investigate the Maw and find out what it is."

About forty million questions crowded Ben's mind. He opened his mouth to try to articulate at least sixty-three of them, but Tadar'Ro interrupted.

"I told Jacen Solo not to go. And I give the same message to Luke Skywalker and Ben Skywalker."

"Why not? If there's something wrong there—" Ben began.

"There the Mind Drinkers dwell," Tadar'Ro said. "It is a dangerous place for those who use the Force."

Ben looked at his father. Luke nodded slightly.

"We embarked on this journey to find out what happened to Jacen Solo to turn him into Darth Caedus," Luke said, "and also to see if we can find out anything about the strange mental illness that is crippling the Jedi Order one by one. Tadar'Ro . . . we have to go investigate this."

Despite the intensity with which he had warned them, Tadar'Ro did not seem surprised at their decision. Perhaps, after knowing four humans, he was starting to figure out how stubborn they could be.

"So said Jacen Solo. And I will give you the same parting gift I gave him: a riddle. *The Path of Enlightenment runs through the chasm of Perfect Darkness. The way is narrow and treacherous, but if you can follow it, you will find what you seek.*"

Ben and Luke exchanged glances. "No other clues?"

"As you told my people earlier . . . you must figure it out for yourselves."

Despite everything, Ben found himself grinning. He had no idea that the Aing-Tii had such a sense of humor.

"And for Ben Skywalker, I have another gift. One that is not quite so difficult to understand."

He had been carrying one of the *Vor'cha* stun sticks attached to a belt around his waist. Now he reached to unfasten it, offering it to Ben.

"You and your father were attacked with such a weapon. I deeply regret that attack. Now the weapon is yours. I know you will wield it carefully. It can render your enemy unconscious, even through armor."

"Lubed!" Ben said, grinning, as he accepted the stick. He bowed to Tadar'Ro. "Thank you, Tadar'Ro. Thank you for everything."

Luke caught Tadar'Ro's eye and smiled a little. Then, before Ben knew what was happening, there was a sharp pop of displaced air. The *Vor'cha* stick simply vanished from his hands to reappear in his father's. He gaped for a second, and then realized that while he had been studying so hard to learn flow-walking, Luke had readily mastered the other known Aing-Tii Force technique. He laughed a little as Luke tossed the stick back to his son.

Tadar'Ro bowed to both Skywalkers. "Travel safely. May you learn what you must."

"May the Force be with you," Luke said.

Amusement bathed them. "It is always with everyone," Tadar'Ro said, nodded to them, and turned to go.

Less than an hour later, they were ready to depart. Ben had even had a chance to grab a sanisteam and a nerf steak. He slipped into the chair beside his father, moving quietly as Luke was recording a message.

". . . and based on all this, we've decided to head to the Maw," Luke was saying. "I'm not sure when we'll be out of the Rift and you'll be able to receive this, but I thought you should know as soon as possible. Ben and I will get to work on the riddle, but if any of the Masters figures it out before we do, I promise I won't be insulted.

I hope to talk to you soon, and I hope all is well back home."

He punched a button and sent the message, then turned to Ben. "Ready to talk to these Mind Drinkers who supposedly dwell in the Maw?"

"Sure," Ben said, lifting the *Vor'cha* stick. "I think we can handle them."

Chapter Twenty-five

KESH.

LADY RHEA HAD SPOKEN WITH LORD VOL, AND THE *Eternal Crusader* had been summoned back to Kesh. As they entered orbit, Vestara realized that the whole armada had been recalled. Currently in orbit around a world that, two years earlier, had never even seen an operational space-faring craft were more than two dozen starships.

Vestara, Lady Rhea, and a few other crew took a small transport to Tahv. The sharp delight Vestara took in the fact that she was no longer on the outside, wistfully looking in, but almost always brought in on every major decision and planning session had not faded over the last two years. She was aware of the responsibilities of such an honor, and never took it for granted.

She recalled the first time she had stood in these Council Chambers, frightened but resolute. How naïve she had been then. She smiled a little and shifted position, then stilled as Lord Vol began speaking.

"A short time ago, many of us felt a very strong rippling in the Force. We sensed a presence that we immediately realized would be a threat to us. Ship was able to identify that presence as the current Grand Master of the Jedi—Luke Skywalker."

A soft murmur went through the room. Lord Vol held

up his hand for silence. "The information Ship has given us on this Skywalker is sobering. He is, however, far from his home base. We do not know to what end. Still, I am not about to overlook an opportunity when one drops as perfectly into our hands as ripe fruit. Skywalker is several light-years away, but still within our ability to reach. Over the last day, I have been in contact with Lady Rhea." He nodded to Vestara's Master, who stepped forward.

"When Ship came to us with the news of the near extinction of the Sith," she said, her voice clear and strong, "we did not fall victim to despair. We acted. Vessel by vessel, we are assembling a fleet with which we will eventually take back the galaxy from the Jedi, who spread like vermin throughout system after system. Such is our goal.

"Some will say, one man cannot hold a whole galaxy together. True. But one man can lead and inspire. If the head is cut off, the body will follow. Luke Skywalker has done much to fight the Sith, the dark side. He was at one point the last Jedi, and now he has re-created the Order with hundreds of them." She was so disgusted by this she was almost spitting the words. "And now, somehow, he has broadcast his presence into the Force. And we can take him down.

"Lord Vol and I have handpicked a single strike team to bring against this Skywalker. He—"

"A moment," said Yuvar Xal, Ahri's Master. "The Grand Master of the Jedi cannot possibly be simply wandering off alone. He must be on a mission of great importance, and it is logical to believe that he has many vessels under his command. A single strike force would do nothing against that."

"There was something about his presence—I do not think so. For whatever reason, my instincts are telling me that he is, if not alone, at least unaccompanied by

any sort of fleet," Lady Rhea said. Vestara understood
what she meant. There had been a sense of isolation in
Skywalker's presence.

"Regardless, if such does turn out to be the case, we
will be able to make that determination and call for re-
inforcements. A huge fleet will announce our presence.
One or two smaller vessels will be able to glean information much more readily," Lady Rhea continued.

Xal looked unhappy, but fell silent.

"Now," Lady Rhea continued. "We—"

It rocked through them like a wave. Vestara actually
stumbled. It was at once almost overpowering and nour-
ishing. Pure dark-side energy crackled through the
room, piercing their hearts, like an embrace that was
welcomed but too tight to be truly comfortable. Vestara
extended a hand, as if she could physically reach out
and touch whatever it was that was permeating her entire being. She wanted it, ached for it, felt tears suddenly
stinging her eyes—

And then a rush of joy flooded her.

Ship. He was all but singing, a devoted pet racing to
his beloved master, following that call of the dark-side
energy.

"No!" cried Vestara. "Ship!"

She blinked, recovering as the strange pull suddenly
ended. Lady Rhea was staring at her.

"Vestara, what is it doing?"

Vestara licked lips suddenly gone dry. She felt intensely, terribly bereft. Abandoned, left behind, empty.
Her connection with Ship had always been acknowledged as the strongest among any of the Sith. He had
contacted her first, and had maintained that level of—
intimacy, almost—through the last two years. Now he
had left them, left her, without even a twinge of regret or
a farewell.

"He—he's gone," she said in a voice that trembled.
"He's following that—that—call."

For a dreadful moment, everyone was still. Horror,
anger, and anguish flooded into the Force. And then
Lord Vol rose. His body was frail, but his power was
not, and he gut-punched them with his determination.

"We had planned to send a strike force after Luke
Skywalker," he said. "Now we have a more important
mission—follow Ship and recover it."

Him, Vestara thought. *Ship's male.*

"The strike force will prepare to launch after Ship as
soon as you are prepared under the command of Lady
Rhea."

Lady Rhea turned her eyes to Vestara and nodded. Excitement and fear both clutched at Vestara, but she
forced them back. If she was to be of any use on this
mission, she would need to be calm, be in control of her
emotions, not let them dominate her.

They would find Ship, and find out what had been so
compelling that he had felt it necessary to abandon
those he had once come to.

Leia and Han sat on Allana's bed, tucking the covers
gently in around her. The little girl was proving to have
a backbone of durasteel, given how well she bounced
back from things. She seemed to have recovered fully
from the incident at the Livestock Exchange and Exhibition, except she seemed unusually thoughtful. Whenever
Han or Leia tried to gently coax her into talking, she
said she was fine and smiled at them.

But tonight, she looked up at them just before they
each leaned in turn to kiss her forehead. "I have been
thinking," she said.

The pair exchanged glances and sat down on either
side of her bed. "About what, honey?" Leia asked.

"About . . . what happened at the show."

Leia reached and stroked the girl's soft, round cheek. "Go on."

"You . . . you had to kill some of the animals to save people."

Leia nodded. "That's right."

"But they were just animals. They had been bred to be mean."

"It wasn't their intention, not like with sentient beings," Leia said, wondering where this was going. "That much is true. But a threat to a being is the same, whether it's done with intention or not."

"But . . . the nexu. She had cubs."

Ah, now Leia understood. "Yes, she did."

"And you killed her. Because she was hurting people. So now the cubs have no mother, no one to look after them." She lifted her calm gaze to theirs. "I think we should take responsibility."

"What?" Han exploded.

"One of the cubs. Radd Minker said you could tame them if you found a good trainer for them. We took their mother away. We should take care of at least one of them. It's the right thing to do. It's justice."

Han gave Leia a what-the-stang-do-we-do-now look. Leia suspected she had a similar expression on her own face. But she was also unspeakably proud of their granddaughter. Her instincts, her moral compass—they were dead-on. She was an amazing little girl, and would grow into a remarkable woman.

"You're right, honey. It is the right thing to do."

Han's eyebrows shot up. "I thought we were getting her a nice little kybuck," he said. "You know . . . gentle, small, no mouthfuls of sharp teeth."

"We might not be able to keep one for ourselves," Leia continued as if she had not heard Han at all, "but we can certainly make sure they all go to good and loving homes."

"Or how about a tauntaun?" Han said, desperation creeping into his voice. "Threepio can give it a bath every other day."

"Can we *try* to keep one?" Allana asked, slightly wistful, also ignoring Han.

"We'll see," Leia said.

Tahiri sat alone in her apartment, mechanically forking what passed for dinner into her mouth, chewing and swallowing. It was technically eating, but she paid no attention to the process. Her mind was elsewhere.

She wondered how Jaina Solo was doing. Several days had passed since that reporter Javis Tyrr had done his "exposé" on the evils of the Jedi. As part of the team that had been responsible for nabbing Seff Hellin, Tahiri was relieved that Daala had agreed not to extradite him or Natua Wan. But it was clear that the Chief of State was smarting, and had decided to do everything she could to humiliate the Jedi if she couldn't have her prize.

The interview with Jaina was painful to watch. Knowing the other woman as well as she did, Tahiri could *feel* Jaina straining to utter acerbic responses to the utterly inane questions Tyrr was asking. Or—which would probably please the Solo daughter even better—pop the reporter one. She was sorry, too, for Cilghal and Tekli, although both came off well. The former's quiet dignity and composure made Javis Tyrr look tawdry, and the latter's obvious distress and extreme cuteness were certain to make any viewer root for her.

The only reason Tahiri was not on holocam with them was that she was no longer officially a Jedi, and therefore Jaina Solo had not been ordered to give her name. For that, Tahiri was intensely glad. There were days when her decision to keep apart from the Order completely felt like the right one. And others when it felt utterly and completely wrong.

She put down the fork, stared at the half-eaten food, and rested her face in her hands for a long moment. She thought back to the words Seff Hellin had hurled at her, thinking she was a doppelgänger: *Murderess, traitor, pathetic slave to her emotions—that's what she is.*

They'd hurt. They'd hurt more than she would ever have expected. They'd hurt because they were true. She had been all those things . . . and perhaps still was the latter. She had told Jaina she was trying to figure things out, and she was. Jaina had responded at the time with a hug, and later showed faith in Tahiri by asking her to participate in the Darkmeld conspiracy. Maybe there was a way back from this after all.

The door chime sounded. Tahiri sighed, shoved aside the half-full plate of food, and padded to the door on bare feet.

Three GA officers stood outside. Two had weapons. The third was dressed in a suit and carried a datapad atop which was folded a small card.

"Tahiri Veila, you are under arrest on the charges of obstruction of justice, complicity in the murder of Admiral Gilad Pellaeon, and treason."

Read on for an excerpt from
Star Wars®: Fate of the Jedi: Abyss
by Troy Denning
Published by Del Rey Books

BURIED DEEP INSIDE THE JEDI TEMPLE ON CORUSCANT WAS
the Asylum Block, a transparisteel cube standing in its
own hidden atrium, bathed in artificial blue light and
surrounded by tidy rows of potted olbio trees. Through
a second-story wall, Leia Solo could see Seff Hellin
kneeling in his cell. He was in the corner, staring at his
bloody knuckles as though surprised that hammering at
a fusion-welded seam might actually damage them. In
the adjacent cell, Natua Wan was endlessly scratching
at her door lock, trying to slip her splintered talons into
a magnetic seal that a nanoscalpel could not have
breached.

Seeing the pair in such a state made Leia's heart ache.
It also terrified her, for both of Corran Horn's children
had fallen victim to the same condition. Now, with
Temple scientists no closer to identifying a cause, she
was beginning to fear that this strange insanity might
claim an entire generation of Jedi Knights. And that was
something she would not allow—not when every new
case reminded her how confused and helpless she had
felt losing Jacen to the madness of the Sith.

The golden outline of an access portal appeared in the
invisible barrier field that enclosed the atrium. With
Han and C-3PO following behind, Leia stepped into the
leafy-smelling interior and was not surprised to feel a
subtle pang of loss and isolation. The olbio trees were

filled with ysalamiri, small white reptiles that hid from their native predators by creating voids in the Force. The adaptation was an invaluable tool to anyone who needed to incarcerate rogue Force-users—and all too often lately, that included the Jedi themselves.

As the portal crackled shut behind them, Han leaned close and warmed Leia's ear with a whisper. "I don't think cutting them off from the Force is helping. They look crazier than ever."

"Seff and Natua are not crazy," Leia reprimanded. "They're ill, and they need our understanding."

"Hey, nobody understands crazy better than me." Han gave her arm a reassuring squeeze. "People are always calling *me* crazy."

"Captain Solo is quite right," C-3PO agreed. The golden protocol droid was standing close behind the Solos, his metallic breastplate pressing cold against Leia's shoulder. "During our association, Captain Solo's sanity has been questioned an average of three times per month. By the psychiatric care standards of many conformist societies, that fact alone would qualify him for a cell in the Asylum Block."

Han shot a frown over his shoulder, but turned back to Leia with his best smirk of reassurance. "You see? I'm probably the only one in the whole Temple who receives on their channel."

"I wouldn't doubt that," Leia said. She gave him a wry smile, then patted the hand grasping her arm. "But thanks—I just wish you really *did* know what's going on with them."

Now it was Han who grew serious. "Yeah. Seeing 'em slip away like this brings bad memories. *Really* bad memories."

"It does," Leia acknowledged. "But it's not the same thing. By the time anyone realized what was going on with Jacen, he was *running* the Galactic Alliance."

"Yeah, and we were the enemy," Han agreed. "I just wish we could have stuck Jacen in a deten—"

"We *would* have, had there been some way to take him alive," Leia interrupted. They didn't turn down this lane often, but when they did, it devastated her—and she couldn't let herself be devastated now. "Let's just focus on the Jedi we *can* save."

Han nodded. "Count me in. I don't need anybody else's family getting caught in the kind of plasma blast we did."

Han was still speaking when Master Cilghal and her assistant Tekli appeared, walking between two rows of potted olbios. In their white medical robes, the pair made a somber impression: Cilghal a sad-eyed Mon Calamari with a high-domed head, Tekli a diminutive Chadra-Fan with her flap-like ears pulled tight against her head fur.

Cilghal extended a web-fingered hand first to Leia, then to Han, and spoke in her rippling Mon Calamari voice. "Princess Leia, Captain Solo, thank you for coming. I trust you were able to find someone to watch Amelia on such short notice?"

"No problem," Han said. "Bazel is keeping an eye on her."

"Bazel Warv?" Tekli squeaked.

"Yeah, Amelia just loves the big guy." Han smiled. "I'm beginning to think that girl's going to marry a Ramoan when she grows up."

The glance that Tekli shot up at Cilghal was almost imperceptible, as was the answering dip from the Mon Calamari's near eye—but not quick enough to escape the practiced gaze of a former diplomat.

"Is that a problem?" Leia asked. "Bazel has always been very good with her."

"I don't believe there's anything to worry about," Cilghal said. "It's just that the only link we've been able to establish between patients is one of association."

"What kind of association?" Han asked.

"Age and location," Tekli supplied. "All four victims were among the students hidden in Shelter."

Leia nodded. Shelter was the secret base where the Jedi had sequestered their young during the last part of the war with the Yuuzhan Vong. Located deep inside the Maw cluster of black holes and cobbled together from the remnants of an abandoned weapons lab, it had been a gloomy place to care for young Jedi—and now, it appeared, perhaps a dangerous one.

"Are you thinking environmental toxins?" Leia asked.

"We decontaminated the place pretty well," Han added. "But I suppose we could have missed something— the Imperials were making some strange stuff there."

Cilghal spread her hands. "It's impossible to say. At the moment, all we have is a simple observation." She lowered an admonishing eye toward her assistant. "The sample is too small to establish a statistical correlation."

"True, but it's the only firm link we have among all four," Tekli countered. "And whether it's causative or not, Bazel *does* associate closely with both Valin and Jysella."

"Yeah, along with Yaqeel Saav'etu," Han said. "I've heard Bazel call the four of them the *Unit*."

Leia raised a brow. "Did this Unit include Seff or Natua?"

"Not that I ever heard," Han said.

Tekli confirmed this with a shake of her golden-furred head.

"You see?" Cilghal asked. "There are plenty of facts and connections—but which are significant? Are any?"

"If anyone can sort it out, it's you," Leia said. "In the meantime, there's nothing wrong with being careful."

"Of course not," Cilghal said. "So if you'd rather return to Amelia right away—"

"No, I don't think that will be necessary," Leia interrupted. "Artoo-Detoo is there, and he has standing orders to contact us if anything starts to look out of the ordinary. And we're very eager to help you."

"Yeah." Han glanced toward the cell block. "Judging by the looks of those two up there, you need it more than ever."

"Thank you." Cilghal turned and waved them toward the cell block. "But actually, the reason I asked you here is that Seff has begun to improve."

Han looked doubtful. "So he *didn't* tear up his hands punching walls?"

"He did," Cilghal admitted.

"But he *has* stopped," Leia noted. "Is that the improvement?"

Cilghal nodded. "A few days after we isolated them from the Force, both Seff and Natua began to exhibit symptoms of violent psychological withdrawal. Seff's present calmness suggests he may have entered a recovery phase."

"Wait a minute." Han cast an uneasy look toward Leia. "You're saying they're *addicted* to the Force?"

"Only that there's some connection," Cilghal said carefully.

"We're wondering if the Force acts as some sort of carrier for the madness," Tekli explained. "Or maybe a trigger."

Cilghal fixed an admonishing eye on her assistant. "That's all speculation at this stage, of course." The other eye swung toward Leia—a Mon Calamari ability that Leia still found a bit unsettling. "So far, we haven't been able to confirm either the withdrawal or the recovery."

"And that's why you need us?" Leia surmised.

Cilghal nodded. "We'd like to conduct a furtive encephaloscan to determine just how calm Seff truly is—"

"And you want us to distract him," Han finished.

"Would you mind?" Cilghal asked. "We can't establish a baseline stress pattern unless we keep his attention focused elsewhere. And you're the best con artists in the Temple."

"On *Coruscant*," Han corrected, a bit too proudly. He hitched a thumb toward C-3PO. "But Goldenrod here isn't going to be much help tricking anyone. Why'd you want *him* along?"

"Natua has been hissing as she works," Tekli explained. "I'm beginning to think she's talking to herself."

"That's entirely possible," C-3PO offered. "The phonetics of many reptilian languages include sibilant root patterns. I'd be happy to assist you in identifying the language, if you wish."

"A translation would be much more useful," Tekli said. "It might be helpful to know what she's saying."

"See-Threepio is entirely at your disposal," Leia said to Cilghal. "As are Han and I."

Cilghal thanked them and led the way to the Asylum Block. Tekli disappeared into the control room to retrieve a pair of stun sticks for the Solos and a tranquilizer pistol for Cilghal, then announced that she would join them with the encephaloscanner once Seff was distracted. Leia and Han secured the stun sticks in the small of their backs, under their belts, then followed Cilghal to a small turbolift and ascended to the second-story catwalk.

The cells arrayed along the catwalk were clearly designed to confine rather than punish, with flowform couches, holographic entertainment centers, and privacy-screened refreshers. Judging by the muffled screel of fingernails coming through the second door, the distinction of purpose was no comfort to Natua Wan.

The first door stood open. Inside the cell, a tall, powerful-looking human Jedi sat meditating, with an upturned palm resting on one knee and a wrist stump on the other. On the floor beside him rested an artificial hand, palm-up, with the thumb and middle finger touching. Dozens of surgeries and skin grafts had repaired his burn scars to the point where his face looked merely plastic instead of horrific, but his ears remained flat and misshapen, and his short blond hair betrayed its synthetic origins in its coarse, bristly nature.

As the group approached his door, the Jedi's blue eyes popped open, fixing first on Leia, then Han. "Princess Leia, Captain Solo," he said. "It's nice to see you again."

"You, too, Raynar," Han said. "You doing okay in here?"

"Very well," Raynar said. "Thank you."

A sad reminder of the price young Jedi too often paid for their service to the galaxy, Raynar Thul had gone missing on the same strike mission that had claimed the life of the Solos' youngest son, Anakin. He had reappeared years later, badly disfigured, insane, and directing the expansion of the Killik Colony into the Chiss territories. Fortunately, he had not proven too powerful to capture alive, and he had been living in the Asylum Block for more than seven years now while Cilghal helped him put his mind back together. Had Natasi Daala been the Galactic Alliance Chief of State at the time, he would probably have been frozen in carbonite, as Valin and Jysella Horn were—and that angered Leia. Anyone whose mind came undone because of what they had suffered for the Alliance deserved to be nurtured back to health, not labeled a "danger to society" and hung up like wall art in some Galactic Alliance Security blockhouse.

Leia stopped at the entrance to Raynar's cell. "Cilghal has told us how much progress you've made." Actually, she had told the Solos that all that remained was for *Raynar* to realize that he was recovered. "Is there anything you need?"

"No, I'm free to visit the commissary myself," Raynar said. He glanced toward the adjacent cell, where Natua was still scratching at her door, then grinned a bit mischievously. "Unless you care to do something about all that racket? It's enough to drive a man crazy."

"No problem," Han said, reaching for the control pad on the exterior of the cell. "It'll be quieter if we close this—"

"On second thought," Raynar interrupted, "I may be growing fond of the noise."

Han smirked. "I *thought* that might fix your problem."

"You should apply for therapist credentials, dear," Leia said drily. She turned to Raynar. "But seriously, Raynar, if the noise bothers you, why don't you just change your quarters?"

Raynar's eyes widened as much as his rigid brows would allow. "Leave my cell?"

"The door *has* been open for quite some time," Cilghal said. "And if matters continue to deteriorate with the younger Jedi, we may be needing your room."

"There are plenty of empty quarters up on the dormitory level," Han prompted.

Raynar retrieved his artificial hand, then rose and stepped toward the door. "Would I be welcome?"

"That depends," Han said. "Are you going to do your own chores?"

"The days when I considered myself above doing chores are long past, Captain Solo." Raynar's tone was more distracted than indignant, as though he was so consumed in thought that he had failed to notice Han was joking. He stood at the door considering his options, then shrugged and began to reattach his artificial hand. "I don't know if I'm ready—I don't know if *they* are."

Before Leia could suggest that there was only one way

to find out, Raynar turned away and started toward the interior of his cell. Cilghal shook her head in disappointment, Han sighed, and Leia bit her lip in frustration.

"Relax—I'm just going to pack," Raynar called over his shoulder. "I *have* been here awhile, you know."

Leia's relief was bittersweet. She was happy to see Raynar leaving his cell, but it made her wistful as well, because incarceration and rehabilitation had never been a possibility for her son Jacen. He had been too powerful to capture and too menacing to leave free, and in the end there had been no choice except to hunt him down. Leia would go to her grave wondering how she had not seen him falling until it was too late, whether she had missed some flash of opportunity to save him—and she knew Han would, too.

Once Raynar had retrieved a small duffel and begun to pack his few possessions, Cilghal smiled and thanked both Solos, then started down the catwalk again. As they passed the next cell, Natua stopped scratching at her door locks and pressed herself to the transparisteel, her narrow eyes fixed on Han. A ruddy flush began to creep up her delicate face scales, and she slid a hand along the wall, reaching out in his direction.

"Captain Solo." Even through the electronic speaker that relayed her voice to the catwalk, Natua's voice was soft and cajoling. Leia was just glad that the Falleen's powerful attraction pheromones were safely trapped inside her own cell. "Please . . . get me out of here. They're hurting me."

"Not as much as you're hurting yourself," Han said, pointing to the crimson streaks that her bloody fingertips were leaving on the wall. "Sorry, Nat. You need to stay here and let them help you."

"*This* isn't help!" Natua slapped the wall so hard that the resulting *pung* caused C-3PO to stumble back into the safety rail; then she began to curse in the strange hissing language Tekli had mentioned earlier. *"Sse-orhstki hsuzma sahaslatho Shi'ido hsesstivaph!"*

"Oh my—Jedi Wan is promising to kill Captain Solo and his fellow imposters in a terribly unpleasant way," C-3PO explained. "Fortunately, it appears she hasn't thought through her plan very well. I don't even *have* intestines."

"Then you recognize the language?" Leia asked.

"Of course," C-3PO said. "Ancient Hsoosh is still the Language of Ceremony in the best houses of Falleen."

"Language of Ceremony?" Han echoed. "Like one they'd use to make formal vows?"

"Precisely," C-3PO said. "The elite classes have kept it alive for more than two thousand standard years to distinguish—"

"Threepio, that's not important at the moment," Leia interrupted. She could tell by the way Han was clenching his jaw that he was truly disturbed to have a mad Jedi making death vows against them. A lecture on the history of ancient Hsoosh might be enough to make him yank out C-3PO's inner machinery. "Wait here and let us know what else Natua has to say."

C-3PO acknowledged the command, and Leia and Han followed Cilghal to the next cell. Seff was still kneeling in the far corner, facing away from them with his battered hands resting on his thighs. The slow, steady rhythm of his breathing—apparent from the barely perceptible rise and fall of his shoulders—suggested he was meditating, perhaps trying to calm his troubled mind and make sense of what had been happening to him.

Cilghal glanced back down the catwalk toward the turbolift, where Tekli was waiting with what looked like a meter-long recording rod that ended in a large parabolic antenna. When the Chadra-Fan nodded her readiness, Cilghal stepped closer to Seff's cell and rapped gently on the wall.

Seff answered without looking away from the corner. "Yes, Master Cilghal?"

His voice came from the small relay speaker near the door, and when Cilghal answered, she angled her mouth toward the tiny microphone beneath it.

"How did you know it was me?" she asked.

"It's . . ." Seff struggled with an explanation for an instant, then said, "It's *always* you—or Tekli. And Tekli wouldn't reach that high when she knocked." He shrugged. "So, no, I haven't developed the ability to touch the Force through a ysalamiri void-bubble."

"But you *do* seem to be feeling better," Cilghal said.

"I'll take your word for it." Seff remained facing the corner. "I don't have a clear memory of how I was feeling before."

Cilghal rolled a hopeful eye in Leia's direction, then spoke to Seff again. "Do you remember why you're here?"

"That would depend on the meaning of *here*. I remember trying to rescue Valin Horn from a Galactic Alliance Security facility, and being ambushed by someone who looked a lot like Jaina Solo." Seff stopped and shook his head. "I assume I'm in the Asylum Block inside the Jedi Temple detention center, but none of it makes much sense."

"It probably *shouldn't* make sense," Cilghal said. She smiled in a relief that Leia did not quite share. "I'm afraid you've been suffering from paranoid delusions lately."

Seff's head and shoulders slumped in a fairly convincing manner, and he continued to look into the corner without speaking.

"Seff, you're going to get better," Cilghal said. It was something any good mind-healer would say to a patient—whether or not it was true. "This is an encouraging sign."

Leia couldn't read Mon Calamari faces well enough to know whether Cilghal was being sincere, but she *did* know that she wasn't convinced. She didn't like the way Seff continued to hide his face. And if he was having trouble remembering what had happened to him, how had he known earlier that it was always Cilghal or Tekli who visited him?

Cilghal continued speaking into the relay microphone. "Seff, you have visitors. Would it be okay if we came inside?"

"Visitors?" Seff finally looked away from his corner. "Absolutely. Come inside."

Before Leia could express her concerns, Cilghal reached over and entered a code to deactivate the lock. As the door slid aside, Leia glanced toward Han and was relieved to see the same wariness in his eyes that she felt in her gut. If Cilghal was being too optimistic, at least there would be someone else ready to jump on Seff.

"Princess Leia, Captain Solo . . ." Cilghal waved them into the cell. "After you."

"The *Solos*?"

Sounding less surprised than cynical, Seff rose and turned toward them. To Leia's surprise, there were no alarming glints in his eyes, no suspicious mouth twitches, nothing obvious to suggest that Cilghal's apparent relief was anything but warranted.

Seff raised his brow in an expression of astonishment that seemed rather rehearsed. "What are *you* two doing here?"

"We just wanted to check up on you," Han said, holding out his hand and crossing to the corner so Seff would not have an excuse to approach the door. "Good to see you're feeling better."

As Seff took Han's hand, Leia winced inwardly and readied herself to spring into action at the first hint of trouble. But Seff merely remained in the corner and looked slightly bewildered as they shook hands.

Leia moved her hand away from the stun stick in the small of her back and went to stand with Han. "You *do* look much better than the last time we saw you."

Seff's eyes shifted in her direction. "From what I'm gathering, that wouldn't be difficult."

He flashed a self-deprecating smile, and Leia began to wonder if all of the betrayal and disappointment she had suffered over the decades was beginning to make her too suspicious.

"Do you *remember* when you saw the Solos?" Cilghal asked. She remained just inside the door, as though her presence was an unpleasant requirement and she didn't want to intrude. "Aside from here on Coruscant, I mean."

Seff frowned for a moment, and Leia thought he was going to say that he couldn't recall.

But then he flashed that hangdog smile again and said, "Wasn't it on Taris, at that pet show?"

"That's right," Han said. He clapped a hand on Seff's shoulder and slipped smoothly around to the other side, so the young Jedi would have to face away from the door as they spoke. "The one where the ornuk took the grand prize."

"Han, it wasn't the *ornuk*," Leia said in a reproachful tone. She slipped around to Seff's other side and stood opposite her husband, so they had the young Jedi flanked on both sides and could quickly redirect his attention with a gentle hand on the shoulder. "It was the chitlik."

Han scowled. "What are you talking about? It was that big ornuk. I should know. It nearly bit off my ankle!"

Leia rolled her eyes and—seeing by Seff's slack jaw that their distraction was working—shook her head vehemently. "That was the cannus solix! You would have known that, if you hadn't been off starting fights when the judges explained the difference."

"Hey, I didn't start that fight," Han countered, the edge in his voice so sharp that even Leia wasn't sure he was acting. "Is it my fault if—"

"How many times have I heard *that*?" Leia interrupted. Across the cell, she could see Tekli standing in the door, pointing the funnel-shaped antenna of the portable encephaloscanner at the back of Seff's head. "According to you, it's *never* your fault."

"That's right—it *never* is." Han turned to Seff. "You were at the show, kid. Who did they arrest?"

But Seff was no longer paying attention to Han. He was looking at the same corner he had been facing when they arrived, staring at a wavy blur in the transparisteel that Leia did not recognize as a reflection—until she realized why Seff had known it was Cilghal knocking earlier. Hoping to draw his attention back to her, Leia laid a hand on his shoulder.

"Seff, please forgive us," she said. When he continued to watch the reflection, she squeezed hard. "After you've lived together as long as we have, you develop a few tender—"

Leia did not realize Seff was attacking until she felt his arm snaking over hers, trapping her elbow in a painful lock that she could not slip without snapping the joint. She whirled away, screaming in alarm, and barely managed to keep him from grabbing the stun stick secured in the back of her belt. In the next instant Han was between them, bringing his own stun stick down across Seff's shoulder.

Seff pulled back, dragging Leia into the path of the strike. He still took most of the blow across his biceps, but she was jolted so hard that her knees locked and her teeth sank deep into her tongue.

Incredibly, Seff did not drop. He drove Han back with an elbow to the face, landed a side kick to the gut that sent Han slamming into the wall, then launched himself across the cell at Tekli and Cilghal.

"No, you won't!" Seff landed two meters away and nearly fell as his leg buckled beneath him. "I won't be copied!"

Both of Leia's legs and one arm had turned to noodles, but she still had one good arm with which to grab her stun stick.

By that time, Seff was only a pace from Tekli and Cilghal.

The *phoot-phoot* of a tranquilizer gun sounded from the doorway. Seff stumbled again, one arm trying to slap the darts from his chest as he struggled to keep his balance. He took one more step, then Leia activated her stun stick and sent it spinning into the back of his legs. He crashed to the floor just centimeters from Cilghal's feet, then lay there twitching and drooling.

Cilghal turned to Tekli. "You may as well deactivate the scanner." She sighed. "I think we've learned what we came to find."